UNDER A RIVIERA MOON

HELEN MCGINN

Boldwood

First published in Great Britain in 2025 by Boldwood Books Ltd.

Copyright © Helen McGinn, 2025

Cover Design by Alice Moore Design

Cover Images: Shutterstock

A CIP catalogue record for this book is available from the British Library.

Paperback ISBN 978-1-80280-622-9

Large Print ISBN 978-1-80280-621-2

Hardback ISBN 978-1-80280-620-5

Ebook ISBN 978-1-80280-624-3

Kindle ISBN 978-1-80280-623-6

Audio CD ISBN 978-1-80280-615-1

MP3 CD ISBN 978-1-80280-616-8

Digital audio download ISBN 978-1-80280-618-2

This book is printed on certified sustainable paper. Boldwood Books is dedicated to putting sustainability at the heart of our business. For more information please visit https://www.boldwoodbooks.com/about-us/sustainability/

Boldwood Books Ltd, 23 Bowerdean Street, London, SW6 3TN

www.boldwoodbooks.com

For George, Xander and Alice

1

PRESENT DAY

'On the floor in five, if that's okay with you?' Maggie addressed the young man in the make-up chair. He nodded without looking up, eyes fixed on the phone in his hand. Behind him, the make-up artist rolled her eyes dramatically. Maggie winked at her. 'Great, see you out there.'

It was almost seven in the morning, and they were already behind schedule. Rehearsals were due to start any moment and so far, only one presenter had turned up. Maggie called for her assistant producer, a frighteningly confident twenty-something with perfect skin, hair, teeth and nails.

Maggie hoped the bronzer she'd applied before leaving the flat was going some way to reassuring people that she wasn't in fact dead. 'Any sign?'

The twenty-something shook her head. 'I'm going to send one of the runners to the hotel. She's not picking up and I can't get hold of her agent either. You're probably not going to like this but look...'

Maggie squinted at the phone screen being held in front of

her to see a picture of the presenter in question coming out of a well-known London nightclub looking worse for wear. 'Seriously?' Maggie glanced at her watch. 'We're not live for another hour or so, we'll just have to start rehearsals without her. Put her straight into the dressing room when she gets here and let me know as soon as she does.'

'Got it.'

Sometimes Maggie felt more like a glorified babysitter than a TV producer, an award-winning one at that. Almost two decades in the business and even when she thought she'd seen it all, so-called 'talent' still managed to surprise her with their behaviour. 'I'll go and have a word with Max and give him the heads-up that he might be doing this one alone.' Maggie made her way back to the make-up room, her best everything-is-under-control look firmly on her face. The one thing she didn't want anyone to do was panic. Not yet anyway.

Twenty minutes later, the one presenter they had in the building was running through rehearsals for the low-budget Saturday morning children's entertainment show Maggie had fallen into producing whilst in between other jobs. Creating rehearsed chaos on a weekly basis was exhausting and the frighteningly early starts really didn't help matters. Sitting in the dark room in the gallery, the wall of screens in front of her capturing every angle of the action taking place on the studio floor, Maggie watched as the lone presenter went from camera to camera, reading the autocue and delivering every word perfectly. He might not be very likeable in real life, but Maggie had to admit this one was pretty good.

'She's here; I've put her straight into make-up.'

Maggie turned to see another runner at the door. 'Thanks, I'll be there in a minute. How is she?'

The runner grimaced.

'That bad, huh?' Maggie stood up, grabbed her coffee and made her way back across the studio to the make-up room. She knocked on the door, opening it slowly.

The chair swivelled round to reveal a young woman curled up in a camel-coloured velour tracksuit, sunglasses on her face, hair piled up on top of her head in a messy bun. 'Hey, Mags.' The woman's voice was gravelly, her late night obviously having taken its toll.

'Susie, what happened to you?' Maggie turned the chair back round to face the mirror.

Susie took off her sunglasses. 'Nothing!' She tried to smile but her face crumpled and she started to cry.

Maggie turned to the make-up artist. 'Can you give us a minute?' she whispered. Once the door closed, Maggie stood behind the chair and looked at Susie in the mirror. 'You know I can't put you out there in this state.' She spoke softly. Years of experience had taught her that the best way to handle this sort of situation was as calmly as possible. No matter what, there was a show to be made.

'Maggie, please. I'm so sorry, I don't know what happened last night. I swear I wasn't even drinking.' Susie spoke between sobs.

Maggie reached forward and pulled out a tissue from a box on the counter, passing it to her. 'Listen, I know you love this job and you're good at it. Very good, to be honest. But you can't do it like this. So, I'm going to send you home now, say you're not well. Next week you are going to be here and deliver the best show you've ever done. And you won't ever do this again, agreed?'

The young woman nodded, her eyes falling to the sodden tissues she held in her hand.

'Good. Now, go home, sleep it off and we'll speak on

Monday.' Maggie squeezed her shoulder gently. 'I'll get someone to order you a cab.'

'Thank you,' whispered Susie. 'It won't happen again, I promise you.'

'I know it won't. Go, before anyone else sees you. And it might be a good idea to stay in tonight too.'

Susie nodded.

'I've got to go.' Maggie turned and left the room. Before she'd even closed the door, someone else was asking for her on the floor. She spoke into her headset. 'There in a moment.' By the time she got back in the studio, all hell had broken loose. People were standing on chairs and tables and the children who'd been sitting watching from the sofa when Maggie had last seen them were now screaming hysterically. 'What's going on?' Maggie surveyed the scene.

Her assistant producer looked utterly panic-stricken. 'One of the kids opened the cage backstage, the one with the pet rats in.'

Maggie instantly looked down at her feet, wondering why she'd agreed to the feature in the first place. She hated rats. She called for the floor manager, an unflappable man called Gary who'd been in the business even longer than she had. He soon appeared from behind the bank of cameras, brandishing a broom.

'Where's the guy in charge of the bloody things?' Maggie continued scanning the floor for rodents.

'He was outside having a fag, apparently,' said Gary.

'Right, get the kids out of here. We've got—' Maggie glanced at her watch again '—about half an hour before we need the floor cleared.'

Gary nodded. 'You know what they say, Maggie?'

'If you say anything about children and animals, Gary, I swear to God...'

'I wouldn't dare. We'll get it sorted.'

Maggie made her way back to the gallery, slipping into the darkness of the room. Out on the studio floor, people heard your every word, saw your every move. Not even a whisper went unnoticed. But in the gallery the madness was on the other side of a screen. Here, you could hide away from everything.

Sometimes it felt like she'd watched her own life from a gallery, seeing events unfold from afar. If only she could go back and give the younger Maggie direction, speaking gently into her ear. The problem was, younger Maggie wouldn't have listened. She thought she knew it all back then. What was it they said about the arrogance of youth? At least you were full of optimism, fearless of what lay ahead. Now she'd been knocked about by life, had the tales to prove it. She looked at the monitors, watching the carnage. The urge to walk out was strong but Maggie knew she couldn't leave everyone in the lurch. It was bad enough already and in any case the television world was a very small place. One bad job and your name was mud. She'd seen it happen to others and it wasn't a pretty sight.

Somehow, they'd got through the morning and made it to the end of the live show without too many hitches; everything that could have gone wrong had done so in rehearsals. What's more, the young presenter had really pulled it out of the bag managing to hold the show together without his usual co-host.

Maggie thought about Susie, wondered if her earlier warning would sink in, but it was out of her hands now. She'd tried to skip the usual post-show drinks in the local pub round the corner from the studio, her early start having caught up with her. All she really wanted to do was head home to her flat, put on a tracksuit and curl up on the sofa with a good book for the afternoon. But Gary was having none of it, roping her in to join the rest of the crew 'just for one drink'.

An hour and a half later and on her third gin and tonic, Maggie found herself sitting on a stool at one end of the bar listening to Lottie, one of the researchers on the show. She was pouring her heart out about her current dilemma involving her flatmate (who she clearly loved) and the flat-mate's boyfriend (who she clearly didn't) and whether it was right or not to let a friend know if you didn't like their partner.

'I'd say it depends on how close you are,' said Maggie, reaching for the open packet of crisps on the bar. 'What you don't want to do is say something uninvited. If she asks your opinion, then you should tell the truth. But otherwise, unless you think there's something seriously wrong with them, it's dangerous ground.' Maggie took a sip of her drink.

'Are you speaking from experience?' The young woman looked at Maggie, raising an eyebrow as she did so.

'At my age, everything is spoken from experience.'

'How old are you?'

'I'm forty next month.'

'Oh.'

Maggie laughed. 'You think that's old?'

'No, I just...' Lottie shifted on her seat. 'What's your story, Maggie?'

'What do you mean?' Maggie was taken aback by her question. Astute, yes. But unexpectedly direct, especially from someone so much younger than her.

'I mean just that. How long have we been doing this show together, three months? And I don't know anything about you.'

'Are you always this nosy?' Maggie smiled, amused by Lottie's approach.

'What can I say? I'm a researcher. I was born nosy.' Lottie shrugged her shoulders.

Maggie thought about it for a few seconds before speaking. There were two ways she could answer this question. The first was honestly. But that also meant going into details and she wasn't ready to do that. She'd barely been able to process what had happened to her in the last few years, let alone talk to someone she didn't really know about it. Reminding herself she now had a fair bit of gin in her system, she decided against that first option and instead, she went with the second. 'There's not much to tell, to be honest. Pretty standard, I'd say.'

'How did you get into TV?'

'By accident.'

Lottie laughed. 'Definitely standard.'

'I trained as a lawyer, actually.'

'Really?'

Maggie looked a little embarrassed. 'Yep, I know. I was all set for a life as a corporate lawyer; finished my training and everything. I started my first job and after about three months I knew I'd made a huge mistake. I just couldn't spend the rest of my working life behind a desk arguing on someone else's behalf. I had to do something else, but I didn't have a clue what that was. I was waitressing to earn some money when an opportunity came up to help on a TV show. One of the other waiters had worked in production and asked if I'd be interested. I took it, desperate to do something. Twenty years later, here we are.'

'And you've worked your way up to producing?' Lottie's eyes glistened.

Maggie nodded. 'Took a while and I've done some terrible jobs in my time but yes, that's essentially it. Persistence is key. That and a bit of luck, being in the right place at the right time. Now I can't imagine doing anything else. How about you, what are you planning after this job?'

'No idea.' Lottie took a large gulp of her drink. 'Don't get me wrong, this is fun. But I want to be a writer. I'm working on my own stuff, hoping to put on a play next year.'

'Really? What kind of play?'

'Well, I haven't written it yet. Work in progress, you know?'

Maggie looked at the young, clearly ambitious woman. For a moment she longed to swap places and be the one with her life ahead of her. The list of things she'd do differently was long. For a start, she wouldn't have spent so many years trying to save her marriage.

'Hey, are you okay?'

Maggie glanced up to see Lottie looking at her, her face concerned. 'Oh, yes, Sorry. I was miles away.'

'I think there's more to your story than you're letting on.' Lottie lowered her voice.

Maggie nodded slowly. 'There is. I'm just not ready to tell it yet.' She put her hand on Lottie's arm and squeezed it gently. 'But thank you for asking.' She quickly wiped at a tear that threatened to fall, then smiled back. 'I think I'm going to get going, I've already stayed way longer than I meant to.'

'You sure I can't get you another?'

Maggie slipped off the stool and hooked her bag over her

shoulder. 'Thanks, but honestly, I can't. I've got plans later so… see you next week?'

As she crossed the park on her way to the tube station, Maggie felt a rush of guilt. She didn't have plans. In fact, it had been months since she'd socialised at all outside work. Not seeing people was just easier for now; no need to pretend she was fine.

The September sun shone brightly. People passed, chatting and laughing. Groups sat on the grass, the debris of their long-gone picnics around them. Everyone was seemingly still in summer mode as far as Maggie could tell. She tried to look on the upside of having an evening all to herself. She could have a long bath, read her book, watch anything she wanted, eat whatever she fancied. Maybe she should go and see an old film at the cinema? Like she used to with Jack…

Her old life, the one where she was married to someone she loved and who loved her right back. In a split second she was there, remembering the way he would look at her, telling her they could get through anything.

By the time Maggie got to her front door she was holding back tears, biting her lip hard to stop them falling. She got inside as fast as she could, not wanting to bump into any of her neighbours. Before walking up the stairs to her flat, she picked up the small pile of post that had been left for her, too distraught to notice the handwritten envelope on the top. Once inside, she shut the door, dropped her bag on the floor and went into the kitchen to make herself a cup of tea. She opened the sash window and within seconds Tiger, her beloved cat, appeared on the windowsill, meowing loudly.

'Oh, don't give me that,' said Maggie, stroking him under the chin. 'You didn't miss me at all.' He began to purr as she tipped some of his food into a bowl and put it on the floor.

'There you go, you dirty stop out.' She watched as he weaved between her ankles before sniffing the food and turning his nose up. 'You have to be kidding me, that stuff cost a small fortune.' Tiger looked up at her disdainfully. She flicked the switch on the kettle, scanning the back gardens of her neighbours below as she waited for it to boil. Next door, a couple of children shrieked with delight as they bounced on a trampoline. On the other side, an elderly couple tended to their immaculate flowerbeds. Maggie had been in the flat for a few months and was yet to meet any of her neighbours properly. In their old house, she'd known the people on both sides well but here, everyone seemed to keep to themselves. Tiger nudged her arm, having jumped up onto the kitchen counter. Maggie looked at her cat, his head raised in expectation, eyes closed. She tickled him gently as the sound of water on a rolling boil filled the kitchen.

Taking her tea to the sofa, Maggie sat down, the pile of post in her lap. She discarded the flyers advertising various food delivery services and was left with a white envelope, her mother's writing on the front. She loved the fact that despite modern technology, her mother wrote to her at least once a month with news from home. She opened the letter, reading it as she slowly sipped her tea. There were the usual updates: the weather, what had been happening on the farm. She turned the page to see her mother's familiar signature. She thought of home, the old farmhouse she grew up in. She imagined her parents in the kitchen, sitting in their usual chairs at the kitchen table, a fire going in the grate. Suddenly she wanted to be back there.

Reaching for her phone, she typed out a message on the family WhatsApp she'd insisted on setting up, knowing her father would see it even if her mother didn't.

> I thought I might come back for a few days.
> Have you got any plans? x

She pressed send. A few moments later her phone pinged on the table. She picked it up and read the message on the screen.

> We can't wait to see you. Dad x

Maggie sighed. Yes, it was time to go home.

2

___

PRESENT DAY

Maggie had woken early and was on the road well before most, especially on a Sunday. Tiger had protested at being put in his cage at first but settled quickly once on the passenger seat. Maggie packed her laptop so she could stay on top of things whilst away, but she wasn't due back in the studio until Friday; it felt like a minibreak. Not that visiting her parents really counted as a minibreak but for now, familiar surroundings were all Maggie wanted.

Hitting shuffle on her current favourite playlist, a mix of folk, rock anthems and some classic hip hop thrown in for good measure, Maggie set off on the familiar route feeling better than she had done for a while. Getting out of the city was like coming up for air. As she left the suburbs and hit open motorway, she lost herself in the music, singing loudly. Every now and again Tiger would make his presence known with a paw through the cage door to get Maggie's attention. She stopped for coffee after a few hours, then again for a sandwich and a packet of crisps a few hours after that, before pushing on through the Northumberland landscape with its big skies and finally into the Scottish Borders. Catching her first sight of Eildon Hill as she made her way towards her hometown of Melrose always made her feel like a kid again. Along with her parents, she'd walked that hill almost every Sunday morning as a child and seeing the outline on the horizon never failed to transport her back to that time in an instant. Crossing the River Tweed over the old stone bridge, she wound her way up the hill on the other side and turned off the road onto the track leading to the farm. The sun was still bright, just a few clouds in the sky. The house came into view, its whitewashed walls and bright blue door looking exactly as it always did. The last of the roses hung around the door frame and as Maggie pulled the car up in front of the house, out came her mother. Dressed in her familiar uniform of jeans, an old white cotton shirt with the sleeves rolled up and a clay-splattered navy apron over the top, she wore a beaming smile on her face. A small black and white Jack Russell and an old black Labrador followed close behind.

Maggie opened the car door. 'Hey, Mum.'

'Darling, you must be exhausted. Come inside, I've just put the kettle on. All good?'

'I'm fine, Mum, thank you.' She got out and hugged her mother. 'It's so lovely to be home.'

Her mother hugged her back hard. 'We've missed you. We've been worried about you.'

'I know you have, I'm sorry. I just got busy with work.'

'Did you get my last letter?' Her mother looked at Maggie, smiling hopefully.

'I did, thank you. I love your letters, Mum. I think you might be one of the only people left who writes them.'

Her mother looked her daughter straight in the eye. 'How are you doing?'

Maggie nodded. 'Getting there.' She reached down and stroked the Labrador, now leaning against her legs. 'Hey, Juno.'

There was a loud meow from the passenger seat. Maggie went round to open the door. 'Let me bring Tiger in. He'll be happy enough once he's back in your kitchen.'

They chatted as Maggie's mother made up a tray with a pot of tea, a jug of milk and three mugs. Maggie sat watching from the old kitchen table, covered in the usual debris of books, old newspapers and a pot filled with pencils and pens. It always amused Maggie that her mother, a celebrated ceramicist and something of a local celebrity, prized that pot Maggie had made for her many years ago at school over anything she'd made herself.

Maggie's father appeared at the door, still in his farm overalls. 'Sylvie, you didn't tell me Margaret was here!'

'Michael, how many times do I have to ask you not to come in here in those boots, they're filthy!' Sylvie threw him a look.

Maggie got up and went to her father. 'Hi, Dad.'

He hugged his daughter then held her face in his hands before kissing her forehead. 'Let me get these boots off before she banishes me.' Her father rolled his eyes and laughed. 'Is that tea?'

'It is. Do you want some cake?' Sylvie reached for a battered old biscuit tin on the side.

'Ooh, yes please,' chorused father and daughter.

They sat eating fruit cake with their fingers as they caught up on Maggie's news. She told them about her latest job, including the disastrous morning she'd had the day before.

'When does that finish?' Her father spoke through a mouthful of cake.

'I've just finished so I've got a bit of a break before the next one.' Maggie wrapped her fingers around her mug. 'There's a job that's come up, it's a two-month project but I think Jack might be working on it too, so I haven't committed yet.'

'Isn't that a bit unfair?' Her mother looked at Maggie, one eyebrow raised.

Maggie sighed. 'It's just the way it goes, Mum. We always knew this would happen; we work in the same industry.'

'But why can't you take the job and Jack find something else?' Maggie's father bristled.

'Dad, honestly. It's not a problem. We'll work it out as we go. I'm not sure I'd want to take it anyway. The job involves pop stars from the nineties competing to get back into the charts with a live show every Saturday night. I swore never again after the last time I did something like that, so I'll only take it if nothing else comes up. Which it usually does, touch wood.' Maggie put her fingers on the kitchen table, feeling the familiar grooves in the wood under her fingertips. The hours they'd spent round that table as a family, the three of them but always with people coming and going. Over the years various friends, often fellow artists, had come to stay for a few days and would still be there a month or so later. At times it had felt like a commune; Maggie loved it and being an only child, she'd never had to vie for attention. There was always someone to talk to in the kitchen.

'I'm sure it will,' said her mother, reaching for Maggie's empty plate. 'Another slice?'

'If it's alright with you, I might just walk down to the river after that drive.' Maggie got up from her chair, attracting the attention of the two dogs curled up in a basket by the range cooker. She looked at them. 'You heard the word "walk", didn't you?'

'Oh, do take them, they'd love that.' Sylvie gathered the

empty mugs and walked to the sink. 'Michael, did you take that pie out of the freezer?'

'I think so, let me go and check.'

'Just to take it out and put it on the top.' Sylvie waited until he'd left the room. 'He's getting so forgetful.'

'How is he?' Maggie leant against the wall, watching her father through the large kitchen window as he crossed the yard to the barn.

'Not too bad, all things considered. But we do have to keep an eye on it. Regular check-ups, that sort of thing.'

Neither wanted to say the word 'dementia' out loud but it sat there, like an unwanted guest.

'You will tell me when it gets worse, won't you?'

'He's alright, really. As long as he's here at home with me, he's happy. There is something I need to talk to you about, though. I was going to tell you in my next letter but now you're here it makes things a bit easier.'

'What is it?' Maggie felt panic rise in her chest.

'Nothing bad, don't worry.' Her mother gestured for Maggie to sit back down. 'I got a letter recently, from an old friend of my mother's. I've not heard from her for years, not since your grandmother died.' She picked up a letter from a pile on the table and slipped open the envelope. Putting her glasses on, she unfolded the piece of paper carefully. 'It's from a woman called Allegra; they knew each other in Paris.'

Maggie looked surprised. 'I didn't know she lived in Paris. What was she doing there?'

'Studying photography at an art college – her parents lived there for a couple of years – and Allegra was her best friend there. American, very glamorous by all accounts.'

Maggie tried to imagine her grandmother as a teenager in Paris. They'd adored each other and Maggie used to love visiting her as a little girl, making the long journey south with her parents in the car to stay in her cottage by the sea. Widowed at a young age, her grandmother had brought up her mother for much of her life on her own. Maggie had been in her late teens when she'd died and still missed her dreadfully. 'What does the letter say?'

'Allegra lives in France now. She left the US and retired to Cannes after her husband died apparently. She says she's been going through some old boxes that hadn't been touched for years and found one belonging to my mother. It's got some of her photographs and her old camera. She says she thought about sending it but wondered if we might like to go and collect it instead, given it's obviously got sentimental value. She didn't want to just put it in the post without asking me first.' Maggie's mother looked up from the words on the paper, a small smile on her face. 'Obviously I can't leave your father here on his own...'

'You want me to stay here and look after him?' Maggie couldn't hide the reluctance in her voice, much to her instant embarrassment.

'No, Maggie, I want you to go and get it.'

'But surely you want to go and see her yourself, don't you?'

Her mother looked out of the window. 'I would love to, really. More than anything it would be lovely to talk to her about her time with my mother... but I really can't. As I said, your father has good days and bad days and for now I want to be here for all of them.' She sat down and reached for her daughter's hands across the table. 'Darling, all I'm suggesting is that you think about it. My mother used to talk about this woman all the time. They kept in touch practically until the day your grandmother died. Allegra always sounded so interesting, and she knew all the famous artists, everyone from

Picasso to Warhol apparently. You could stay for a few days; she's offering a room at her house so it's not going to cost much more than the flight there. Which, if you go, I would like to treat you to.'

'Mum, I haven't said I'll go yet and even if I did you don't have to do that.'

'It would be your birthday present and besides, you'd be doing me a favour. I'm not leaving your father so hearing all about it from you is the next best thing. I'd love to see some more of my mother's photographs; I don't know much about her time there. I've always regretted not asking her more about it when I had the chance.'

Maggie hadn't entertained the idea of going anywhere on holiday for a while, certainly not since her divorce. It was years since she'd had a real change of scene. But how could she just drop everything and go? What about Tiger? Then the penny dropped. Was this her mother's way of getting Maggie out of her current rut without being seen to interfere?

'Don't overthink it,' her mother said, gently, squeezing Maggie's hands.

Maggie gave her a sideways glance, a wry smile on her face. 'Don't think I'm not onto you.' She stood up, the dogs immediately at her feet, all eyes on her. 'Back in about half an hour.' Maggie kissed the top of her mother's head.

'See you in a bit. And can you just check your father hasn't forgotten to take that pie out on your way past?'

* * *

Maggie set off along the path that ran along the riverbank, both dogs walking dutifully close behind. She made her way down the familiar narrow road from the house towards the chain bridge that linked them to the Melrose side of the river. The road was lined with old oaks and thick cotton wool clouds hung low in the sky. The sun still shone but the air was beginning to cool. Maggie looked across the dark waters of the Tweed towards the triple peaks of the Eildons beyond. She headed east along the river towards one of her favourite places, a deep holding pool on the bend. Reaching the corner, Maggie made her way across the grass to the water's edge. She picked a spot on a rock overlooking the long, deep pool and sat, watching the water as it swirled and eddied. The dogs made themselves comfortable in the long grass behind her, settling down for a late afternoon snooze. Clearly the fish weren't biting; there wasn't a fisherman to be seen, not even in the shallows further upstream. She kept her eyes on the stout-coloured water, hoping to catch a glimpse of a salmon. Before long, her mind had wandered back to the last conversation she'd had with Jack just a few months before. She'd gone over it so many times in her head and still it didn't make sense.

They'd agreed to meet for a drink to toast their decree absolute. It had been Jack's suggestion and had seemed like quite a good idea at the time. After all, they'd both agreed to a divorce in the first place. Saying no would have seemed churlish. And so there they were, sitting opposite each other at a table outside a pub in Hampstead, both smiling as they raised their glasses. Hard as it was, Maggie was determined to 'do' divorce in a civilised manner.

They'd met on a TV job years before; she was an assistant producer and Jack was a cameraman. The attraction had been instant and three months later, by the end of the gig, she'd moved into his rented flat. Life went by in a blur of work, long lazy Sundays spent mostly in bed or in the pub with friends along with the occasional trip out of London to visit their families. After a couple of years, Jack proposed and Maggie was over the moon. So far, so normal.

After almost three years of marriage, on Maggie's thirty-fourth birthday, they'd been out for dinner with friends and on the walk back home Jack had raised the subject of starting a family. Despite worrying about temporarily losing an income, they decided the time was right. Nine months later, Maggie stood in their bathroom holding a pregnancy test in her hand. It had been the first time she'd been late since she'd stopped taking her contraception pills and she braced herself for the moment she'd seen in so many films, the one where she'd walk out of the bathroom and silently show him the stick, waiting for him to see the thin blue line. He would then look at her, a mix of wonder and disbelief. She'd slowly nod, then smile.

Instead, she stood alone in the bathroom, willing the test to tell her she was pregnant. It wasn't until Jack knocked gently on the door, asking if she was alright, that she realised that line wasn't going to appear, no matter how long she stood there staring at it.

Almost four years, three rounds of IVF, twenty eggs and six embryos later, there was still no baby. Barely a moment went by when Maggie wasn't thinking about getting pregnant and each time treatment failed, she felt the gap between the two of them widen. In that time, they went from talking about almost nothing else but having children to not being able to bring up the subject without arguing. Maggie wanted to keep trying; Jack wanted to stop. By this time, some of their friends had started having their own children. Life had changed so much and yet Maggie was stuck where she was, unable to move forward. Unexplained infertility, they'd been told. No matter how many times Jack tried to convince her no one was to blame, Maggie felt ashamed. Somehow, she'd failed. It was all her fault.

Their separation happened quickly. A filming job had taken Jack away from home for two weeks and, both exhausted after years of disappointment and sadness, not to mention financial stress, they realised life was less painful apart than it was together. The fight in them to see it through had gone and they both knew it.

Jack moved out shortly after and Maggie threw herself into work, accepted every invitation to go for drinks from concerned friends and for the next few months tried her best to shut out the pain of the previous few years. And she thought she was covering it up well right up until the point she went to visit her parents for her mother's birthday.

By this time, Maggie was barely sleeping. She'd lost her appetite almost completely. As they'd sat around the kitchen table on the evening she'd arrived, sitting in familiar surroundings and without the need to put on a brave face, Maggie's defences had completely crumbled. Once she started crying, she couldn't stop. She remembered her father quietly leaving the table and returning with a small whisky in a tumbler. Her mother simply held her hand across the table. Maggie had talked and they'd listened, without judgement. Later, she and her mother had walked along the river to the same spot Maggie was in now. She remembered how they'd sat on the rock, her mother telling her how much they loved her, and that Maggie mustn't lose faith in life.

'Keep going,' she'd said. 'Things will get better, I promise.'

Maggie looked down into the deep waters before her. She'd got so used to living with a feeling of sadness, like a dull ache. Some days were worse than others – passing babies in prams was always hard to bear, even now – and there were times when she'd wondered if she would ever feel truly happy again. But she'd held on to her mother's words and that sadness didn't seem to hurt quite as much as it used to.

She thought about her mother's request, realising it would be churlish to say no. Even if she had no idea who this woman was, it was in the South of France! At the very least she'd be able to see a place she'd always dreamt of. And a change was as good as a rest, as her mother always liked to remind her. Then again, what if a job came up when she was away? Turning down work wasn't something she could easily afford to do.

Maggie glimpsed a flash of silver underneath the surface. She could just make out the shape of a salmon resting near the bottom of the pool. She watched as it moved gently. Then, with a flick of its tail, it was gone.

'Keep going,' she whispered.

By the time Maggie got back to the house it was golden hour and, as ever, her parents were sitting in their usual seats in the garden overlooking the river.

'Make yourself a drink and come and join us,' said her father.

'I will,' called Maggie. 'I'm just going to grab a jumper.' She went into the kitchen, the smell of their supper wafting from the range. The table had been cleared, a pile of plates with some cutlery placed on top of their faded old linen napkins at one end. She poured herself a glass of wine from the chilled bottle of Macon Villages she found in the fridge door and grabbed her jumper from the back of the chair. Stepping outside to join them, she was hit by the familiar scent of lavender and lemon balm hanging in the air.

'How was your walk?' Her mother lifted the brim of her old straw hat.

Maggie sat on the grass between them and was soon joined by the dogs, Juno leaning against her body with his full weight as Labradors do. 'It was so lovely. There wasn't a soul to be seen down by the river.'

'See any fish?' asked her father.

'One, actually. Quite big, too. Can I do anything to help?'

'No, it's all done. Just keeping it warm until we're ready to eat. Did you have a think about running that errand for me?' Her mother looked at Maggie hopefully.

'Errand?' Her father raised his eyebrows.

'I told you, Michael. The box of my mother's things.' Sylvie smiled at him.

Maggie could tell from her mother's measured tone that she'd obviously told her father more than once.

'Oh yes, I remember.' He nodded but Maggie didn't think he remembered at all.

'Tell me about her and Allegra again, Mum?' Maggie hoped this would save her father from having to ask what she was talking about.

Sylvie took a sip of her whisky and soda. 'If I remember rightly Allegra was a beautiful American, very tall with auburn hair. My mother on the other hand was quite short with thick dark hair; apparently they made quite a pair. Spent most of their time hanging about in the best jazz clubs in town. Not that my mother's parents knew that of course.' Sylvie laughed. 'This was a time when you had all the greats playing in Paris from John Coltrane to Charlie Parker and my mother was mad about her music. I grew up on those jazz records thanks to her time in Paris.'

'Have you still got any of them?'

'Yes, they're all in the cupboard in there.' She gestured to the conservatory.

Maggie loved how her parents still listened to vinyl, oblivious to how on trend they were. 'What brought them back here?'

'I'm not entirely sure. I know they left quite suddenly because there was some unrest in the city. There were lots of protests going on at the time.'

'Student protests?' Maggie sat back on her elbows, stretching her legs out on the grass.

'No, this was a few years before the student uprising. Something to do with the Algerian war. I know she was devasted to leave. She adored Paris. Where are you going, Michael?'

'To put one of those records on. I'll turn the speaker into the garden.'

'Not too loud, darling. We don't want to upset the neighbours again,' Maggie's mother called after him. 'Last time I went out in the evening and left him alone, the neighbours on both sides messaged me to ask us what was going on. I got home to find The Allman Brothers blasting from the speakers. I don't think he realised how loud it was. They weren't cross really, just worried.' She sighed.

Maggie reached for her mother's hand. 'I'm so sorry, Mum. It must be so hard. I wish I was here more to help.'

'You being here now is enough.'

The sound of a piano, trumpet and double bass soon drifted from the house into the garden, carried on a gentle breeze.

Maggie thought of her grandmother, imagining her dashing around Paris with her friends. She'd never even been to a jazz club. She took a sip of her wine and listened to the music, wishing for adventure of her own. If only she was brave enough...

3

PARIS 1961

'*Un crème, s'il vous plait.*' The young woman looked up at the waiter, unable to keep herself from looking at him a little longer than she needed to. Thankfully her eyes were hidden by a pair of black sunglasses, shielding them from the bright Paris sunshine. He merely nodded and turned, a perfect split-second display of Parisian insouciance. Being American, she wasn't used to it. Even New York seemed like a friendlier place than here – and that was saying something.

Allegra Morgon had been in the French capital for about a week and was feeling desperately homesick. Not that she would ever admit that to her parents. As far as they were concerned she wanted them to think she was having a marvellous time, if only to make them regret their decision to send her away so suddenly. Looking back, she knew she'd been the author of her own misfortune. She'd been on her third and final warning from the headmistress at her school back in Manhattan. Deciding to skip class to go and meet her boyfriend, the one her parents had forbidden her to see,

hadn't been the best decision she'd ever made. And it definitely hadn't helped that the person who'd caught them sitting
under a tree with a half-drunk bottle of bourbon beside them
was her own mother.

What Allegra hadn't anticipated was being sent to another
country to stop her from seeing that boyfriend ever again but,
in their wisdom, that's what her parents had decided was best.
Allegra was shipped off to Paris at just eighteen years of age to
learn French at an expensive language school before she
caused them any further embarrassment. Her mother was
quite the socialite with a spotless reputation, their Upper East
Side apartment frequently filled with the great and the good
of New York City. She hadn't even had time to say goodbye to
her friends. Now here she was, sitting outside a pavement café
in the sunshine, waiting for her mid-morning coffee. Not
exactly a harsh punishment but she was homesick, none-
theless. She missed having people to talk to. Much as she'd
tried to make friends on her course at the college, she was
struggling to fit in.

The waiter returned with her coffee on a tray and put it
down on the table, replacing the ashtray with a clean one as
he did so. 'Merci,' said Allegra, giving him what she hoped was
a winning smile. He didn't even make eye contact. She sighed,
quietly amused. Being tall with long, auburn hair, she was
used to attracting attention. Realising at an early age she was
never going to blend in, she'd long ago stopped trying.
Instead, she used it to her advantage. But here in Paris, no one
seemed that bothered. She picked up her cup and watched as
people passed along the street, stopping to pick up their bread
from the boulangerie opposite or to look at the dresses in the
shop window next door. No one seemed to be in a hurry here,
not like they were back home.

A deafening screech of tyres in the road right in front of her made her jump, spilling hot coffee onto her hand. A woman – young, with thick, dark hair cut into a striking bob – stood stock-still halfway across a pedestrian crossing. The books she'd obviously been holding had fallen to the floor, the front wheel of a scooter just inches away from her legs.

'What the bloody hell do you think you're doing?' the woman shouted at the driver, her cut-glass English accent impossible to miss.

The driver got off the scooter and started shouting at her in French, waving his hands dramatically. Allegra watched as the woman started picking up the books, the man still shouting angrily. She couldn't believe he wasn't apologising or even asking if the woman he'd almost run over was alright.

Getting up from the table, Allegra started walking towards them. She addressed the man. '*Arrêtez, monsieur*... please stop shouting.' She wished she had more French words in her vocabulary.

He looked at Allegra, his face red with anger. He said something she didn't understand but she continued speaking, her tone firm. 'This wasn't her fault. You should've stopped. She was crossing the road.'

'Please, it's okay. I'm not hurt.' The woman looked at Allegra, her eyes glistening. She carried on picking the books up from the floor.

'Here, let me help you.' Allegra bent down. The man went on, his voice getting louder. 'Hold on one minute,' she whispered to the woman before standing up and turning back to the man. She towered over him. '*Monsieur, vous êtes un chauffard*.'

He gawped at her, mouth like a fish. Allegra simply held his stare.

'*Je m'en fiche!*' He shrugged. '*Pas fute-fute.*' He tapped his head as he said it, then walked back to his scooter. They watched as he rode off without so much as a backward glance.

'Thank you,' said the woman, brushing back her dark hair from her flushed face. 'What did you say to him?'

'I called him a road hog. I learnt it from a taxi driver. Here,' said Allegra, gently helping her to her feet. 'Are you okay? Do you want a glass of water? Or can I buy you a coffee? I'm just having one.' She gestured to the café on the corner.

'I think I'd better.' Her voice shook slightly.

Before they'd even sat down the waiter was back with a tray and two small glasses.

He put the glasses on the table. 'Brandy, on the house. I saw what happened.'

'*Merci*, that's really kind.' Allegra felt bad for writing him off earlier.

He smiled, then disappeared back inside.

'Sit down, take a moment.' Allegra held out her hand for the woman. 'I'm Allegra.'

'I'm Elizabeth, pleased to meet you. You're American?'

Allegra smiled. 'And you're English, right?'

'I am. Although I could understand every word he was saying. What a pig.'

Allegra laughed. 'I didn't think he was being very complimentary.'

'No, he wasn't. Honestly, you'd think I would have got the hang of it by now but crossing Paris streets never gets easier.'

'Do you live here?'

Elizabeth nodded. 'We've lived here for almost two years. My parents teach at the Sorbonne and I'm studying at art school here. I was just on my way to the bookshop by the river.' She picked up the book on the top of the pile, brushing off dirt from the cover.

'I heard someone talking about a fabulous bookshop the other day.'

'Yes, I love it. I'd rather sit and read books in there than in a classroom any day.' Elizabeth picked up her brandy and swirled it in the glass before taking a large sip, shuddering slightly. 'I was taking these back for a friend. We're always swapping books. So, what brings you to Paris?' Elizabeth fixed her with her huge eyes.

Allegra held her glass between the tips of her fingers. She was about to reply with her stock answer but something about this woman made her feel at ease. So, for the first time since being in Paris, she decided to be completely honest. 'My parents, except they didn't bring me here. I was packed off after getting kicked out of school back in New York. I don't think they knew what else to do with me. I'm just here for a year, not even that.'

Elizabeth raised one dark eyebrow. 'What did you do?'

'Nothing that bad really but I hated school over there. Mind you, it was a little extreme to send me to the other side of the world! Do you like it here?'

'It took a while to get used to it, but I love it now. How are you finding it?'

'I haven't really done much apart from walk from my apartment to the college and back so far. That's why I thought I'd come up this way, walk along the river. Get to know the city a bit.'

'Where's your apartment?'

'Just off Boulevard de Montparnasse.'

'You live in the 14th?' Elizabeth's eyes widened.

'I do. Is that bad?'

'No, it's amazing! I'd love to live there. So many great bars and clubs and you've got all the best cinemas and markets right on your doorstep.'

'I do?'

'Have you really not been out yet?' Elizabeth looked genuinely shocked.

Allegra laughed. 'I only just got here, to be fair.'

'Well, that's a terrible waste.' Elizabeth picked up her glass. 'At least I know how I can repay you now. Do you have plans tonight?'

Allegra shook her head.

'Perfect, walk with me to the bookshop now and I can introduce you to my friend. He also lives in Montparnasse, not far from you. And then later, if you like, we'll take you somewhere that'll change how you feel about Paris. Deal?'

Allegra picked up her glass and held it to Elizabeth's. In that moment, they went from strangers to friends and for the first time since she'd got there, Allegra was glad to be in Paris.

* * *

Allegra and Elizabeth walked through the narrow, cobbled streets of the Latin Quarter, past shops, bistros and bars, towards the Seine, before turning left onto Rue de la Bûcherie. There, in the corner, was a small bookshop, with several rickety-looking tables and chairs outside. People were sitting drinking coffee, or something stronger despite the relatively early hour. Most had their head in a book.

'Elizabeth!' A man with a shock of white hair shouted his greeting from the doorway of the bookshop.

'Hi, George.' She held up a book of collected poems by Sylvia Plath. 'I loved this one so much, I've read it three times over.'

He gestured at a book in the shop window. 'Have you read Ted Hughes' latest collection?'

Elizabeth pulled a face. 'Too dark for me.'

George laughed. He looked at Allegra, standing just behind. 'Who's this?'

'This is my friend Allegra. She just helped put me back together after practically getting run over.'

'Nice to meet you.' Allegra extended a hand.

'New York?' He smiled warmly at her.

'Yes, how did you know?'

'I'm from New Jersey originally.'

'This is your shop?' Allegra peered inside, the walls and shelves stacked with books from floor to ceiling. There was barely room to move. She was enchanted by what she saw.

'Go on in, look around.' George gestured for her to step inside.

'Follow me,' said Elizabeth. 'The library upstairs is one of my favourite places in the whole city.'

Allegra followed Elizabeth, past the heaving shelves and up a narrow staircase, the paint worn off the wood by the footsteps of a thousand readers and writers before them. They walked past rooms lined with more books; chairs nestled into corners wherever space allowed. Walking through a low door in the wall, they reached a room at the front of the shop overlooking the river. Allegra could see the soaring towers of the Notre-Dame Cathedral, the stained glass of the huge rose window catching the light of the sun.

Elizabeth took a seat on a bench that ran the length of the

room and put her books down beside her. She glanced at her watch. 'Etienne will be here any minute now. I said eleven; he's normally on time.'

'Who's Etienne?' Allegra was running a finger along a line of books, stopping at a biography of Steinbeck.

'We met when I first got here. I was kind of forced on him as he's at the same art school here in Paris too. His aunt also teaches at the Sorbonne and knows my parents. Anyway, we've become good friends. You will love him.'

'Boyfriend?' Allegra looked at Elizabeth, one eyebrow raised.

'No, that's Luc. You'll meet him later. You'll love him too.'

Just then, a young man walked through the low door, ducking his head as he did so. He stood up, his frame tall, his shoulders broad. 'Hey, Betty.'

'I do wish you wouldn't call me that.' They kissed on both cheeks.

'Sorry, Elizabeth.' He winked at her, then turned and extended his hand to Allegra, fixing her with his deep blue eyes. 'Hello, I'm Etienne. Pleased to meet you.'

It took a few seconds for Allegra to engage her mouth to speak. Light brown hair fell to the top of his cheekbones, his mouth wide. He wore a battered brown jacket, a faded blue shirt and jeans. A long, crumpled scarf hung loosely around his neck.

'Bonjour,' she managed, eventually.

'So, what have you got for me?' Elizabeth looked at the book in his hand.

Etienne held it up. 'I think you're going to like this one. It's by a famous French photographer, part of the surrealist crowd.' He turned to Allegra. 'She's a very talented photographer, did she tell you?'

'I wouldn't say that.' Elizabeth looked vaguely embarrassed.

'You are! You need to show your friend some of your work.'

'I'd love to see. What do you like photographing?' Allegra walked over to look at the book, now in Elizabeth's hands.

'Anything, really. People, places. But to be honest Paris is such a beautiful backdrop, it's hard to take a bad photograph in this city.'

'Anyone can take a photograph but to capture a real moment, emotion even, that takes skill, and you have it.' Etienne looked at Elizabeth, his face serious.

'Well, that's very kind of you to say so, thank you.' Elizabeth was blushing now. 'But let's change the subject, shall we? Can you believe Allegra also lives in the 14th and she's not even been to a club yet?'

'Are you serious?' Etienne turned his attention to Allegra. 'What have you been doing?'

'I've not even been here for a week.' Allegra shrugged, slightly embarrassed.

'That's no excuse. Okay, so I heard—' Etienne lowered his voice '—Dizzy is playing tonight at the Bal.'

'At the where?' Allegra looked from one to the other.

'It's the best jazz club in Paris right now and it's practically on your doorstep,' said Elizabeth.

'You have to come,' said Etienne, placing his hand gently on Allegra's arm.

She turned her face to his, his gaze so friendly and warm. It was impossible to say no. 'I'd love to, thank you.'

'Great,' he said. 'We have a plan.'

For the next hour, they sat like cats in the sun, stretched out on the benches under the bookshelves as they chatted and pored over the pages of various books. Allegra found herself drawn to the art books and Etienne talked her through some of the artists, his knowledge and passion for the subject obvious from the way he spoke about them.

'The funny thing about this guy,' said Etienne, pointing at a picture of an artist Allegra had never heard of, 'is that he was doing this kind of thing years ago. They say Warhol is exhibiting here in Paris soon.'

'Really?' Allegra had definitely heard that name before. She knew he was causing quite the stir back home in New York.

Etienne nodded. 'Yes, and he credits this guy—' Etienne tapped the page in front of Allegra '—as one of his greatest inspirations. Duchamp was making art out of everyday objects long before this lot. Where you live, in Montparnasse, is where most of the artists moved to when Montmartre got too expensive.'

She found herself watching his jaw as he spoke, forcing her concentration back to his words. Allegra moved to get a closer look at the picture. 'Is that... a urinal?'

'Yes, it was one of his most famous works. It's called *Fountain*. Confused the whole of the art world back then. He lived in New York for a while and eventually kind of retired from art. He became a chess player, a very good one at that. His wife once got so cross with him playing chess so obsessively, she glued all the pieces to the board.' Etienne laughed at the thought.

'Hey, have you seen the chess players in the park?' Elizabeth swung her legs out from underneath her, moving to the window. 'We should go. Do you play?'

Allegra shook her head. 'No, but I'm happy watching.'

'I'll teach you,' said Elizabeth. 'I'm rubbish but I love it and the only way to get better is to play.'

They gathered their things and made their way back down the stairs to the front of the shop, waving their goodbyes to George as they left. Winding their way back through the streets, Allegra chatted easily with Elizabeth and Etienne and as they strolled in the warm September sun, she didn't feel such a stranger in the city.

4

PARIS 1961

It was already past nine o'clock in the evening when Allegra found herself knocking on the door of Etienne's apartment on Rue Delambre. She'd spent much of the afternoon with him and Elizabeth, walking through the Jardin de Luxembourg. They'd stopped to watch the boats on the lake from deckchairs before moving on to see the chess players by The Orangery. It was, as both Elizabeth and Etienne had promised, an incredible sight. Every single table was taken, each one with inlaid squares making up a chessboard. The players moved their pieces in turn at lightning speed. Every now and again a player would get up and another would take their place.

'Winner stays, loser walks,' said Etienne, answering the question Allegra was just about to ask.

Before long, a small crowd had gathered around one particular table. One of the players was old, with a heavy grey beard and the other was young with long, curly dark hair. Neither took their eyes off the board at any point. At first the assembled crowd spoke in hushed tones but before long, each play was met with cheers or gasps, depending on whose side the spectators were on. Finally applause broke out as the young man offered his hand.

'Who won?' Allegra was spellbound but couldn't make out from either player's expression who was the victor.

'He did,' said Elizabeth, nodding towards the elderly gentlemen who slowly got up from his chair and shook his opponent's hand, before reaching for his walking stick and shuffling off through the crowd.

They walked on through the park heading south, past statues – including a replica of the Statue of Liberty much to Allegra's amusement – and people playing pétanque wherever space allowed.

'This might not be the grandest garden in Paris, but it's my favourite,' said Elizabeth. 'There are so many corners to it and it's just so quiet and calm, even though we're in the middle of the city.'

As they'd neared the southern edge of the park, Elizabeth had left them to walk back up to her parents' apartment, instructing Etienne to walk Allegra back to hers. As the couple made their way along the elegant tree-lined avenue towards the fountain at the end, Etienne asked Allegra about her life back home. She'd been purposefully sketchy with the details, not wishing him to know too much about her at this stage. By contrast, he'd happily talked about his family and his home in Provence, not far from Saint Tropez. Allegra had heard of it thanks to a film she'd seen a few years before starring Brigitte Bardot, but the way Etienne spoke about it made it sound like a slice of heaven. His parents were farmers – at least, that's how he described them – but they also had vineyards, selling their grapes to a local co-operative winery.

'The landscape is beautiful, unspoilt. Just fields and trees and mountains in the distance. Nothing like here,' he said, gesturing to the buildings they now passed as they walked along the narrow back streets towards Allegra's digs.

'So why are you here if you love it so much there?'

'I will go back one day but before I do, I want to learn and travel and experience the world. Isn't that why you're here too?' He turned and looked at her.

She swallowed hard. 'Yes, I guess so.' How could she possibly tell him she was only here because her parents had literally forced her? Standing in front of a man she could barely take her eyes off in a city she was falling in love with, she thought of her life back home. Even a month ago she couldn't imagine ever leaving New York. For the first time in her life, Allegra was grateful to her parents. They might have only sent her away to save face, but that morning had opened her eyes to a whole new world, and she was more than ready to embrace it.

'I think this is you?' Etienne pointed ahead at the yellow stone building on the corner.

Allegra looked up. 'Yes, I'm that one up there, on the fourth floor, second window in.' Her heart sank a little. How she wished they could carry on walking and talking.

'What are you doing now?'

'Well, I have got a bit of work to catch up on but...' She tailed off.

'How about I show you some more of the city? Maybe some paintings I think you might like?'

It was as if he'd read her mind. 'I'd love that.' Allegra smiled at him, hoping he wouldn't be able to tell how much her heart was racing. What was wrong with her?

'Perfect.' He looked at his watch. 'We have plenty of time. I think we start with a gallery just round the corner, it's a former artist's studio belonging to Antoine Bourdelle, a famous

French sculptor. They've just opened a new hall and I've been meaning to go for weeks.'

'Oh, I love sculpture,' Allegra lied.

'And then if you like we can go and see one of the greatest paintings of Paris I've ever seen in my life. It's hanging in a gallery by the river. It's about half an hour if we walk.'

Allegra nodded. 'That's sounds... nice.' She wanted to kick herself in the shins. Why was she sounding like such a drip?

For a second Etienne looked worried.

'No, I really would like to,' she said, mentally pulling herself together. 'I honestly can't think of anything I'd rather do right now. The alternative is sitting in my room up there, attempting to write an essay.' *Wishing I was with you*, she wanted to add.

His face broke into a wide smile. 'Then let's go.'

They stood side by side, gazing at a canvas painted with swirling colours – deep blue, red, yellow and green. It was almost child-like. In the centre, a naked couple lay in a boat, wrapped in each other's arms.

'I thought you said this was the greatest painting of Paris, but isn't that a gondola?' Allegra tipped her head to one side.

'Look around the couple, what else do you see?' Etienne turned to her.

She could feel his gaze on her as she looked at the painting. At first, she couldn't take her eyes off the couple in the centre of the painting but the more she looked, the more she saw. To the right of the figures in the boat she could make out the shape of the Eiffel Tower, the Notre-Dame Cathedral and another building she recognised but couldn't place. A haloed moon hung in the sky as they floated on a deep blue sea, surrounded by musicians. As the moments passed, Allegra felt calmed by the image, it's tenderness slowly revealing itself.

'Who painted it?'

'Marc Chagall. It's called *The Concert*.'

'It's beautiful,' Allegra whispered.

'They say he paints dreams.'

She knew he was looking at her as he spoke and she lifted her head to meet his gaze. Allegra closed her eyes and quickly opened them again, fearing this may all be a dream. To her relief he was still standing in front of her, now smiling.

'Are you okay?' His brow furrowed.

She wanted to kiss him but didn't dare. 'You know when I said I loved sculpture? I lied.'

Etienne laughed. 'I could tell.'

'But I love this.' She gestured to the painting in front of them. 'Can I see your paintings?'

Etienne shook his head. 'I wish you could but I'm not very good to be honest.'

'You're at art school here aren't you?'

'Yes, but I study sculpture. That's why I wanted to take you to the Musée Bourdelle.'

Allegra grimaced. 'And now I've told you I don't like it. I'm so sorry.'

'Listen, I'm happy you love this painting. We can tackle sculpture next. The sculptures we saw were quite brutal, I think. Perhaps Rodin might be more your style.'

'*The Kiss*?'

'You know it?'

'I wouldn't say I know anything about it. I just saw it in a book at school once.'

'Then I want you to see for yourself. His sculptures look

quite different in real life.' He smiled at her hopefully. 'I think you'll see it in a different way.'

'I think you might be right.'

Eventually, they left the museum and wandered slowly back down the Rue Vanneau, the late afternoon sun still warm on their faces. They chatted easily, Allegra's guard now fully down. She felt like she'd known him forever, not just a few hours.

Before long, they'd reached the corner of her apartment building.

'Okay, I'm going to leave you here, but promise you will come tonight? We will eat at mine first, then go to the club,' said Etienne.

'Yes, of course. Can I bring anything?'

He took out a pen and a small notepad from his pocket and jotted down his address, holding the lid of the pen in his mouth. He shook his head, then tore the page out of the book and handed it to her. 'No need, just come around nine.'

Allegra laughed. 'Nine o'clock? What time do we go to the club?' The idea of starting the evening so late amused her.

'It won't get going until about eleven.'

'Eleven?' Her eyes widened, wondering how on earth she was supposed to stay awake that long.

'I thought you lived in the city that never sleeps?' Etienne nudged her arm gently.

'Not in the bit I live in.' She thought of her parents' apartment, of the gilded life they led. Her mother used to tell her that money didn't buy happiness, but it gave you freedom. Allegra had never understood what that meant. The last thing she'd felt living with her parents in that enormous apartment on the Upper East Side was freedom. In fact, she'd felt trapped in a life she didn't want. They had everything and nothing.

Possessions were more important to her parents than any real emotional connection as far as Allegra could tell. She felt happier standing on the corner of this street in Paris with a man she'd only just met than she'd ever done in New York.

Allegra looked at the piece of paper in her hand to see he'd drawn her a little map.

'Just go left out of here, then cross the boulevard and walk down Rue de la Gaité. We live above the bistro next to the theatre. I'll hang this scarf—' he gestured to the one around his neck '—from the balcony so you know which one we are. Press the bell, the one with my name next to it.'

Allegra scanned the page. 'What name am I looking for?'

'Beaumont. Etienne de Beaumont.'

Allegra extended her hand. 'Nice to meet you Etienne de Beaumont, I'm Allegra Morgon.'

'Nice to meet you too, Allegra Morgon.'

He took her hand in both of his and shook it, smiling. He held it for a moment.

Allegra felt the heat rush to her cheeks. What was happening here? She'd never been so lost for words.

Later that evening, as Allegra made her way to Etienne's apartment, the piece of paper with his address clutched firmly in her hand, she looked down at her outfit and wondered for the hundredth time if she was underdressed for a jazz club. She had no idea what to wear and given her limited options had gone for the safety of black, her favourite colour. She wore slim trousers that finished just above the ankle with a soft knitted black sleeveless top and flat ballet pumps, her long hair pulled back in a loose ponytail at the base of her neck and tied with a bright red scarf. She'd applied some kohl around her eyes but had struggled to see exactly how it looked in the tiny mirror above the sink in her room.

The other girls on her floor were all dressed up for a dance being held at the college so Allegra had done her best to slip out unnoticed. She could hear them talking excitedly about the night ahead, specifically which boys would be there. It was like being back at school in New York and, frankly, she couldn't wait to escape. Walking along the street towards the main road ahead, as Etienne instructed, Allegra could feel the butterflies in her stomach building. She knew Elizabeth would be there, along with her boyfriend Luc. As she reached the bistro, tables spilling onto the street, she looked up and spotted Etienne's scarf hanging from the balcony as promised. The window doors were open and Allegra could just make out the sound of music coming from the room above. Standing on the doorstep, she took a deep breath and pulled gently at her ponytail before pushing the button next to his name. She looked up to see Elizabeth standing on the balcony, waving down at her.

'He's just coming,' called Elizabeth.

Allegra nodded and smiled, determined to hide her nerves. She listened as the sound of footsteps behind the door got closer, then waited as the lock turned. The large door opened and there was Etienne, a tea towel thrown casually over his shoulder. He gestured for her to come inside, kissing her on the cheek as she did so.

'We live so close we're practically neighbours! Follow me, everyone is here.'

Allegra followed him up the narrow wooden stairs, watching as he took two at a time. 'I feel bad that I didn't bring anything but you did tell me not to.'

Etienne waved her concern away. 'We have everything we need, come and see.'

She followed him into his apartment, a small room with

white walls and wooden rafters and double doors at one end opening onto a tiny balcony. Bookshelves lined the wall on either side and to the left stood a two-ring stove next to a sink. As Allegra walked further into the room she saw that it was L-shaped with a bed pushed up against the far end, a small hand-basin in the corner. The fireplace was filled with more books and a huge painting hung above it showing a couple floating above a town, a small red house below them. Allegra thought it must be by the same artist they'd seen earlier that day. In the middle of the room was a table, far too big for the space, covered in a red and white checked tablecloth like the ones she'd seen on the tables in the bistro downstairs. On it sat various bowls filled with bread, salad, big tomatoes and a board with cheese and charcuterie. An empty jam jar held a bunch of dried flowers and alongside sat an open bottle of red wine.

'Here, let me get you a glass.' Etienne picked up a small empty tumbler and filled it with wine.

Elizabeth came in from the balcony and crossed the small room to give Allegra a hug. 'Did you have a lovely afternoon? I had a feeling Etienne wasn't going to let you go. Did he drag you round that sculpture place he loves so much?' She laughed, winking at Etienne.

'I didn't mind it actually,' Allegra said, laughing too.

Etienne jokingly scowled at Elizabeth. 'Some people like that stuff.'

'I think you're just being polite,' said Elizabeth, reaching for Allegra's hand. 'Now, come and meet Luc.'

Just then, a man appeared from the balcony. He had blue eyes, sandy hair and a moustache, and was older than she'd expected when Elizabeth had mentioned a boyfriend. He smiled at Allegra and raised a hand in greeting. 'Hey, Allegra.

I've heard so much about you already. Mostly from him.' Luc nodded in Etienne's direction.

'Don't embarrass him, Luc,' said Elizabeth. 'Now you're here, Allegra, let's eat. I'm starving.'

They sat round the table, the warm evening breeze blowing gently into the room. As they ate and drank, Allegra was quizzed on life in America. Having not been, the others were all under the impression that New York was the coolest place on earth. She was only too happy to tell them it wasn't a patch on Paris as far as she was concerned. Then, having once again sidestepped some of the more personal questions – there was no way she wanted to own up to living in an apartment in New York at least twenty times the size of the room she was in now – Allegra asked them to tell her all about the jazz club they were going to that night.

'I'm not sure I can really put it into words but this place is a feeling,' said Etienne. 'If you get it, you will feel it here.' He held her hand and placed it gently in the middle of Allegra's chest.

She thought her heart might leap out of her ribcage right there and then.

'Everyone comes together to play, to dance and sing. It's just magical, Allegra.' Elizabeth's eyes shone as she spoke.

'Have you had enough to eat?' Etienne turned to Allegra.

'Thank you, I have.'

'More wine?' Luc reached for the bottle.

'I think I'll just finish this.' Allegra picked up her glass feeling a little light-headed. She wasn't used to drinking red wine and it had gone down rather too easily.

As if sensing how she was feeling, Etienne suggested they go to the balcony for some air. They stood side by side looking out across the crowded street, the faces of people below glowing in the light of the streetlamps.

'So, are you ready to see another side of the city?' Etienne took a cigarette from a packet in his pocket and lit it, blowing a thin line of smoke into the night air.

Allegra reached for his mouth and took the cigarette between her long fingers. She watched as the smoke curled up gently. She took a puff and handed it back to Etienne, trying not to cough as she did. It was much stronger than anything she'd ever smoked back in New York. She'd occasionally stolen some of her mother's long, thin cigarettes, which tasted of toothpaste, to have with her friends in the park after school.

'I really am,' she said, looking up into his eyes. What she really wanted to tell him was that she'd never felt like this about anyone in her life. But it was too soon, she told herself. She barely knew him even if it didn't feel like that. Allegra smiled.

'What is it?' Etienne asked.

'Nothing, really. I'm just very glad I met you.'

His eyes shone in the dim light. 'I'm glad I met you too.'

She thought for a moment he might kiss her but instead he just lowered his eyes and smiled. Maybe she was reading this all wrong and he was just being friendly? Her limbs felt light, as if she might float off the balcony at any moment. Allegra had never wished to be wrong about something more in her whole life.

5

PRESENT DAY

The drive back down to London had been miserable, with rain all the way. Maggie didn't even have Tiger to keep her company. Having decided that if she was going to go to Cannes it would be sensible to leave her cat with her parents for the time being, Maggie had left promising to let her mother know one way or the other in the next few days. As a freelancer, the thought of going abroad, even for just a short break, had been enough to give her sleepless nights.

It was dark by the time Maggie arrived back in London and once she'd got in the door, the only thing she wanted to do was collapse into bed and watch something mindless on her laptop before falling asleep. She hadn't even taken her coat off, when her phone starting pinging with messages. She rummaged in her pocket for it and looked at the screen. It was Jack's number. Tapping on it, she read the last one.

Please call me

Maggie's heart lurched in her chest. Had something

happened to him? She opened the others, all similar in their urgent tone.

> We need to talk
>
> Where are you?
>
> Can you speak?
>
> Call me pls

She'd missed three calls from him too. She looked at the screen, a faint feeling of nausea coming over her. Sitting down on the sofa, her hands shaking, she called Jack back. He answered immediately.

'Maggie?'

It still hurt to hear his voice. 'Jack, what is it?'

'Are you on your own?'

'Yes, why? Please, you're scaring me. Is everything alright?'

'I'm fine. It's just... well, I wanted you to hear this from me.'

Maggie closed her eyes slowly, bracing herself. 'Hear what?'

'I'm engaged.'

'Oh.' She couldn't hide the surprise from her voice.

'To Lottie.'

'Lottie the teenage researcher?'

'Maggie, she's not a teenager. She's twenty-five.'

'Same thing. Hang on, I saw her recently on a job.' Maggie remembered talking to her at the bar, thinking how sweet – and young – she seemed. 'She didn't mention you.'

'She didn't know we'd been together.'

'Married.' Maggie rolled her eyes.

'Okay, married. Anyway, she didn't know when she met you.'

Maggie knew it was bound to happen to one of them sooner or later. She just hadn't been expecting it so soon.

Jack spoke again, his voice quiet and low. 'She's pregnant and I wanted you to hear it from me and not from anyone else.'

Maggie felt as if someone had punched her hard in the stomach. Twice.

'Pregnant?'

'I'm so sorry, Maggie. I know this will come as a huge shock. It has to me too.'

She literally couldn't believe what she was hearing. 'But I thought...'

'Maggie, can I come and see you?'

'Absolutely not.' Maggie shook her head, trying to stop the tears.

'Please, I think it would be a good idea.'

'Jack, I don't need you to come and comfort me. It's fine.'

The truth was Maggie felt as far from fine as she ever had but the last person she wanted to see was Jack.

'We only just found out yesterday but she's told a few people already. Someone just messaged me to say congrat—' Jack stopped himself. 'I wanted to tell you first.'

'How thoughtful.' Maggie knew it was a low blow, but she couldn't help herself. After all those years of trying – and failing – to have a baby, all that heartbreak and bitter disappointment, Jack had met someone else and boom! He was a father-to-be. Maggie had never ever felt so alone.

She looked at a red wine stain on the carpet, something she'd been meaning to tackle since she'd first moved into the flat. 'I've got to go.'

'Maggie, wait...'

She hung up and sat in silence. Her phone screen faded to

darkness and Maggie let it drop to the floor then sat back and closed her eyes. She imagined Jack seeing the scan for the first time, stroking Lottie's swollen belly, making plans. She remembered how it felt standing in the tiny spare room of their old flat, the one they'd hoped would be a nursery one day. They'd even dared to buy a cot with one of the pregnancies, but it had remained in its box after yet another miscarriage. Jack eventually returned it to the shop, only to be told they couldn't provide a refund, just a credit note which they would never spend. The thought of swapping a cot for some scatter cushions and a new set of kitchen knives was too painful.

She was woken from her half-sleep by the sound of her phone ringing. Realising it was now dark outside, she looked at the time. It was nearly eleven o'clock at night. Seeing her mother's name, she realised she'd totally forgotten to let her parents know she'd got back safely, as she usually did at their insistence.

'Mum, hi.' Maggie tried to sound bright. 'I'm so sorry, I totally forgot to message you.'

'We were worried. How was the drive?'

Maggie was happy to hear her mother's voice but as much as she wanted to tell her what she'd learnt from Jack, she didn't want her parents to worry about her. 'All fine, apart from the rain.'

'You sound tired, darling.'

'I know, I fell asleep as soon as I got home. That's why I didn't message.' Maggie felt awful for lying but she could feel the tears coming back and desperately didn't want her mother to hear her cry. 'I think I'm going to just get into bed, can I call you tomorrow?'

'Yes of course, sleep well.'

'You too.'

She sat back and looked about the empty room for a moment, wondering what to do next. Everything felt heavy, from her limbs to her eyelids but nothing felt as heavy as her heart. Thinking of Jack moving on to a life they should have had together was almost unbearable. Deep down she wondered if they would ever have recovered, even if they had gone on to have children, whether their own or perhaps even adopted. Now she'd never know. It was as if someone had taken her life plan and ripped it up right in front of her eyes and there was nothing she could do about it.

* * *

The sound of her alarm clock woke Maggie with a start. She shifted and moved her leg, expecting to find the weight of her cat on the bed. It took her a moment to remember Tiger wasn't there. The memory of yesterday's phone call with Jack came crashing into her mind, leaving no room for thoughts of anything else. She sat up and checked her phone. Her head ached from the three huge glasses of wine she'd consumed in front of a terrible film she'd started watching halfway through in the hope of taking her mind off things. To her relief she hadn't responded to Jack's follow-up messages, much as she'd wanted to send him a stream of consciousness about how she felt about his news. However, she had obviously swiped right on a few matches against her better (sober) judgement. Maggie scrolled through the messages she'd received back, most of them suggesting meeting at short notice and certainly not for meaningful conversations.

Pulling on a dressing gown, Maggie padded into the sitting room and rifled through her handbag. She found a packet of paracetamol and popped two into her mouth, washing them down with some water straight from the tap in the kitchen before putting on the kettle.

She heard her phone ringing in the bedroom and went to pick it up. It was her mother.

'Just calling to check you're alright; you sounded so sad last night. Is everything okay?' Maggie couldn't help but smile; her mother really did seem to have a sixth sense. 'I know, I'm sorry. I was just really wiped out from the drive.' She tried to think of something to say to change the subject. Looking around the room, her eyes fell on the envelope on the table that she'd been given by her mother with Allegra's address and details. 'Mum, I've decided I'll go to Cannes. I'm going to book flights this morning.' She was taken aback at her own sudden decision-making but in that moment she knew she had to get away from London as fast as she could, even if it was just for a few days. She didn't want to see anyone she knew, let alone anyone Jack knew. This trip was the answer.

'Really?' Her mother sounded ecstatic. 'Let me know how much and we'll send you the money.'

'Mum, you really don't have to do that.'

'I want to. I told you, you're doing me a favour.'

'Well, if you're sure... thank you.'

'I'll let Allegra know you're coming. I've given you all the details.'

'I'll book it now.'

As soon as she was off the call, Maggie opened her laptop and searched for flights, fighting back the fat tears that threatened to fall onto the keyboard as she typed in details. Suddenly she couldn't wait to get on a plane, away from it all, as fast as she possibly could.

6

PARIS 1961

After clearing the last of the plates from the table, Allegra, Etienne, Elizabeth and Luc finished their drinks and headed back down the narrow stairs and onto the street. The pavements were still crowded with diners and drinkers as they made their way through the back streets towards the jazz club. Elizabeth and Luc walked ahead, arms around each other's shoulders, talking in the hushed tones of lovers as Allegra and Etienne walked side by side just a few paces behind.

'Look, there it is.' Etienne pointed ahead.

Allegra saw a red sign with white neon writing on the corner of the next street, the words 'Bal Blomet' signalling the entrance. She felt a buzz of excitement. 'I've never been to a jazz club before.' She watched as her new friends were greeted warmly by the doorman before he opened the door. As soon as he did so, the sound of music spilled out from inside.

'Here,' said Etienne, holding out his hand. Without thinking, she placed hers in his. 'Now whatever you do, don't let go until we make it across the room to the bar on the other side. Otherwise, I might never see you again.' He grinned at her and turned, leading her down the dark stairway. The music grew louder as they neared the bottom of the stairs. A black curtain was pulled to one side to reveal a dance floor packed with people, the band on stage at the far end. The heat of the room hit her with force, the noise unlike anything she'd ever heard before. A sea of bodies moved in all directions on the dance floor and the band played a furious tune, the smell of smoke and sweat and alcohol heavy in the air. A man playing the trumpet on stage stood at the front, his eyes squeezed tightly shut, his cheeks blown out so much Allegra thought they might just burst. Beside him, another man seemed to be wrestling with the piano keys but somehow the sounds he was making worked perfectly with that of the trumpet. At the back, a drummer sat calmly behind his kit, gently nodding his head and watching the crowd in front of him.

'Over there,' she heard Etienne call in her ear, gesturing to Elizabeth who was by a table on the far side of the club. They skirted the dance floor, occasionally moving to make room for a couple in full spin, faces flashing past with laughing, open mouths. Reaching the others, Etienne pulled out a chair for Allegra and asked her if she'd like something to drink.

'Whatever you're having,' she said, unsure what else to say. Elizabeth shouted at Allegra over the noise but Allegra couldn't hear. She just nodded and smiled, then watched as Luc took Elizabeth's hand, leading her on to the dance floor. Within a couple of beats, they were moving together to the music. Elizabeth beamed with delight as Luc spun her first one way, then the next. Allegra felt almost breathless just watching, the music pulsing through her body. It was like being in an underground world, one that felt a million miles away from the real one despite its proximity.

She felt a tap on her shoulder and looked up to see

Etienne, a small glass in his hand. She reached for it and took a sip, the taste of something strong and sweet hitting her palate. She almost choked.

'It's rum punch,' Etienne said in her ear. 'It gets better after the first, I promise.' He laughed and sat down beside her, watching the crowd move to the music. 'Isn't it amazing?'

Allegra leant towards him to speak into his ear. She could smell him, a dusky, sweet scent that felt both strange and familiar all at the same time. She closed her eyes for a moment, reminding herself that he was, still, a relative stranger. 'I've never seen anything like it.'

'Do you want to dance?' He looked at her hopefully.

Allegra shook her head. 'I don't know how.'

He reached for her hand. 'I'll show you.'

She took another gulp of her drink and swallowed hard before taking his hand and following him to the dance floor. The band had just started playing a new song, this one more frantic than the last. The dancers seemed to move more quickly as one, the throws and spins of the couples more daring than before.

Allegra gripped on to Etienne's hands as if her life depended on it. At first, she felt stiff and awkward but as Etienne guided her, holding on to one of hers and placing the other on her back to steady her, she began to relax. With each spin she grew a little braver and as the song built to its crashing last few bars, Allegra threw herself into the dance like never before. In one final move, Etienne caught her just as she felt she might lose her footing. They stood breathless as the crowd erupted in joyous applause. For a second their eyes locked, then Etienne pulled her body towards his.

'I thought you said you couldn't dance!' He laughed, brushing her hair from her shoulder.

'If it weren't for you, I'd have gone through that wall,' said Allegra, suddenly embarrassed.

Before they could catch their breath, another song started and the crowd moved to a new beat. This time, a saxophonist joined the band on stage much to the assembled crowd's delight, playing like his life depended on it. On and on they danced, united in joy as the music pounded as fast as their hearts.

* * *

It was almost four o'clock in the morning by the time Allegra and Etienne emerged back out onto the street. Having tried – and failed – to find Elizabeth and Luc as the crowd on the dance floor began to thin out after the closing bars of the last song, they'd been among the last to leave the club. The cool air hit Allegra's cheeks as she stood for a moment, adjusting to the quietness. It had obviously rained whilst they'd been inside, the road now dark and wet.

'Here,' said Etienne, putting his jacket around Allegra's shoulders.

'Thank you.' She felt suddenly awkward, the gesture unexpectedly intimate.

'I don't know about you, but I don't think I'm ready for my bed yet. How about we walk up through the park to La Dame de Fer?'

Much as Allegra didn't want the night to end, she didn't have the energy for more dancing. 'I don't think I can face another club.'

'It's not a club,' Etienne laughed. 'I mean the Eiffel Tower.'

Allegra looked nonplussed.

'We call her the Iron Lady, La Dame de Fer.'

'Ah, of course!' Allegra sighed. 'Yes, let's.'

They started walking along the quiet street, sidestepping the puddles reflecting the lights of night-time Paris. After their closeness on the dance floor, his hands holding her body to his, Allegra thought it funny to be simply walking alongside him as if nothing had happened.

'So, you didn't answer my questions earlier when I asked about your life back home. Now you know me a bit better, can I ask you again?' He looked at her in the half-light and put an unlit cigarette between his lips.

Allegra shrugged. 'I guess. What do you want to know?'

'How about why you don't want to talk about it?' He stopped to strike a match.

She looked at the cobbled stones beneath her feet. 'It's complicated.'

'Try me,' he said, his face momentarily illuminated by the small naked flame.

'Long story short, I got kicked out of school. My parents didn't know what to do with me. Or, rather, they didn't want me embarrassing them any more than I already had, so they sent me over here to study for a year.'

'Why did you get kicked out?'

'I got caught skipping school.'

Etienne looked surprised. 'That's it?'

Allegra immediately felt foolish. When he put it like that, it did seem a little amateur. 'I'd been cautioned a few times. Drinking in the park, that kind of thing.'

'Didn't you like school?'

'Hated it.'

'And will your parents come and see you whilst you're here?'

'I doubt it.' She shrugged her shoulders, hoping she at least sounded more nonchalant than she felt.

'Do you have any brothers or sisters?'

'No, it's just me. How about you?'

'Two sisters, both older. So, it must be quite intense?'

Allegra laughed. 'What do you mean?' She wasn't used to such intrusive questions.

'I mean, just you and your parents. You know, you must have all the attention, all the time. My sisters and I used to constantly fight for our parents to notice us. Still do.' He laughed.

'I've never really thought about it like that but now you say it, it is a bit like that. Nothing I did was ever good enough. Maybe that's what made me go the other way. If I disappointed them first, I could just get on with it. What about yours?'

'The opposite really. I think I could do anything and they'd be, like, well it's your life. I suspect they are hoping that I'll go back to the farm one day, perhaps take over, but I'm not sure that's what I want to do. We'll see.'

'The farm sounds so wonderful, though.'

'It really is. Let's go this way.' He pointed up ahead. 'Then we can walk through the park.' Etienne led them down another side street before turning left onto a wide tree-lined avenue. There, up ahead and simply lit by spotlights on the ground, stood the famous Paris landmark.

Allegra gasped. 'It's magnificent.'

'Shall we walk up? It's not far, it'll only take about ten minutes. But the view from right underneath is worth it.'

For a moment Allegra wondered how many other girls Etienne had walked through the park with at this impossibly romantic hour. The light was still flat but sunrise wasn't far off.

'If you're thinking I do this a lot, you're wrong.' He looked down at her, his hair falling to his cheekbones.

'Not at all,' she said, hoping the expression on her face didn't betray the fact that yet again he seemed to know exactly what she was thinking.

'I mean, I do this a lot but on my own. Paris at this time of day is so quiet and the light on the river in the morning is just beautiful. I love it.'

They walked through the park, the trees on either side silent witnesses to their conversation.

'So, what do you want to do?' Etienne asked, not for the first time.

'Now?' Allegra replied playfully.

He gently nudged her arm with his elbow. 'In life.'

'I have no idea. Girls like me aren't expected to do anything, really. Except marry someone rich and throw parties. That's what my mother did. My parents aren't interested in me actually doing something with my life other than being pretty.' Allegra caught herself. 'Oh God, I'm sorry. That sounds so conceited. It's just that's all that seems to matter to them.'

'Well, for what it's worth I think you are. But the only one who can determine what you do with your life is you, Allegra.'

'It's not as easy as that, believe me.' She stopped walking and turned to look at him. 'Why am I telling you all this? I don't even know you and I'm pouring my heart out.'

'Blame Paris.' Etienne smiled.

'Maybe it's the rum punch.'

Etienne looked at his watch. 'That was hours ago.'

Soon they neared the base of the mighty iron tower, the brownish red of the iron stark in the dawn light. Craning their necks, they stood right underneath and looked up through the structure.

'It's hard to believe anyone even had the idea to build such a thing,' said Allegra.

'You could say that about any art, really. But that's the point. People do it to communicate an idea, a message, whatever you want to call it.'

'Isn't it just to have something nice to look at?'

'Now you sound like you describe your mother. Don't you want art to make you think? Perhaps even challenge your thinking? Some art is meant to provoke you.'

Allegra thought for a moment. 'What else should I see whilst I'm here?'

Etienne grinned. 'How long have you got? I could take you to a museum every week in this city for as long as you're here and still we'll have only seen a tiny bit.'

'Let's do it then.'

For a moment he didn't reply and Allegra could have kicked herself. That had been way too forward, too presumptive.

He grinned and held out his hand for her to shake. Relieved, she took it. Etienne was clearly thrilled. 'Once a week, we will go to a museum and I will show you something by a different artist each time. But you must promise me one thing.'

'Go on.'

'You have to tell me what each piece makes you feel.'

She screwed up her nose. 'Really? What if I don't feel anything?'

'Then you explain why. No right or wrong answers but talking about it is the point of art. At least, I think it is.'

'Fine, agreed. Now that we have a deal, I want you to promise me something.'

Etienne looked at her, his head to one side, one eyebrow raised. 'Go on.'

'Whatever happens between now and the time I go back to New York, please know this has been one of the best nights of my life. And I'm going to come here again on my birthday next year, which is the 14 May by the way, at exactly this time...'

Etienne glanced at his watch and laughed. 'You mean five o'clock in the morning?'

Allegra squeezed his hand. 'I'm being serious. I'm going to come and stand here at five o'clock in the morning on the day of my birthday, just to remind myself this really happened. I want you to be here too.'

He put his hand to her face. With his thumb, he gently wiped under her eye. She saw the black smear on his skin.

'Oh no, my kohl. I must look a mess.' Allegra laughed.

He nodded. 'A very beautiful mess.' He took her hand again. 'Come with me, I want you to watch the sunrise from the best spot in Paris. It's just over on the other side of the river.'

They walked on towards the Seine and crossed the wide bridge, the cool dark waters flowing below them. The cobbled streets were all but empty, with just a few cars passing as they walked the length of a long ornamental lake. Reaching the end, Etienne put his hands on her shoulders and turned her around to face the Eiffel Tower once more. Behind it on the horizon, the sun was starting to come up, throwing a warm orange glow over the landscape in front of them. The lake was still, reflecting the light as if it were a mirror.

Allegra sighed. 'It's magical.'

Etienne reached for her hand. 'It's Paris.'

* * *

She was woken by the sound of banging on her bedroom door from the girl in the room opposite.

'What time is it?' Allegra's voice was husky, a result of the smoky club the night before.

'It's after two o'clock and you've got a visitor downstairs,' said her neighbour before turning and going back into her room, slamming the door.

Walking slowly down in her dressing gown, Allegra was met by Elizabeth who insisted she throw on some clothes and come and fill her in on all the details of the night before.

Minutes later they sat at a small round table on the pavement at the café opposite Allegra's building. Elizabeth ordered two coffees and Allegra, sunglasses firmly on, asked for a croissant.

'What do you mean, he didn't even try and kiss you?' Elizabeth's question drew glances from the couple at the next-door table.

Allegra looked embarrassed. 'There were moments when I thought he might, but he didn't.'

'Wow, he must have it bad.'

'What do you mean?' Allegra picked up the warm croissant now in front of her and tore off the end, folding it carefully into her mouth.

'Well,' said Elizabeth, 'it's obvious he really likes you.'

'Really?' Allegra couldn't help but smile. 'How can you tell?'

'For a start, he barely left your side and didn't stop talking. He's usually much quieter. And then...' She paused. 'There was the dancing.'

'Surely he loves dancing!' Allegra thought of Etienne spinning her with ease, turning her first one way, then the other. She remembered the feeling of his hand on her back and she shivered at the thought.

'He usually stays at the table. He always says he loves the music but is happy to leave the dancing to others. Last night, I thought he might never stop.' Elizabeth picked up her small coffee cup, blowing on it gently.

'By the way, where did you two go? We looked for you everywhere at the end.'

Elizabeth took a long sip of her coffee and replaced the cup slowly. 'I went back to Luc's.'

Allegra tried not to show her surprise. 'Oh, right. Do your parents know about Luc?'

'You must be joking. They'd absolutely kill me. I had to climb back into our apartment through my bedroom window this morning.'

'How old is he?'

'Twenty-two. But that's not the bit they'd worry about.' She lowered her voice. 'He's a communist.'

Allegra raised her eyebrow. 'Is that so bad?'

'He's one of the leaders of the biggest student protest groups.'

Allegra still couldn't work out what Elizabeth was saying. 'Sorry, I don't get it.'

'My parents are both lecturers at the university. They'd be furious if they knew I was hanging out with him. Honestly, I think I'd be on the next boat back to England.'

'But... why is it so bad?'

'They'd be sent home too if the board at the university ever found out I was fraternising with a communist.'

'Really?'

'Yes, really. It would be so frowned upon.'

'Is it worth the risk?' Allegra was wide eyed.

Elizabeth smiled. 'Absolutely. I love him.'

'Wow, okay.' Allegra carefully peeled off another strip of croissant and held it between her long fingers. 'Can I ask you a question?'

'Sure.'

'How do you know?'

'That I'd be sent home?'

'No, how do you know you love him.'

Elizabeth sat back and sighed. 'I just know.'

'But, like... what's the feeling?'

'You haven't been in love before?'

Allegra shook her head. 'Never.'

'What about Etienne? Do you think you could fall in love with him?'

'I'm not sure what to think. He had every opportunity to kiss me last night, but he didn't.' Allegra looked at the flaky pastry in her hand before putting it into her mouth. She chewed slowly, savouring the buttery taste.

'Well, I happen to think he's smitten.'

Allegra hoped her friend was right. She thought of the sunrise they'd watched together that morning, smiling to herself.

'Looks like you're already falling,' said Elizabeth, reaching for the leftover flakes on Allegra's plate.

7

PRESENT DAY

Maggie stepped out of the train station in Cannes and into the heat of the day. She'd landed just after ten o'clock in the morning, then taken a surprisingly quick train from Nice to Cannes. It was all so unfamiliar, she kept having to remind herself it was real rather than something she was watching on a screen. Not wishing to pitch up at her host's house too early, Maggie decided to take a walk along the famous Boulevard de la Croisette before heading for the Old Town where Allegra lived.

Walking down the street towards the Croisette, she glimpsed the glittering sea ahead. The sky was a beautiful bright turquoise blue and grand white stone hotels lined one side of the boulevard, designer shops nestled in between. Tall palm trees stood on either side of the road which was busy with cars and people. Maggie felt like she was in a film set rather than an actual place. Billboards on the beach side were plastered with iconic faces, from Marilyn Monroe to Sophia Loren adding an air of faded grandeur. Walking towards the Palais des Festivals, she glanced up at the concrete steps leading to the cinema, thinking how much smaller it looked compared with all the pictures she'd seen of various film stars walking the most famous red carpet in the world.

Reaching into her bag, she pulled out a folded piece of paper with her mother's instructions on them so she could remind herself of the name of the street she was heading to. Looking up, she saw the hill on the other side of the old port with the Gothic church and clocktower at the top as Allegra had obviously described it to her mother.

She crossed a main square, leaving the boats behind her. The streets quickly narrowed and within minutes Maggie was walking along the cobbled streets of the Old Town, a world away from the glitz of the Croisette. The colours of the buildings were different here, pale yellows and pinks sitting alongside darker ochre tones, all with painted shutters. The cafés were quieter here too, the pavement tables taken up by locals rather than tourists. Up and up Maggie went, pausing every few streets to check her bearings and make sure she was still heading towards the church at the top of the hill. Just then, the sound of bells rang out. She glanced at her watch; it was almost midday.

As if on cue her stomach rumbled, reminding her that she hadn't eaten anything since the so-called energy bar she'd managed to snaffle from someone at a stand giving them away at St Pancras train station that morning. Deciding she needed something proper in her stomach before turning up on a stranger's doorstep, she looked at the board outside the little restaurant she found herself in front of. The list of starters and mains was short but within seconds Maggie saw exactly what she wanted: steak frites with Béarnaise sauce. As she settled down at an empty table, a waitress came straight over with a basket of bread and a small jug of water. She asked Maggie if she would like a menu and Maggie replied with her order using the best French accent she could manage.

'Would you like some wine?' The waitress reverted to English, much to Maggie's embarrassment. Her accent obviously wasn't as good as she'd hoped.

'Erm, yes, but I don't know...' Maggie looked at the wine list, desperately searching for a name she recognised at the top end of the menu.

'How about a glass of the house red? It's from a vineyard near here, it's very good.' The waitress smiled.

'Yes, that would be lovely. Thank you.' Maggie handed her the menu, relieved that was over. She sat back and sighed. It all felt so surreal, to be on her own in a strange town. But if it was her way to forget what was happening back at home, Maggie had to admit it was working. She'd barely given Jack and his impending fatherhood situation a second thought that day. Just as her mind started wandering off down a rabbit hole of what ifs, the waitress came to the table with an empty tumbler and a small carafe of red wine. Maggie took a sip, the thick bramble fruit flavours hitting her taste buds like a jackhammer. She shook her head a little.

'You like it?' asked the waitress as she laid out Maggie's knife and fork.

Maggie nodded. 'Yes, it's just a little stronger than I expected.'

'It's the Mourvedre grape.' The waitress smiled. 'It's a bit of a beast.'

'I'll keep going,' Maggie replied, laughing.

She sat back and watched the world go by as she waited for her food, enjoying the sights and sounds of a new place. It took a while to arrive but from the first taste of fresh baguette, thick with cold, unsalted butter to the last bite of her steak smothered in the tangy, unctuous sauce, Maggie savoured every mouthful. Just as she was wiping the last of the Béarnaise on her plate with a few remaining salty frites, her phone rang. She looked at the screen, seeing it was a number she didn't recognise.

Maggie answered. 'Hello?'

'Bonjour, is that Maggie?'

As soon as she heard the accent, Maggie knew who it must be.

'Allegra?'

'Yes, hello! Are you okay? I was just a bit worried as I know you haven't been here before and I thought you might have got lost.'

Maggie looked at her watch. She'd been there for well over an hour. 'I'm so sorry Allegra, I didn't realise the time. I'm just round the corner, I just had to get something to eat. I hope you don't mind.'

'Not at all, I'm glad you're here. Where are you?'

'In a restaurant just below your house, I think. It's called Café Suquet.'

'Oh God, whatever you do don't drink his house red, it'll strip the enamel from your teeth.'

Maggie almost choked. 'Okay, thank you.' She didn't dare confess she'd done exactly that. 'Listen, I'll just finish here and then I'll be with you.'

'Great, see you in a bit.'

Maggie paid the bill and started up towards the church again. The streets narrowed and turned to steps as the hill grew steeper. The sun was still strong in the cloudless sky and Maggie's limbs felt heavy as she climbed. As she neared the top, the wall on her right curved round and behind it was the church, its clocktower looming high over her. On the other side stood tall, thin houses, three or four storeys high and so close together they seemed to lean into each other for support. All had small balconies around their upper-floor windows with painted shutters, most of them firmly shut. Maggie's eyes were drawn to one particular house, salmon pink in colour with pale green shutters thrown wide open. She could see clearly into the first-floor room, right through to the large floor-to-ceiling window on the other side.

A woman came out onto the balcony. She was tall, wearing a long, emerald-green kaftan, silver hair falling to her shoulders. 'Well, are you going to come in?' she called down, smiling. She waved and pointed to the door on the ground floor. 'Come on up, it's open.'

Maggie waved back and walked to the door. She pushed it open to reveal a narrow stone staircase, the door to the room on her left closed. The walls were painted the colour of egg yolk and Maggie's eyes were immediately drawn to the painting at the top of the stairs. Walking up the stairs, she glanced at the signature in the corner of the canvas.

'I sincerely hope you're Maggie,' said the woman, laughing gently.

Maggie extended her hand. 'Nice to meet you, Allegra. Is that—' Maggie gestured to the painting '—a Picasso?'

'It's a print, darling. But yes, it is. Come on in, please.'

Maggie's eyes widened as she looked at the signature in the frame. She followed the woman into the first-floor room, a simple sitting room with white wooden floorboards and two long pale blue velvet sofas on either side. Bookshelves lined one wall and every shelf was full. The low square table between the sofas was stacked with more books and ornaments and a huge bowl of roses in various pink hues spilled out of the centre, filling the air with their scent. More paintings covered the opposite wall, all different in size and style. Maggie wanted to have a proper look, but Allegra was beckoning her up another flight of stairs around the corner.

'We'll go straight up to your room. I'm sure you're desperate to get out of those clothes and into something more comfortable.'

Maggie looked down at her denim cut-offs. She'd only brought a couple of dresses and a few more T-shirts to last her whilst she was here. 'Oh no, I'm fine. Really. But thank you.'

'Well, in that case let's go straight up to the terrace. I've got some refreshments up there. You had an early start, didn't you? Your room is just in there; pop your bag down and follow me.'

Maggie did as she was told, putting her bag on the bed in what was obviously the guest room. The bed took up most of it, covered in a duvet that made it look like a giant marshmallow. There was a plain wooden dresser in one corner and a small sink in the other.

'You'll be far too hot under that; just fold it up and put it on the floor. There's a sheet underneath. And a bathroom there,' said Allegra, pointing to another door opposite. 'One more floor.'

Maggie followed her up a small wrought iron spiral staircase, wondering how on earth Allegra managed these stairs every day. She was already short of breath. They reached the top floor where a small galley kitchen sat to one side, the rest of the room taken up with a table and chairs, a small battered brown suitcase sitting in the middle of it. More paintings covered the walls; Maggie quickly scanned them to see if she recognised any other signatures before following Allegra through the kitchen to a short staircase with a tiny door at the top, so low she had to duck her head to get through it. Stepping onto the roof terrace, Maggie stood up and turned to see one of the most beautiful views she'd ever laid eyes on. She could see right across the whole town to the bay with the old port and the hills beyond. Turning to her right, she looked out over the ocean then down to the church and across the other side of the town to the mountains in the distance. Maggie looked down at the patchwork of rooftops below. 'This is incredible,' she gasped.

'I always think it looks like an impossible puzzle from here. But somehow it works,' said Allegra, following Maggie's gaze. 'And the more you look at it, the more you see. Come and take a seat.' She walked over to an L-shaped sofa shaded by a large umbrella. Behind it was another table and chairs covered by a cane roof.

'You must be so fit with those stairs.' Maggie's heart was still beating faster than usual.

Allegra sat down. 'I know, the whole house is upside down really. There is another kitchen downstairs on the first floor, but I hardly ever use it. I like to be up here.'

Maggie smiled. She took in this stranger's face, with her bright green eyes, the lines on her face indicating that she'd laughed more than she'd cried in her life. It felt strange but entirely normal to be sitting here with her and Maggie couldn't quite put her finger on it, but it felt like they'd met before.

Allegra leant forward and poured out two large glasses of iced water from a pitcher. She handed one to Maggie. 'Here you go.'

'Thank you.'

'So, Maggie, your mother mentioned you're here for a couple of days.'

'Yes, I've got to fly back the day after tomorrow for a job,' Maggie lied.

'And you haven't been to Cannes before?'

'No, never.' Maggie looked around at the view again. 'It's beautiful. How long have you been here for?'

Allegra sighed. 'Well, I can't believe it but over twenty years now.'

'Really? But you're from the States originally?'

Allegra's face hardened a little. 'Yes, I lived in New York as a kid. I moved back after the year I had with your grandmother in Paris and stayed until coming here. Were you close?'

Maggie nodded. 'I adored her.'

'You look just like her.'

'How funny, my mother says the same. She says it's the eyes.'

'Exactly. Your grandmother had the same big brown eyes. The same shape, too.' Allegra gently touched Maggie's face. 'You remind me of her. Except you're much taller than she was.'

'Mum tells me you both had a wonderful time in Paris together.'

'Yes, we did.' Allegra laughed. 'Not that our parents had a clue what we got up to. I mean, those were the days...' She tailed off.

Maggie detected a sadness in Allegra's voice. 'I don't want to be a burden to you at all and obviously I'm here to pick up the box of my grandmother's things but given I've got some time here, is there anything I can do to help if you're clearing out?'

Allegra looked at her with surprise. 'Clearing out?'

'I'm sorry, I thought that was what you were doing. I'd assumed that's why you came across her box of belongings.'

Allegra laughed. 'Darling, I'm not going anywhere. I've only got me to worry about so I'm staying right here.'

Maggie began to apologise, embarrassed that she'd made such an assumption.

'Please, it's fine. I know it might seem crazy me living here on my own, but I love Cannes and can't imagine living anywhere else, not now. I'm happy here.'

The words landed heavily. How she wished she could say the same of her home. Maggie swiftly changed the subject to avoid the tears she felt might come otherwise.

'I'd love to hear more about your time in Paris with my grandmother. Have you looked through the box?'

'I've only peeked inside. That's when I saw her old camera on the top and decided it was just too precious to put it all in the post and that perhaps your mother would like the opportunity to collect it.'

'I'm sorry you got me instead of her, but she can't leave my father.'

'I know, she explained. I'm sad not to meet her but I get to meet you.' Allegra squeezed Maggie's arm. 'I'll go and get the box.'

Maggie sprang up. 'Please, let me go. I can't watch you doing those stairs again. It'll do me good.'

Allegra laughed. 'If you insist. The box is on the table downstairs. It's a small suitcase I bought for her, but that's another story.'

8

PARIS, 1961

For the next few weeks, barely a day went by when Allegra and Etienne weren't together. As soon as classes were over, they would meet in a park or café and Etienne would take Allegra to see a different painting or piece of art in a new part of town. They walked everywhere, under the increasingly autumnal skies, talking about what they'd seen. At first, Allegra had found the whole art appreciation thing awkward but with Etienne's encouragement, she began to trust her judgement and grew in confidence when it came to conveying what she felt when looking at whatever was in front of her that day.

But there was still one thing bothering Allegra – Etienne hadn't tried to kiss her yet.

'Are you being serious? Not even once? Do you want me to say something?' Elizabeth asked Allegra one lunchtime between classes, as they lounged on the benches at the bookshop.

'God no, don't you dare...' Allegra clocked the mischievous look in Elizabeth's eyes.

Her friend laughed. 'Okay, fine. I won't, I promise. But it is rather strange. He's never really been one for taking it slowly.'

'I don't think I want to know.' Allegra couldn't help but notice the number of girls who seemed to know Etienne, waving or saying hello as they passed them on the street. Most of them had a certain look in their eye, a knowing one at that.

Elizabeth sat up and leant against the window. 'Are you coming tonight? Luc says the band playing there are one of the best around.'

Since their first visit to the jazz club, Allegra had lost count of how many times they'd been, each time quite different to the last. The music was always intoxicating, the atmosphere one of pure, united joy as people of all ages, colours and walks of life danced together until they could barely stand, spilling back out onto the street in the early hours of the morning.

Which made her classes at college something of a struggle. Allegra had already been called in to see the principal to ask why she'd been absent from class. Ms Miller, the formidable woman who ran the language school, was clearly used to dealing with young American girls who'd just arrived in Paris, miles away from their parents for the first time. She'd given Allegra a stern telling-off and warned her that any more absences would mean having to inform her parents, and neither of them wanted that, did they? Allegra had nodded – and she meant it. The one thing she really didn't want was to get kicked out and sent back home to her parents. Allegra was absolutely not ready to leave.

'I've got a test tomorrow so I'm going to have to give it a miss tonight. I'm sorry.'

Elizabeth sighed dramatically. 'Well, it obviously won't be any fun without you but if you must... what's your plan after your test tomorrow?'

'I'm meeting Etienne.'

'Of course you are.' Elizabeth winked at her friend.

Allegra blushed.

'I wish Luc wanted to see me every minute of the day, but he seems far more interested in his stupid student group.'

'I thought you liked all that stuff?'

'I do admire it, I suppose. But he's with them all the time. He's talking about organising some kind of big protest, not that I'm supposed to know about it.'

'What about?'

'No idea. I'm not allowed anywhere near his meetings. I literally get thrown out of the apartment.' Elizabeth was clearly quite offended by this.

Allegra didn't like the sound of it. 'Doesn't that bother you?'

'Kind of, but he says it's for my own protection.' Elizabeth swiftly changed the subject. 'So, what are you going to see with Etienne tomorrow?'

'I never know until we get there.'

'How romantic!' Elizabeth clapped her hands with delight.

'I do love it but to be honest if he doesn't kiss me soon...' Her words tailed off. She'd never had to make the first move before and really wasn't sure how to go about it. Surely it couldn't be that difficult. But then again, Allegra didn't want to look like a fool.

The friends parted with promises to catch up at lunchtime the following day and Allegra made her way back to her apartment, deciding to take a longer route and walk along the river before heading south. Browning leaves crunched on the pavement beneath her feet. Paris had a different feel to it now that the warmth of summer had gone but the colours of autumn suited the city beautifully. She had every intention of returning to her room to study but as she headed away from the river down Rue de Varenne back towards her apartment, she passed a stone archway with enormous iron gates. She remembered Etienne telling her about the Musée Rodin, where all the artist's works were displayed in an old Parisian mansion house where he once lived. And here she was, standing right outside it. Barely a month before, Allegra would've walked straight past. Now she wondered if she should spend just an hour in the museum, especially now she wasn't going out later.

The mansion stood at the far end of a large cobbled court-yard, manicured gardens on either side. Allegra paid for her entrance ticket at a small booth at the top of the stone steps and walked into the museum. With its polished wooden floors and high ceilings, she was surprised to find the sculptures not behind glass but right there in front of her, placed simply on plinths or tables. She made her way slowly through the rooms, each one displaying different sculptural takes on the human form in various materials – clay, stone or bronze – along with sketches and paintings hung on the wall. It took a while for Allegra to notice but the more she studied them, the more she realised some were more erotic in content than she first thought. She moved slowly through the museum, taking her time as she studied the pieces, wondering what the artist was trying to convey with each one. She stepped into the large room at the back overlooking the garden, huge windows flooding it with light. There in the middle of the room sat two stone figures the colour of milk, entwined in each other's arms. Sunbeams fell across their bodies, throwing shards of light across their smooth curves. Their almost featureless faces were turned towards each other as they kissed. Their intimacy felt impossibly real to Allegra, enough to make her feel she should almost leave them alone. She stepped back and sat on a bench just to the side of the door, wanting to commit the image to her memory so she could take it with her.

It was only when a security guard came and tapped her on the shoulder that Allegra realised the museum had all but emptied out and she was going to be among the last to leave. She walked back through the gate onto the quiet street, the sun now low in the sky. Never in her life had she taken herself off to a museum of any kind and now here she was, wanting to know more about the artist and the stories of the subjects behind his art. Most of all, she couldn't wait to talk to Etienne about it. Allegra smiled to herself as she walked back to her tiny apartment. Who even was she?

* * *

For once her student digs were quiet. Allegra was relieved; the corridor outside her room was usually like a human highway with people coming and going from each other's rooms, their voices carrying under her door. But that evening, she seemed to have the place to herself. Allegra's plan had been to have an early supper in the student dining room, then head back to her room and study for the test. But as she sat at the desk staring at a textbook, her mind was elsewhere. The clock ticked loudly and the hours passed and still Allegra couldn't focus on what was in front of her. Instead, her mind repeatedly returned to the image of the embracing couple she'd spent so long looking at that afternoon. She loved the way his hand had sat so gently on the top of her thigh, her arm wrapped around his neck as if pulling herself up towards him, urgent yet tender at the same time.

The sudden tap at her window made Allegra jump. She went over and looked down onto the street below to see Elizabeth standing there, waving her arms frantically.

Allegra opened the window and called down. 'Hey, is everything alright?'

Elizabeth looked down the street one way and then the other before calling up in a loud whisper, 'It's Luc.'

'Wait there, I'm coming down.' Allegra threw on a jumper and slipped on her shoes. When she opened the front door, Elizabeth darted inside and grabbed Allegra's arm. 'He's been arrested.' Her voice was shaking.

'Why? What's happened?'

Elizabeth wiped tears from her face. 'I don't know exactly but you know I said he was organising a protest? Well, it happened earlier this afternoon and the police came and broke it up. They took some of them away in police vans, Luc included. He sent one of his friends to come and find me to tell me. He must think I can help but the only way I can is if I tell my parents. And I just can't do that.'

'Is him protesting really so bad?'

Elizabeth sighed. 'He's an activist; he opposes the war in Algeria. That's what this is all about. If my parents knew...'

'Surely it's a good thing that he's standing up for what he believes in, isn't it?'

Elizabeth lowered her voice. 'Some of my parents' friends, other academics, have been sent home because they've been accused of sympathising with the wrong side, at least as far as the French government are concerned. They could lose their jobs, and it would all be my fault. He's been arrested before, but they've never held him for this long.'

For the first time since being in Paris, Allegra was suddenly aware of a darker side to the city. 'What can I do to help?'

'Come with me to Etienne's. Maybe he's heard something.'

Allegra nodded. 'Wait here, I'll just get my coat.'

9

PRESENT DAY

Maggie carefully climbed the stairs holding the small brown suitcase in one hand, the other firmly on the handrail. She handed it to Allegra before sitting back down next to her on the rooftop sofa. The sea breeze had picked up, a relief from the considerable heat of the earlier afternoon sun.

Allegra sat up and placed it carefully on her knees before popping it open and lifting the lid. Inside was a pile of photographs, a leather camera case on top. Allegra picked it up and handed the camera to Maggie. 'Your grandmother loved that so much.'

Maggie took it, running her fingers over the faded leather, scratched and worn. She opened it and looked inside. Given her limited knowledge of vintage cameras, she guessed this one had probably been quite smart for its day. It felt so strange to be holding something that had clearly been so precious to her beloved grandmother.

'She took some really beautiful photographs using that camera,' said Allegra over Maggie's shoulder. 'Always had such an eye.'

Maggie placed it gently on the table and peered back inside the box. The photograph on the top was face down, a pencil scrawl on the back. She looked closely. 'What does that say?' She held it by the tips of her fingers and gently lifted it out. 'Rue de la Gaité – 1961.' She looked at Allegra.

'Turn it over.'

Maggie did so. The black and white image in front of her showed two people at a table covered in a checked tablecloth in what looked like a small apartment. A man was looking straight into the camera, smiling. He had light coloured hair combed back and a small moustache. He looked in his early twenties, as far as Maggie could tell. Next to him sat a very beautiful woman, her dark hair drawn into an elegant-looking ponytail, dressed in a black sweater. She was glancing down at her plate, a fork in her hand, smiling. In the middle of the photograph was an arm holding out a bottle of red wine, half full, no label. The table was covered in plates and bowls and in the middle sat what looked like a jam jar holding a small bunch of flowers. The window behind was open and above their heads on the wall was a painting that appeared to be by Renoir from the small corner Maggie could see. She studied the photograph for a moment, then turned to Allegra.

'Is that you?'

Allegra peered at the photograph. She raised an elegant eyebrow and nodded.

'You were beautiful,' whispered Maggie.

Allegra laughed gently. 'Yes, that was taken in a man called Etienne's apartment; he lived above a restaurant in that street. That's why all the stuff on the table wouldn't look out of place in a restaurant because it was actually from the one downstairs.'

'My grandmother obviously took the photograph. Who's that?' Maggie pointed at the smiling man at the table.

'That's her boyfriend at the time, Luc.'

Maggie looked more closely. 'Was their relationship serious?'

Allegra sighed. 'Your grandmother was mad about him. He was older than her, quite a bit older in fact. Her parents didn't know about him; she didn't think they'd approve.'

'And if that's you and my grandmother took the photograph, who's this?' Maggie pointed at the arm holding the wine bottle.

Allegra paused for a moment. 'That's Etienne, my boyfriend back then. We spent hours around that little table. Luc and Etienne would make us dinner, usually something scavenged from the restaurant. Every now and again they'd manage to get their hands on some steak or chicken and we all felt terribly sophisticated and spoilt.'

Maggie handed the picture to her and took out the next photograph. Again, it was face down. She read the writing on the back, squinting to make out the faded words. '"Place Dauphine – 1961". Where's that?' Maggie turned the photograph over. The image in front of her made her gasp. There, in a faded black and white photograph, was an image of a couple kissing on a park bench. The young man in the photograph had his arm around the woman's shoulder, pulling her towards him. Her face was partly obscured but the passion between them in that stolen moment was obvious. 'That's not my grandmother, is it?' Maggie almost didn't know where to look.

'No, it's not. That's Etienne.' Allegra pointed at the man in the photograph, then moved her long finger down until it rested on the young woman in the photo. 'And that's me.'

'Wow, Allegra.' Maggie looked at her. 'What a photograph.'

'I know, she was very talented.'

'Allegra, I'm not talking about the composition. I'm talking about you in the picture. You both look like you're madly in love.'

'We were. I remember that day like it was yesterday.'

'Is there another photograph of Etienne? I want to know what he looked like. I can't see your faces properly in this one.'

'I'm sure there'll be one in there.'

Maggie handed the photograph to Allegra and picked up the next one, reading the words on the back aloud. '"Etienne – 1961".' She turned it over to see a young man standing in a cobbled street, a book in his hands. He wore small glasses and appeared to be reading the back cover, his hair hanging forward slightly as he did so. Just to the side of him was a scooter propped up by its stand and in the foreground, Maggie could make out a rack of clothes. Below was a small pile of bric-a-brac. She showed it to Allegra. 'That's him?'

The old woman nodded, her eyes glistening. 'That's him.'

'Where was this taken?'

'I'm not sure which one that was but we used to go to one of the many flea markets nearly every weekend. The first silk scarf I ever owned was bought from one of those markets. It was from Dior and had a map of Paris printed on it.' She smiled at the memory.

'Do you still have it?'

Allegra shook her head.

'Shame. It would probably be worth a fortune nowadays.' Maggie looked at the picture again, taking in the features of the young man in the centre of the shot. 'He looks lovely.'

'He really was.'

'Can I have a look at that other one again?' Maggie took

the photograph of the kissing couple from Allegra and gazed at it. 'I mean, this is almost certifiable.' She laughed.

'I've not seen that photograph for years,' said Allegra.

'Didn't my grandmother give you a copy?'

'Yes, she did… but I don't have it any more.' Allegra was quiet for a moment. 'How about we save some of these until later? We could walk down to the beach. It'll be quieter now and we could have a quick swim if you like; the water is still warm at this time of year.'

'I'd love that,' said Maggie, placing the photographs back in the case. 'I'll grab my swimming stuff.'

'I'll meet you downstairs. Wait for me on the bench outside the front door.'

Maggie went to her room and put on her bikini, throwing a T-shirt and a pair of denim shorts over the top, then went downstairs and sat in the shade on the bench opposite the front door as instructed. The gentle breeze carried the scent of the pine trees surrounding the church at the top of the hill and Maggie listened to the quiet voices of the tourists on the other side of the wall, oblivious to her as they wandered around. She looked up at the windows of the houses on either side of Allegra's, all closed with the shutters pulled across.

Maggie thought back to the young woman in the photograph, the image of the entwined couple so hopeful – and yet so sad. She was desperate to know what happened between them but didn't feel she could ask. Not yet anyway.

Allegra appeared at the door, a straw basket over her shoulder and a wide-brimmed straw hat on her head. 'We'll go this way,' she said, waving to the right. The two women made their way down the steps and through the narrow streets from the Old Town towards the port, walking along the road past the old harbour where fishing boats bobbed on the water alongside small yachts. Further out on the other side of the harbour sat a row of gleaming white superyachts, blacked-out windows adding to their arrogant appearance.

Allegra was greeted by various restaurant owners as she passed, giving each of them a wave and exchanging a few words in French.

'Do you eat out a lot?' Maggie asked.

'Not as much as I used to. I like going to the food market and seeing what's good. I've got some cheese and charcuterie for us later. I picked up some figs this morning too, they've just come in. Couldn't resist.'

Maggie's mouth watered at the thought. Fresh figs! She couldn't remember the last time she'd eaten one.

They crossed the boulevard towards the beach, the restaurants quiet with just a few tables taken in each. Allegra walked ahead down some steps to reveal a perfect sandy stretch dotted with sun loungers, most of them empty.

'Here's a good spot.' Allegra dropped her basket onto the sand and pulled out a thin hammam towel, laying it on an empty lounger. She lifted the green kaftan over her head to reveal long bronzed limbs.

Maggie peeled off her T-shirt, wishing she'd whacked on some fake tan before she'd come. By the time she'd wriggled out of her shorts, Allegra was already in the water, ducking under the waves and coming up to stand just a few metres out from the shore.

'Come straight in, it's beautiful,' called Allegra.

Maggie walked into the water, the cool temperature of the sea causing her to hold her breath for just a second. She waded in up to her waist, then closed her eyes and dived into the waves, the sound of the rush of water filling her ears. She came up to the surface and stood, treading water beside Allegra. Looking back at the beach, she could see the hill with the clocktower and pine trees rising behind the hotels along the front. 'This is glorious,' she exclaimed, taking in the view. 'How often do you swim here?'

'I used to come every day but now it's just when the sun shines and the water is calm.' Allegra smiled. 'I'm going to swim to that buoy and back.' She pointed at a small yellow buoy just a little further out. 'Are you coming?'

Maggie nodded. 'Definitely.'

They swam out, the sun on their faces. Maggie felt weightless as her limbs moved through the water, her mind free of the thoughts that had been consuming her since that phone call with Jack. When they got back to the shore, Allegra suggested they dry off on the sun loungers with a glass of wine. She beckoned a waiter over as Maggie got comfortable, stretching out on the pale green and white striped cushion as she looked out to sea.

'Bonjour, Freddie. *Deux verres de rosé, s'il vous plait.*'

'Do you know every waiter in Cannes?' said Maggie, watching as Freddie returned to the bar to get their drinks.

Allegra laughed. 'Not all of them. Freddie's a favourite though. I sometimes have a coffee here if I swim in the morning but this late in the afternoon, it's time for wine.'

Maggie's skin prickled as the sun dried the sea salt. 'What made you move to Cannes in the first place?'

'I came back after my husband died. I didn't mean to stay quite so long but I just haven't got round to leaving yet.'

'Came back?'

'When I lived in Paris, I came down to visit the area and fell in love with it.'

'Was it very different then?'

'Parts of it, but the Old Town hasn't changed that much.

Although of course, you didn't have all these hotels.' She gestured to the row of modern buildings behind them.

The waiter returned with their glasses of rosé, the chilled pale pink wine glistening in the late afternoon sunshine.

Allegra held her glass to Maggie's. '*Santé.*'

Maggie clinked her glass against Allegra's. '*Santé* and thank you for having me. I've had a lovely time already.' She took a sip, the cold wine filling her mouth with the taste of rhubarb and red cherries. 'Was it Etienne who brought you here first?'

'His parents lived about an hour from here. Probably less nowadays; the roads were terrible back then.'

'And Etienne brought you to Cannes?'

'Yes, we came down by train from Paris one weekend and spent an afternoon here before driving to his parents' house. It sounds quite mad given I'd come from a big city on the other side of the world but there was just something about Cannes... I fell in love with the place. I think my heart never left.' Allegra looked out towards the calm blue sea, then turned and smiled at Maggie. 'It just took me a while to figure that part out.'

10

PARIS 1961

Allegra and Elizabeth sat at the table at Etienne's whilst he made them all something to eat. It was around nine o'clock in the evening and there was still no word from Luc.

'I just want to know he's alright,' said Elizabeth.

'I'm sure it will all be fine,' said Allegra, hoping she sounded more confident than she felt. Her friend looked pale and tired.

Etienne joined them at the table, putting an omelette in front of each of them. 'He'll be back soon. When he does, how about we get out of Paris this weekend?'

Elizabeth sighed. 'I definitely need to get away.'

Paris had been a whirlwind since Allegra had met Elizabeth, then Etienne. Weekends had been spent exploring the city's parks and flea markets during the day and pretty much every jazz club in the 14th arrondissement at night. The idea of leaving Paris hadn't even occurred to her. 'Where would we go?'

'We could go down for the party we have at home to celebrate the end of the harvest. It's this weekend,' said Etienne.

Elizabeth's eyes widened. 'You mean go to your parents' house?'

'Yes, why not? We can take the night train from here and be in Cannes by the morning.'

'Assuming Luc's not still in prison,' said Elizabeth quietly.

Etienne filled a small tumbler with white wine and passed it to Elizabeth. 'Betty, he's not in prison. He's at the police station and they'll have to release him soon. He hasn't done anything wrong.' His voice was calm and reassuring. He poured another glass and passed it to Allegra. 'Come on, it'll be fun. And don't forget Monday is a public holiday so we could have a few days and then be back in Paris in time for class on Tuesday.'

Allegra looked at Elizabeth hopefully. 'What do you think?'

Elizabeth was about to speak when there was a knock at the front door downstairs.

'I'll go,' said Etienne.

Elizabeth and Allegra listened as first one set of footsteps went down the stairs, then soft voices and two sets came back up. The door to the apartment swung open and Etienne came back into the room.

'Look who I found downstairs.' He pointed at Luc, standing behind him.

'Did I miss much?' said Luc, a broad grin on his face.

'Luc!' Elizabeth jumped up and ran to him, throwing her arms around his neck and burying her face in his chest. 'You bloody idiot!' she said, her voice muffled by his thick coat.

'I'm sorry,' said Luc. 'I didn't mean for you to worry.'

'Are you okay? What did the police say?' said Allegra.

Luc shrugged. 'Nothing much. We just had to wait until

they let us go. The protest was peaceful so they couldn't charge us with anything.'

'What did you do to your head?' Elizabeth reached out to touch the side of his face by his hairline, a spot of dried blood just visible.

Luc brushed her hand away gently. 'I must've just knocked it. I'm not sure.'

'Can you please stop doing this? You could get seriously hurt one day.' Elizabeth looked at him with pleading eyes.

Luc shook his head. 'I wish I could but until they stop the war, we can't give up.'

A short silence followed.

Etienne handed Luc a tumbler of wine and topped up the remaining glasses. 'We were talking just before you got back and we've had an idea.'

'*You've* had an idea,' said Elizabeth, before taking a sip.

'Okay, fine.' Etienne rolled his eyes at her. 'I've had an idea.' He sat back down at the table next to Allegra. 'How about we get out of Paris and go to my parents' house this weekend?'

'The Domaine?' Luc's eyes lit up, despite the dark circles underneath them. 'I think that's a very good plan.'

Etienne glanced at the clock. 'Hey, you know what? The train leaves in an hour and a half.'

'Then why don't we just go tonight?' said Luc.

'Because my parents would kill me,' said Elizabeth, laughing.

'And I've got a test tomorrow,' added Allegra, then instantly felt a little foolish.

Luc rolled his eyes.

'I tried,' said Etienne, laughing. 'I'll go to the station

tomorrow lunchtime and see if I can book us a sleeping carriage together.'

'Together?' Allegra realised she'd said the words out loud, much to her horror.

'There are six beds in the carriage so we might have to share but it'll be quite comfortable. The motion of the train sends you to sleep, and you wake up in time to see the Mediterranean through the window,' said Etienne. 'It's the best way to get there. If we drive, we'd barely have a day before we'd have to leave again for Paris.'

'Is the train expensive?' Elizabeth wondered.

'Not if you go in the cheap carriage. It's hardly Le Train Bleu – not that I'd know, I've never been on it – but it still gets you there,' said Luc.

'What's the Train Bleu?' asked Allegra.

'The Blue Train runs from Paris to the Riviera but it's a little more luxurious. It's got a dining car and bar and is apparently the most beautiful way to travel. Maybe one day...' said Etienne wistfully.

'I've seen a painting of *The Blue Train* by Van Gogh. I saw it today,' said Allegra.

Etienne turned to her. 'You did?'

'Yes, at the Rodin Museum.'

'You went to a museum today?' said Elizabeth, her surprise obvious.

Allegra laughed. 'I know, I don't even know who I am any more. Yes, I went today. And I saw painting of a blue train going over an aqueduct. I wondered what it was and now I know. I went to see *The Kiss*.'

'You went to see *The Kiss*?' A smile played on Etienne's lips.

'I did.' She nodded, trying – and failing – to look serious.

'By yourself.'

'By myself.'

'And?' said Luc, intrigued.

'Okay, so I know I said I didn't get sculpture before, but this was different.' Allegra felt her cheeks redden. 'It's almost indecent.'

Etienne laughed. 'See? You loved it!'

Allegra knew she was blushing. 'Some of his paintings are rather... graphic.'

'He was fascinated with the body, especially the mystery of the female form,' said Etienne.

'They were very sensual.' Allegra met Etienne's gaze.

The room fell silent for just a moment before Elizabeth coughed gently, reminding Etienne and Allegra they had company. 'That's a plan then. My parents won't mind if I say I'm going with you, Allegra.'

'I guess you won't be mentioning me,' said Luc teasingly to Elizabeth.

She took his hand. 'I'm sorry, you know I can't. They wouldn't let me go if they knew.'

Allegra looked at her watch. 'I should be getting back. I've still got to do some work.'

'I'll walk you back,' said Etienne, standing up. 'You two can let yourselves out; I'll take my key.'

As they walked back along the quiet streets, Etienne told Allegra tales of all the rich and famous people from the past who'd travelled on the Blue Train, from Charlie Chaplin to Coco Chanel. When they reached her door, they stood facing each other, the glow of a streetlamp above casting them in a soft ray of light. For a moment, Allegra thought he was going to kiss her but instead, he simply took her hands and held them in his.

'Until tomorrow,' he said.

Allegra had never wanted to be kissed so much in her life; her body charged with an energy she'd never known. But something stopped her from reaching up to find his lips. She knew that once they kissed, there would be no going back – for her at least. It was infuriating and intoxicating all at the same time.

'Until tomorrow,' echoed Allegra before slipping inside the door.

* * *

The following day had passed slowly for Allegra. Having crammed until gone midnight for her test the following day, she had struggled to focus on the questions in front of her. The minute the bell had gone at the end of the lesson, she ran all the way back to her room, threw some clothes in a small holdall ready to meet Elizabeth at the bookshop as agreed. Etienne and Luc had said they would put together some food for them to take on the train and would meet them at the station at six o'clock that evening, having collected the tickets beforehand.

As she made her way across the Jardin de Luxembourg, she smiled to herself as she walked past the replica of the Statue of Liberty and left the park via the exit near the Medici fountain. This had become one of her favourite corners in all the gardens. The air was crisp and the Paris sky streaked with orange clouds as the sun made its way below the horizon.

Elizabeth was chatting to George, the owner of the bookshop, sitting on the old wooden bench just outside the door when Allegra arrived. She grinned when she spied her American friend. 'Look what George has just shown me,' said Elizabeth. She held out a book for Allegra to see. 'It's about artists in the Riviera. Picasso, Matisse, Renoir... they're all in here.'

Allegra took the book and opened it on a page showing a painting of two white birds on a balcony, an island, palm trees and the deep blue sea beyond.

'This is one of Picasso's paintings of Cannes,' said George, tapping the page. 'It's one of my favourites. Have you been before?'

Both women shook their heads. 'Never,' they said in unison.

'Well then, you are in for a treat. It's one of the most beautiful places on earth. Not quite as beautiful as Paris, of course. Safe travels.'

Elizabeth reached for Allegra's arm. 'Come on, we'd better get going. We're meeting them in half an hour.' She turned to George. 'See you next week!'

'Bye, George, see you soon,' said Allegra, waving as Elizabeth dragged her off.

They set off over the bridge towards the station, chatting excitedly about the weekend ahead.

'Were your parents alright about you coming away?' asked Allegra.

'As soon as I said it was with you and Etienne, they agreed,' said Elizabeth. 'They've never been to the south, so they were really excited for me. I guess you haven't had a chance to tell yours?'

'No, but I'll tell them all about it when I next write.' Allegra had been writing home each week since she'd arrived, as requested by her mother. In return, she'd not heard from them once. Not one letter or phone call. Allegra couldn't bring herself to tell her friend for fear of Elizabeth taking pity, which would no doubt make Allegra cry. 'I'm sure they'll be thrilled to hear about it,' she said, hoping the slight waver in her voice would go unnoticed.

'There's the station,' said Elizabeth. 'It always reminds me of Big Ben.'

Allegra looked up to see a huge clocktower ahead, the stone arches of the building adding a certain grandeur.

They walked into the hustle and bustle of the station, the sound of the gathering crowds reverberating against the steel and glass of the vast hall. A grand staircase swept up one side. 'That's the Blue Train restaurant,' said Elizabeth. 'If we were rich, we'd be dining in there before getting on our train. I told Luc we'd meet them at the bottom of the stairs.'

Etienne and Luc were already waiting, a huge basket covered with a red cloth at Etienne's feet, two baguettes poking out of the side.

'They've just called our train,' said Luc.

'We were worried you wouldn't make it.' Etienne looked at Allegra, clearly relieved.

'Well then, let's go!' Elizabeth kissed Luc firmly on the mouth, then looked around. 'Which platform are we?'

'Over there,' said Etienne. 'Platform H.'

They made their way over to the waiting train, Etienne showing their tickets to the train guard before they all got on. They walked down the carriage to find their couchette in second class, a small cabin with six bunks. They placed their bags on their bunks, Etienne and Luc taking the slightly larger bottom ones at Elizabeth and Allegra's insistence. Eventually the train left the station. Much to their relief, no other passengers had joined them in their little cabin and they opened the windows to watch Paris pass by as they left the city and headed south.

The train picnic was a triumph, Etienne having secured a

feast from the restaurant below his apartment including fresh goats' cheese from Chavignol, some aged Comté, plenty of coarse pâté with some piquant cornichons on the side and a whole block of still-cold butter. There were plump tomatoes, which Elizabeth cut into thick slices before drizzling them with olive oil and sprinkling them with salt, using an old folded-over newspaper as a makeshift platter. Luc had bought some Normandy cider, something Allegra had never tried. The earthy, bitter-sweet flavours took some getting used to but by the time she finished her second glass, Allegra declared she'd never tasted anything so delicious in her life. After they'd cleared their picnic, the four of them settled down to a few games of cards on the floor of their cabin. The gentle rocking and rhythmic sound of the train was soothing and as they rattled through the night, their destination was almost forgotten.

* * *

Allegra woke under the thin sheet on her bunk still clothed. She sat up, the bright light of the morning sun streaming in through a gap at the bottom of the blind. Her head felt heavy. She remembered the cider, the taste of apples still in her mouth. Groggily, she slipped her legs out from the bunk and climbed down the wooden ladder on to the floor. The others were all still fast asleep as far as she could make out. Deciding she needed to go and find a bathroom so she could splash her face with water, she put on her shoes and stepped out of the couchette and into the corridor, closing the door gently behind her.

The view from the window of the train took her breath away. A bright, cloudless sky sat above a patchwork of yellow stone houses topped with terracotta roofs, the blue sea of the Mediterranean beyond, just as Picasso had painted it. The closest she'd been to the coast before then was a trip to The Hamptons one year with her parents to stay with friends of theirs, but here the landscape was different. Everything was brighter, the colours deeper, the light seemingly translucent. As the landscape rolled by, she watched as it changed from small bays to sweeping ones, long stretches of sand one minute then a headland covered with pines before revealing a hidden bay with rocky outcrops on either side.

For Allegra, it was love at first sight.

* * *

As they stepped off the train into the heat of the Riviera, the four friends agreed the first thing they wanted to do was find coffee. Heading down from the station towards the Croisette, they followed Etienne who obviously knew Cannes like the back of his hand.

'We're not being picked up until after lunch so I suggest we go to a café by the harbour, then we can walk up to Le Suquet where the old part of the town is and find somewhere to eat there.' Etienne turned to Allegra. 'But before we go I want to show you something.' He took her hand. 'Follow me.'

They turned left onto the palm tree-lined boulevard and there, up ahead, was an enormous hotel topped with domes on each corner at the front of the building.

Allegra gasped. 'The Carlton!' she exclaimed.

'You know it?' said Luc, looking slightly confused.

'It's the one in *To Catch a Thief*,' said Allegra, staring at it in wonder. She turned to Etienne. 'Can we go in?'

'You have to be staying there to use the bar, but we can always go in. Then at least you can see it inside.'

They walked up the stone steps to the huge front door, the clock above the entrance telling them it was almost eleven o'clock in the morning. The tall white stone portals on either side made it look like a wedding cake and stepping into the lobby through the heavy wooden revolving door, Allegra felt like she was walking into a film set. The white marble floor and huge pink marble columns in the hotel were just as she'd remembered them.

'Can I help you, sir?' A bellboy in a grey suit and peaked cap approached Etienne almost immediately.

Etienne disarmed him with a smile, asking him in French if it was possible to have a coffee in the hotel bar.

The bellboy shook his head and spoke quickly to Etienne.

'As I thought, we can't unless we're staying here,' said Etienne, with a shrug of his shoulders.

'It doesn't matter really,' said Allegra. 'All I wanted was to see the inside.' She swept the room with her eyes.

'*Merci, monsieur*,' said the bellboy, ushering them back towards the entrance.

As the door deposited them back on to the street, Elizabeth sighed. 'What a place.'

'It is but the really beautiful part is over there.' Etienne pointed towards the other side of the bay. 'See that church on the hill? That's the real Cannes.'

They walked along the beachfront towards the harbour and as they got closer, the Old Town came into view. Allegra looked across, a clocktower at one end and a tall stone turret at the other, pine trees lying between them. The buildings lining the front of the harbour were painted in muted shades of pink and yellow with shutters of pale green and blue adding to their appealingly jumbled appearance.

They stopped at a café in the main square for a quick coffee overlooking the old port, before heading up the hill towards the church. Turning up into the twisting cobbled streets, it was a world away from the grand hotels and glamour of the Croisette. Here, the houses were tall and narrow. Pot plants sat on doorsteps and waterfalls of bougainvillea hung down from balconies, their flowers doing their best to look magnificent even though they were just past their best.

The climb was steep and by the time they reached the top, they were all a little out of breath. Allegra looked out across the bay beyond. There were two small islands just off the coast, a smaller one tucked behind a larger one, both covered with trees and dotted with pale stone buildings. Small white sailing boats crept slowly across the water. Below, the town unfolded from the old part immediately beneath them to newer buildings beyond and behind that, hills rose on the other side. Suddenly the Riviera took on a different feel for Allegra. Not just the movie version she'd long imagined but a real place, with its own sounds and scents – what was that? – and even though she was a stranger here, she felt at home.

Eventually they headed back down into the streets of Le Suquet in search of something to eat. It didn't take them long to be tempted into one of the small restaurants on Etienne's recommendation. Taking one of the tables outside, the waiter soon returned with water and a carafe of rosé wine for the table. The menu was on the board and between them they ordered pretty much everything on it, from fresh fish cooked in butter to steak frites, bouillabaisse and ratatouille. Afterwards, they shared a plate of cheese and drank more strong coffee to fortify themselves for the next part of their trip, the drive to Etienne's parents' house.

The journey was around an hour and one of Etienne's sisters, Camille, had offered to come and collect them. They walked to the arranged meeting point in front of one of the modern hotels on the beachfront on the other side of the old port and waited. The beach was almost empty, the tourists long gone.

'Have I got time to put my toes in the water?' asked Allegra.

'Sure,' said Etienne. 'I'll wait here. She should be arriving any minute.'

'I'll come with you,' said Elizabeth. 'Here, hold this for me,' she said, handing her bag to Luc.

Elizabeth and Allegra went down a small flight of stone steps and took off their shoes, crossing the soft golden sand barefoot to the water's edge. The first feel of the Mediterranean Sea on Allegra's skin made her laugh out loud in delight. If she hadn't been about to get into a car she would have happily walked right into the water there and then. She reached for Elizabeth's hand and they stood for a moment, looking out to sea.

'Thank you, Elizabeth.'

'What for?' said Elizabeth.

'For crossing that road. If you hadn't, we'd have never met and I wouldn't be standing here, with my feet in the sand. I'm so happy I could burst.'

'You do realise you're in love, don't you?' Elizabeth grinned knowingly.

Allegra looked back at the boys standing at the top of the steps. Etienne was waving to her, signalling for them to come back. She waved at Etienne, then winked at Elizabeth. 'Maybe.'

11

PRESENT DAY

'Dad, it's Maggie.'

'Darling! How are you? Hang on, let me get your mother.' There was a pause, then Maggie heard her father call out, 'Sylvie, Margaret's on the phone.'

'I do wish you wouldn't call her that.'

Maggie heard her mother's voice in the background.

'Put her on speakerphone so I can hear her. Maggie, how are you?'

'Hey, Mum. It's beautiful here.' Maggie was sitting on the roof terrace at the house, a cold glass of water in her hand. The sun was still warm and the breeze had dropped to a mere whisper.

'How's Allegra?' asked her mother.

'She's wonderful, just as beautiful as you'd said. So glamorous,' Maggie whispered, not wanting Allegra to hear her talking about her. 'We went to the beach earlier. I swam in the Med!' Maggie laughed. 'And the Old Town where she lives is so gorgeous, I'll send you some pictures after this.'

'Have you had a look through the box that belonged to my mother?' said Sylvie.

'Just a few photographs so far. And her camera, of course. It's like opening a box of chocolates, I don't want to eat them all at once. Did Granny ever talk about someone called Luc?'

There was a short silence.

'What's wrong?' asked Maggie.

'She only mentioned him once that I can remember. Allegra will know better than me, to be honest. You should ask her.'

'And there's another photograph of Allegra with her boyfriend at the time, Etienne.'

Maggie's mother sighed. 'I remember that name. Wasn't he one of your grandmother's best friends in Paris?'

'Yes, I think so. Allegra and Etienne were obviously crazy about each other.'

'How do you know?'

'One of the photos in the box is of them. Granny took the picture. It's the most amazing shot.' Maggie reached for her book, the photo tucked carefully in the pages, and looked at it again. The kiss had such a sense of urgency about it, as if nothing else mattered in the world – for them, at least. It must have lasted just a few seconds all those years ago and yet here it was, captured in a faded image forever. She tucked it back in.

'I'd love to know more about their time together in Paris. My mother never really talked about it. Ask Allegra and then you can fill us in when you get back,' said her mother.

'How's Tiger doing?' Maggie asked, feeling slightly guilty for having left him for so long.

'Oh, he's living the life of Riley,' said her father.

'You're mad about him, don't deny it, Michael,' said her mother.

'Well, look after yourselves and Tiger, obviously. Give him a cuddle from me and I'll be back at the weekend to get him.'

'When do you leave?' asked her mother.

'Day after tomorrow.'

'It seems a shame not to stay a bit longer if you're enjoying it,' said her father.

'I know, but it was always going to be a quick visit, with work and everything. Still, I'm so glad I came. It's just beautiful here.'

Maggie said her farewells, promising her parents to send them a few photos from her visit and sat back on the wide cushions, watching as the sun slowly made its way down behind the hills on the other side of the bay. She couldn't get the photograph out of her head. She took a deep breath and let out a long, heavy sigh. Divorced before hitting forty hadn't been the plan yet here she was. And she certainly hadn't been kissed by someone like that. Had she missed her chance?

'Maggie, are you there?'

Allegra's voice came up the stairs, bringing Maggie back to the present. She appeared at the doorway, dressed in a long, flowing pink kaftan painted with exotic orange birds, her silver hair pulled back into a ponytail and a chilled martini glass in each hand. She gave one of the glasses to Maggie and sat down beside her on the sofa, tucking her tanned legs beneath her. 'Did I hear you call your parents?'

Maggie took the glass from Allegra. 'Thanks, yes I did. They said to say hello and thank you again.' She took a sip of the martini, the force of the spirit hitting her palate like a lightning bolt. 'Wow, you don't mess around,' Maggie said, almost choking.

Allegra picked up the cocktail stick from her glass, pulling one of the olives from it with her perfect American teeth. She ate it slowly, then took a sip of hers. 'Crisp, clear and cold, like a martini should be.'

'My parents would love to know more about your time in Paris with my grandmother; they said she didn't talk about it much.'

'We'll come to that, but I want to know more about you first. What do you do back home?'

Maggie took another sip, on second taste not nearly as shocking. 'I work in television. I'm a producer now but I've done pretty much every job going over the years.'

'Do you love it?'

'Mostly, I do. But I needed a break, so this trip came at a really good time.'

'Why, what's going on?' Allegra looked at Maggie, clearly not wanting her to escape the question.

'It's just been non-stop for a while and the nature of the job is fairly stressful.'

'Did you always want to work in television?'

Maggie shook her head. 'I started out as a lawyer but then panicked at being in an office for the rest of my working life, so I bailed. I kind of fell into television but I loved it and never left. I'm still not sure if that was a good thing or not.' She could feel the effects of the drink working on her like a truth drug.

'Well, that depends. I think if you do what you love, then that counts as success more than material gains ever could.'

'Sort of, but happiness doesn't pay the mortgage.' Maggie laughed.

'True, but money doesn't buy you happiness either.' Allegra winked at Maggie. 'You married?'

'Not any more. I was but we split up a few years ago. He's

with someone else now. And they're having a baby.' Maggie looked at her glass, resolving to never drink another martini again.

'That sounds like that's tough for you. I'm sorry.' Allegra sighed.

'Thank you,' said Maggie, forgetting the resolution she'd just made. It felt good to have said the words out loud.

'So, what happened?'

'It's a long story.'

Allegra's reached for Maggie's hand. 'Darling, I've got all the time in the world.'

Maggie told Allegra how she'd met Jack on a production, how she'd loved him, been so sure he was the one. She told her about the years of trying to conceive, of fertility treatments and failed IVF attempts, the heartbreak and pain of those years taking its toll on their relationship. When she recalled the moment Jack had told her he was to become a father with someone else so soon after their relationship ended, fat tears rolled slowly down her cheek.

'I am so sorry,' said Allegra softly, still holding Maggie's hand. 'That's a terrible thing to have to go through. No wonder your heart is broken.'

'Was it that obvious?'

'When you get to my age you can spot it quite easily. I knew you were keeping it to yourself. Much better to talk about it, I find.'

'I blame your cocktails,' said Maggie, laughing through her tears.

'I'm going to fix us another.' Allegra reached for Maggie's empty glass then returned a few moments later, a martini in each hand. 'This is our last, then we'll have some food. No more than two of these, ever. Even Dorothy Parker knew that.'

* * *

The two women talked until the first stars appeared, then went down to the kitchen on the top floor to pick at the platter of charcuterie and cheese Allegra had put together. Afterwards, as they sipped mint tea back on the roof, they took out the box of photographs they had taken back up with them.

Picking up the pictures at the top, Maggie reached in to look at some they hadn't seen. She read the scribbled writing on the back of the photo in her hand out loud. '"Provence, 1961".' Turning it over, she saw a photograph of Luc, Etienne and Allegra sitting at a long table laden with food, under the shade of a tree. Luc was smiling at the camera at the forefront of the picture and behind him, Etienne and Allegra were looking at each other.

Allegra peered closely at it. 'That was taken at the end of harvest, at the harvest feast which was held in one of Etienne's parents' vineyards, not far from the house. All the families who they made wine with at the co-operative came.'

Maggie looked closely at the picture. 'It looks like something out of a film. You obviously only have eyes for each other there.'

'We did. But then,' Allegra sighed, 'everything changed when we got back to Paris.'

'What happened?'

Allegra paused, then spoke softly. 'I haven't talked about this for so long.'

'Much better to talk about it, I find.' Maggie looked at Allegra knowingly.

'Touché, darling.'

12

PROVENCE 1961

Etienne's sister, Camille, had come to collect them as arranged and after exchanging hugs all round, they climbed into the pale blue, slightly battered Citroën DS and set off. They soon left the town behind, heading inland before turning west and into the countryside. Allegra watched through the window as they passed fields of green and gold, the leaves on the vines shimmering in the gentle breeze under a cloudless cerulean sky. Etienne pointed out hilltop villages as they made their way along the increasingly winding country roads towards the house. The drive to the house took longer than expected; the poor state of the roads combined with the number of trucks slowly rumbling along with the last of the grapes meant progress was slow. Not that they cared a jot; it was an adventure and the four friends were in high spirits.

Etienne's family vineyard sat on the slopes of the hills to the west of the bay and as they swept through open iron gates into the drive lined with tall cypress and old olive trees, the car took them right through the middle of the vineyard towards the front of the house.

'Is everything in now?' Etienne asked Camille, looking out at the vines as they passed.

'Almost,' said Camille. 'There's still another parcel of vines to go over on the other side for the late harvest wine. It's not been an easy vintage this year. The yield is pretty small compared with last year, but the quality is looking good.'

Allegra glanced across at Etienne's sister as she drove, all blonde hair and brown skin, dirt under her fingernails. She obviously spent much of her time outside in the vineyard, thought Allegra, thinking how far removed that was from her own life. At least, the one she used to have back with her parents in New York. Everything there had to appear to be perfect. It was a world away from this – and Allegra knew where she'd rather be. *This* was perfect.

Allegra peered out of the window as the house came into view, apricot-coloured stone with light blue shutters, the shade of chestnut trees throwing a pattern of dappled sunlight across the front of it. The house was sizeable but not grand; welcoming rather than overwhelming.

An army of dogs came running out to greet them, barking wildly. A woman, small and blonde, followed behind them. She had the same defined cheekbones and striking eyes as her son's. Etienne greeted her with a hug, and she looked utterly delighted to see him.

'*Ma mère*,' said Etienne, 'you know Luc and Elizabeth and...' Etienne turned to Allegra.

Etienne's mother extended her hands and took Allegra's in hers. 'You must be Allegra. We've heard so much about you. I'm Agnès, so pleased to meet you.' She smiled warmly, kissing her three times on the cheeks before greeting the others in the same way.

A man appeared at the door. Like his son, he too was tall,

with thick dark hair, a weathered face and a wide smile, wearing an old tatty blue jacket and round horn-rimmed glasses. 'Too late to help us pick grapes but here in time for the party!' he said, grinning at the assembled party.

'Papa!' called Etienne. They hugged each other and spoke quickly in French; Allegra couldn't understand a word. He turned to her to explain. 'I'm just apologising for not being here to help this year. It's the first time I've missed a harvest because of starting school in Paris.'

Etienne's father extended his hand to Allegra. 'Hello, I am Nicolas. We are very happy to meet you.' He kissed her three times just as Agnès had done, then turned his attention to Luc and Elizabeth.

Allegra took in the view below the house, over the vine-yards and beyond the heavily wooded hillsides to the deep blue sea just visible in the distance. The smell in the air was earthy, almost herbal and everything was bathed in soft sunlight. She pinched herself to make sure she wasn't dreaming.

'Come inside and Etienne can show you all to your rooms,' said Agnès. She led the way, the dogs following her close behind. They walked through a stone portico, the front door open, into a reception room with a huge flagstone floor. A round wooden table sat in the middle and on it was a large cream vase holding a spray of pink roses, their scent filling the room. The pale walls were covered in paintings of landscapes and still lives. To the left was an enormous fireplace, the remains of an old fire sitting in the grate, cream-coloured candles of varying sizes dotted about the hearth.

A stone staircase sat to the right up to a landing that ran the length of the room and the party followed Etienne up the stairs, dispersing into different rooms as instructed by their host. Allegra and Elizabeth were shown into theirs, a large room with twin beds covered in matching quilted paisley bedcovers and two tall windows overlooking the garden at the back of the house. A free-standing bath sat in front of a small stone fireplace, a pale grey and blue woven rug on the dark wooden floor. A ceramic jug stood on the dresser to one side holding yet more roses, this time cream and peach in colour.

Allegra went straight to the window and looked out over the garden, a neat hedge-lined square with beds full of flowers still in bloom despite the time of year. On either side were orchards of fruit trees and beyond the garden, an olive grove stretched beyond until it dropped away out of sight.

'Isn't it beautiful?' said Elizabeth, sitting down on one of the beds. 'Shall I take this one?'

'Sure.' Allegra nodded without looking, unable to take her eyes from the view in front of her.

'Are you coming down?' Etienne's voice called from the other side of the door.

'Coming!' called Elizabeth. 'Allegra, you ready?'

They made their way downstairs, then followed Etienne through the wooden-beamed kitchen where Agnès and another older woman were busy tending to an enormous stock pot on the stove, the smell of something deliciously slow-cooked in the air, to the back of the house and into the garden. A long table sat under the shade of two chestnut trees, on it a tray with a jug of fresh lemonade and four glasses.

Etienne poured them all a drink. 'Okay, if you're happy, we'll go and help my father down in the vineyard where we're having the party tonight. Drink this first, it's a bit of a walk.'

They set off back down the drive, then took a path off the road into a gently sloping vineyard. The vines were still thick with leaves of green and gold but the bunches of grapes were few and far between. They followed Etienne along the top of the vineyard to a stone hut with a small clearing in front of it where a group of men, including Nicolas, were setting up a long line of trestle tables and putting out chairs.

'Hey, Papa!' called out Etienne.

'Good, you are here.' His father waved. 'I need you to help us set the tables; all the crockery and cloths are in there,' he said, pointing to the hut.

The four friends set to work, laying it as instructed, three long tables each set for forty people.

'So do you host the party for everyone each year?' asked Allegra, still not quite sure how it all worked despite Etienne explaining it on more than one occasion.

'We usually do because we have the largest vineyard and this spot, with the hut, is where it's always been held ever since I can remember. But there are eight other families in the co-operative, so we basically share the winery in the town. We'd love to have our own winery one day but this is how my father wants to do it for now.'

'And building your own winery is expensive, I guess,' said Luc.

'Exactly,' said Etienne. 'Anyway, I'm not here to help that much now.'

'Did they mind you leaving?' asked Allegra, watching as Etienne set out the wine glasses.

Etienne shook his head. 'Not really. They knew how much I wanted to go to Paris and anyway, Camille is the one who'll likely take over running the vineyard eventually. She practically does so now, not that my father will admit it,' he whispered. 'I am very lucky. Not all my friends have parents who are so...' He searched for the right word.

'Supportive?' suggested Elizabeth.

'Understanding.' Etienne smiled. 'It's why I've got to make a success of art school, so they can see it was the right thing for me to do.'

Allegra clocked the trace of guilt in his voice. 'And what about your other sister?'

Etienne stopped what he was doing for a moment. 'Isabelle is married to another winemaker. They have their own winery not far from here just on the other side of the hill.'

'Will she be here this evening?' asked Allegra.

'No,' said Etienne quickly.

Allegra waited for him to expand, but he said nothing more.

'Oh, that's such a shame. I'd love to meet her.'

'Another time, maybe. Once we finish this we can go back to the house and see if we can start bringing some of the food down.' Etienne didn't elaborate on his oldest sister's absence but Allegra sensed there was more to it than he was letting on.

More people arrived carrying platters laden with crudités and charcuterie, bottles of wine and baskets of baguettes, most greeting Etienne with hugs or kisses.

'It's like the biggest extended family I've ever seen,' said Allegra to Elizabeth as they laid folded napkins on top of the plates on the table.

'It really is, isn't it?' Elizabeth laughed. 'I don't think I would have left all this for Paris.'

'I know, same. But I guess maybe it's different when you live here. The grass is always greener, as they say.'

'Shall we walk back up to the house?' said Luc, coming up behind Elizabeth, kissing the side of her head.

'I wouldn't mind grabbing a jumper for later; apparently it's going to get chilly,' said Elizabeth.

'I'll keep you warm, don't you worry,' said Luc, wrapping his arms around her.

As Allegra watched the two of them she wondered, yet again, why Etienne hadn't so much as tried to kiss her. She'd imagined it so many times, both in her waking moments and even in her dreams. The wait was becoming almost impossible to bear. She looked over at Etienne, standing in the shade of an old oak tree, deep in conversation with a much older couple. The old man had one hand on Etienne's shoulder, laughing. She thought back to the time, just weeks before, when she'd first laid eyes on him as he'd walked into the book-shop. She remembered how he'd had to stoop and duck his head to get into the room. Now, she almost couldn't imagine her life before she met him. Her world had seemed so much smaller before he came along and now nothing made her happier than being with him.

'Penny for them?' said Elizabeth, making Allegra jump a little.

'Sorry?' Allegra looked confused.

'For your thoughts. Although seeing where you're looking, I'm not sure I want to know.' Elizabeth gently nudged her friend and grinned.

Allegra dropped her gaze to the floor. Was it that obvious? 'I was just...'

'I'm kidding,' said Elizabeth, laughing. 'Listen, we're going to walk back up.'

'I'll just finish this table. See you back there.' As Elizabeth and Luc headed off into the vines hand in hand, Allegra couldn't help but feel a little jealous.

Etienne, still with the older couple, waved her over.

Allegra put down the last of the napkins and went to join them.

'I'd like you to meet Pascal and his wife, Eve,' said Etienne. 'They own the vineyard just below here. They've been making wine longer than anyone else in this area.'

The couple smiled at Allegra, their eyes bright in their gloriously wrinkled faces.

'They don't speak any English unfortunately.' Etienne turned and spoke to them in French and the woman said something back that made them all laugh.

'I'm not sure I want to translate what she just said to me,' said Etienne.

'Go on,' said Allegra, bracing herself.

Etienne looked at Allegra, his eyes holding her gaze. 'She says I am a very lucky man. You are far too beautiful for me.'

Allegra put her hand on the woman's arm. '*Je suis d'accord, merci.*'

The couple laughed again, louder this time.

Etienne gasped in mock horror. 'I think your French is getting a little too good. Shall we go up to the house and see what else we can bring down?'

They bid their farewells, Etienne promising his father he'd return within the hour, and made their way through the vines back up to the road. The sun was low, thin wisps of orange and pink streaking the sky.

'It's just beautiful here. It must be hard to leave,' said Allegra.

Etienne nodded his head slowly. 'When I'm back here I do wonder why I left. It would be easy to stay. Well, not easy. Making wine might seem romantic but most of the time it's hard work. You are at nature's mercy.' He paused for a moment. 'But I needed to give Paris a try and my aunt, the one who teaches at the Sorbonne, really encouraged my parents to let me go. That's why I must do my best to make a success of it.' He stopped and picked at a leaf on the vine. 'You know what this is?'

'A leaf?' said Allegra, shrugging.

'Very good,' said Etienne, laughing. 'It's Tibouren, a black grape. Quite rare but one of the best for making rosé.' He pointed at the leaf on the vine. 'Look at the indentation here; the shape is quite unusual.'

Allegra looked at the row of vines on the other side. 'Is that the same?'

'Yes, but just down at the bottom here—' he led her along to the end of the row towards another block of vines on the other side of the path '—is something really special. It's Syrah and these vines are almost one hundred years old. They don't produce many bunches when they're as old as this one but what they do usually makes good wine. Really concentrated.'

'How about these ones here, what are they?' Allegra pointed at another row of small vines close to the ground.

'That's Grenache, it's what most of our wine is made from. You can tell by the waxy leaf.' He pulled one from the vine and gave it to Allegra.

She held it in her hand, feeling the texture with the tips of her fingers. 'What will we be drinking tonight?'

'To be honest, no one ever really knows. People bring all sorts of bottles to share. Some are very good, others not so much,' said Etienne, grimacing. 'But when the food is good and you've got the right people around the table, it doesn't really matter. You'll see. Come on, we'd better get going or we're going to be late.' He reached for her hand and pulled her along behind him as they ran through the vines, laughing as they went.

Back at the house, the kitchen was a hive of activity. The long table was covered in huge pots filled with lamb stew, steam coming through the thick cloths placed over the top of them. At one end, Agnès sat behind a mound of sliced toma-toes and the smell of sautéed garlic filled the room. Another woman was putting cheeses onto plates whilst another cut baguettes into slices, tossing the pieces into woven baskets.

'Thank goodness!' cried Agnès. 'I thought your father would be back by now.'

'We've just finished setting up; he'll be back soon.' Etienne picked up an apple from a bowl on the side and was about to take a bite when he stopped and offered it to Allegra. She took it from him and rubbed it on the sleeve of her blouse. 'Thank you.'

'We need to start getting all this down to the vineyard,' said his mother.

'No problem, we can do it. Where are Luc and Elizabeth?' Etienne asked Allegra.

'They should be back here by now; they left before we did.' She suddenly worried she'd blown their cover. Judging by the look on their faces when they'd left, it didn't look like they were in too much of a hurry to get anywhere but away from everyone else.

'Well, we can make a start now,' said Etienne. 'Which car should we take?'

'Is Camille back?' Agnès looked at Etienne, hopefully.

'No, she said she was going to the winery.'

Agnès sighed. 'She's as bad as your father. She'd live in that place if she could.'

'I think they'd both prefer to live in a vineyard,' said Etienne.

His mother laughed. 'I think you are right. Take René instead, we can put this on the trailer.'

Allegra looked around, wondering who René might be.

She'd met so many people already; it was going to be impossible to remember all their names.

'I'll go and get him,' said Etienne.

'What can I do to help?' asked Allegra.

Agnès pointed at the chopping board on the table, her slicing knife still in her hand. 'Thank you, *chérie*. Could you just chop some more garlic? We'll need it for the dressing.'

'Of course,' said Allegra, marvelling at the sheer volume of garlic used in seemingly every dish on the table.

'And after, if you can just get two bottles of the olive oil from the larder, we'll take that down too,' said Agnès.

Allegra glanced at the old woman next to her, bony fingers dicing the fat cloves with such speed and accuracy despite having a conversation with the woman on her other side. She picked up a knife and started chopping, aware that she must look like she'd never actually held a knife before. The pile of chopped garlic next to the old woman grew twice as fast as the one beside Allegra. Still, she liked sitting and listening to the women as they chatted and laughed at each other's jokes, even though she had no idea what they were saying.

Suddenly there was a roar at the door, the smell of engines overriding that of the garlic. Allegra looked up to see Etienne sitting atop a small red tractor.

'That's René?' asked Allegra.

Agnès laughed. 'Yes, that is René. It belonged to Nicolas' grandfather. Still going strong.'

One of the other women said something in French and the others all laughed.

'She said it looks like your Prince Charming needs to work on his mode of transport for you,' said Agnès, translating the joke.

Allegra felt herself blushing.

Etienne walked into the kitchen, leaving the tractor running. 'What shall we take?'

His mother pointed at the pots on the table. 'That can all go now, and we can bring down anything else. Just put it all on the table in the hut when you get there.'

Together, Etienne and Allegra loaded up as much of the food on the trailer as they could, securing it with rope to keep everything from moving about. Etienne climbed up onto the driver's seat and helped pull Allegra up beside him. Then, once his mother had shooed the dogs out of the way, they set off down the drive towards the vineyard, feast in tow.

* * *

By the time Allegra and Etienne got there, guests had started arriving and the table was soon laden with even more plates of cheeses and pâtés, bowls of salads and numerous bottles of wine as more and more people joined the celebration. Lanterns hung from the branches of the trees and lined the long tables, and as the natural light started to fade the lanterns cast their soft yellow glow on the crowd gathered below. Bottles of wine were uncorked and poured into small glass tumblers as people took their places and once everyone was seated, the huge pots of stew were brought out onto the tables and distributed from one end. Numerous toasts to the grape harvest were made – the '*vendange*' as Allegra worked out it was called – each one greeted with great cheers from everyone, young and old.

'Is it always like this?' asked Allegra, as Etienne filled her glass with more rosé, dark in colour. It tasted of wild strawberries. 'It's like the best party I've ever been to. Do you remember when you told me how I'd feel when we were back in Paris, the first time you took me to the Bal?'

'The jazz club?' said Etienne. He put down the bottle. 'Of course I do.'

'You said I would feel it here.' She placed her hand on his chest and looked straight into his eyes, feeling the strong beat of his heart.

'And do you?'

Allegra nodded, holding his gaze.

'You two, over here!' Elizabeth pointed her camera at them.

Allegra went to move her hand from Etienne's chest, but he put his hand over hers and held it there. He looked at her, as if saying a thousand words that only she could understand.

Elizabeth came and sat opposite them. 'Caught on film,' she said, reaching for her glass. She drained it, then picked up Luc's glass.

'Hey, easy,' said Luc, taking it from Elizabeth.

She scowled at him, before taking a piece of bread from a basket on the table. She picked at it, rolling pieces of dough into a ball before popping them into her mouth.

Allegra wondered what had gone on between them. They'd seemed inseparable just a few hours before. She reached across the table and squeezed her friend's arm. 'Hey, come with me to find somewhere to, you know—' she lowered her voice '—pee.'

'Sure,' said Elizabeth, dropping her bread back on to her plate.

'Back in a minute,' said Allegra to Etienne, before getting up and joining Elizabeth on the other side of the table.

As soon as they were out of earshot, Allegra asked if everything was alright.

Elizabeth shook her head. 'I've done something really stupid, Allegra.'

Allegra grabbed her hand. 'What's happened?'

'What do you think happened?'

Allegra's eyes widened. 'You didn't...'

'Sleep with him? No, worse.' Elizabeth put her face in her hands. 'I told him I loved him.'

'But that's great! Isn't it?'

'Not if they don't say it back, it isn't.'

Allegra tried to think of something positive to say. 'Obviously you just caught him off guard. He's clearly mad about you.'

'It seems not as mad about me as I thought he was. And now I feel foolish. I think I'd rather he'd just pretended. Instead, there was a long, unbearable silence after I'd said it.'

'But isn't that better than saying it if you don't mean it?' said Allegra.

'I guess, but right now I'm so embarrassed. I feel like such an idiot.' Elizabeth wiped an angry tear from her face.

Allegra wrapped her arms around her friend and squeezed her tight. 'If he doesn't love you then he's a fool.'

'What do I do now?' Elizabeth glanced over at the table. 'He's talking to Etienne as if nothing happened. Obviously, it doesn't bother him one bit.'

Allegra held her friend by the shoulders, forcing her to look back at her. 'You need to tell him how you feel.'

'Is that what you would do?'

'I think so. But this isn't about me, it's about you. And I don't think you should let this fester. If it's a deal-breaker you need to tell him.'

Elizabeth nodded. 'You're right. But I was so sure he loved me too. It hadn't occurred to me that he wouldn't say it back.'

Allegra felt both sad and cross for her friend. Elizabeth was so open and honest as a person. Allegra knew she'd never put her feelings on the line like that, for fear of them not being reciprocated. Perhaps that's why she'd always kept things to herself, whoever she'd been romantically involved with. Not that she would even call her relationships romantic – until now. She wiped the tears from Elizabeth's face. 'Listen, I know you're heartbroken, but this is what we're going to do. We're going to go and dance, and you are going to absolutely be yourself and have a good time. Okay?' She took Elizabeth's hand, and they went to join the small crowd dancing in the moonlight as the band played.

It was a moment Allegra was to be reminded of years later, when she'd all but forgotten about it. One that, as it turned out, was to change her life in a way she would never have imagined. It was also the night, under a harvest moon, that Etienne kissed her for the first time.

13

PRESENT DAY

'He kissed you that night?' Maggie still held the photograph in her hands. 'Finally!'

'Right?' said Allegra, winking at Maggie.

They both laughed.

'I just hope it was worth the wait.'

'It was the most romantic kiss of my whole life, under that tree—' she pointed at the old oak in the photo '—after everyone had gone home. We'd stayed to help clear up, loading up all the pots and plates onto the trailer. I remember because driving back to the house in the dark on a tractor is not an experience you forget easily. I was quite terrified.'

'Forget the tractor ride, I want to know about the kiss.'

Allegra smiled at the memory. 'Well, I don't think I was the first girl he'd kissed, put it that way. But yes, it was very special.'

'Did Luc and my grandmother make it up?'

Allegra sipped the last of her tea before putting the cup on the table. 'Yes, they did eventually. The trip back to Paris on the train was a little strained, I seem to remember. She still wasn't really speaking to him; awkward when you're sharing a cabin on a long train journey.'

'So, what happened when you got back to Paris?'

Allegra thought for a moment. 'Do you know about the riots that took place that year?'

'Not really,' said Maggie, a little embarrassed.

'Long before the student uprising there were lots of demonstrations in Paris over the war in Algeria. In fact, Algerians were under curfew in Paris, not allowed on the streets after dark. Just after we got back to Paris from Provence there was a huge protest in the city against the curfew and the war. It started as a peaceful protest but people got killed, not that we really knew how bad it was at the time. But the city felt different. Unsettled, you know? We'd been so carefree before, literally thinking about nothing but ourselves and the lives we were living. One night, about a week after that protest, Luc disappeared again. We all assumed that, like before, he'd been rounded up with the other protesting students and would be home in the morning. But he didn't come home the next day, or the next. Your grandmother was absolutely devastated. I remember sitting with her in the bookshop endlessly trying to distract her. We went for long walks in all our favourite parks but ultimately, there was nothing we could do but hope for his return. And, of course, she couldn't tell her parents about it because they didn't know about Luc in the first place and with his political views... she was convinced it wasn't safe to tell them.'

Maggie pulled her cardigan around her shoulders. The air was still warm, but the breeze had picked up. 'Please tell me he came back.'

'He did, eventually. But before he did, your grandmother and her parents went back to England.'

'Why did they have to leave?'

'They got a knock on the door from someone at the university telling them they had to go, immediately. It was all to do with being seen as sympathising with the wrong side as far as those in power were concerned. Her parents were, quite understandably, anti-war along with several other academics at the university. Elizabeth wrote to me and said she'd told them about Luc but by then it was too late. They were on a boat back home the next day.'

'I can't believe I've never heard anything about this,' said Maggie, shaking her head slowly. 'Did you see each other again after she left Paris?'

Allegra looked at Maggie, her eyes pooling with tears. 'No, but we kept in touch by letter for years.'

They both sat in silence for a moment. The clocktower struck loudly, eleven times.

Maggie realised they'd been talking for hours and yet it felt like five minutes. She was tired but wanted to know more. 'Can I ask what happened after that? With you and Etienne. Only if you want to tell me, of course.'

Allegra nodded. 'Yes, but I think we need another glass for that.'

'I'll go and get us one,' said Maggie, picking up the empty mugs. 'What would you like? And please don't say a martini. I don't know how to make one and if I have another, God knows what else I might tell you.'

Allegra laughed gently. 'How about a glass of red wine? There should be an open bottle on the side by the oven; I opened it last night.'

'Back in a moment,' said Maggie, heading for the stairs. She went back into the galley kitchen and started opening cupboards in her search for some wine glasses. She found endless spices and oils, jars of chutney and jams, packets of rice and pasta but no glassware. Heading into the small sitting room, she saw a shelf at one end lined with wine glasses of various size. As she went to reach for some, a framed drawing on the wall just to the left of the shelf caught her eye. It looked very similar to something she'd seen before, a line drawing of a woman's figure, but she couldn't quite place it. It appeared to show a woman standing, taking a robe off over her head. With no more than a handful of lines, the artist had captured the movement of the human body so precisely. Maggie stared at it, thinking how familiar it seemed. She peered closely in the corners, looking for a signature or some initials so she could work out who the artist might be but there wasn't anything as far as she could tell.

When Maggie returned upstairs she found Allegra sitting just as she had left her, her eyes closed. Maggie coughed gently.

Allegra opened them immediately and smiled.

'I'm sorry, I didn't want to make you jump.' She handed Allegra her glass of wine and sat back down on the sofa next to her. 'Are you warm enough? Can I get you a blanket or something?'

'I'm fine, thank you. I was lost in thought, really. It's funny how talking about these things brings back all the emotions as if it were yesterday. I haven't thought about Luc for such a long time. I think about your grandmother a lot, obviously. We were such good friends. We were together such a short time but back then it felt like forever. She changed everything for me. If she hadn't crossed that road that day and nearly got run over, I wouldn't have met her. I'd have been stuck with a bunch of people I'd been trying to escape from. And, of course, I wouldn't have met Etienne.'

'And we wouldn't be here.'

They clinked their glasses.

'Can I ask who that drawing is by, the one downstairs by the shelf where I got the wine glasses? I recognise it,' said Maggie, hoping she didn't sound too pretentious – or stupid.

'Rodin,' said Allegra, as if it was the most normal thing in the world.

Maggie practically choked on her wine. 'Are you serious? As well as the Picasso?'

Allegra laughed gently. 'I already told you, that one's a print.'

'From Etienne?'

'No, from Picasso.'

'Stop it,' said Maggie. She too was laughing now. 'How? When?'

'I'll get to that bit. But first, I need to tell you what happened next.'

14

PARIS 1961

Allegra sat on a green bench in Place Dauphine, waiting for Etienne and Elizabeth. She glanced at her watch; so desperate had she been to escape the confinement of her tiny room that she'd arrived almost half an hour early. She glanced around the now familiar spot. The last of the brown leaves clung on to the spindly branches of the trees, the sand-covered floor below covered with the rest. A few bikes were propped against the trees but the cafés surrounding the square – or triangle, really – were quiet, too late for lunchtime diners and too early for evening customers. The sun was doing its best to find ways through the thick white clouds above, casting sunbeams across the pale stone buildings on one side.

Allegra adjusted her scarf around her neck, tucking it into the front of her navy-coloured wool coat. She took out a letter from her bag, unfolding the thick white pages, her father's familiar scrawl on the page. She'd received the letter the day before, reading the first few lines before folding it up again and putting it back in the envelope. It had taken her all this time to pluck up the courage to read it properly. Dragging her eyes to the page, Allegra began to read. As she feared, her father was calling her back to New York for the winter break. She'd been secretly hoping her parents would let her stay in France given that she was pretty sure she was out of sight, out of mind. But obviously they had other ideas, clearly wanting to show off their Paris-educated daughter at their numerous Christmas parties.

Sitting on the bench, looking at the words in front of her, Allegra realised how much she didn't want to leave Paris. Not now. Perhaps not ever. She was happy here, and the thought of leaving and going back to her parents, even for a few weeks, made her feel wretched.

'Hey, what's that look for?'

Allegra turned to see Etienne's face behind her. He bent down and kissed her on the lips, then came and sat beside her.

'What's this?' He gestured to the letter in her hands.

Allegra couldn't bring herself to meet his gaze, not wanting him to see she was about to cry. 'My parents want me to go home for Christmas.'

Etienne's face dropped, then quickly changed as he smiled at her reassuringly. 'That's good, isn't it? They haven't forgotten about you after all. And it's only for a few weeks, *non*?'

'Yes, but reading this now makes me realise I really, really don't want to go. I want to stay here. I know you're going home to your parents for Christmas, but I'd rather stay on my own in Paris than go home. Elizabeth will be here with her parents so I wouldn't be completely alone.'

Etienne put his arm around her shoulders, pulling her towards him. He spoke gently. 'Is it really that bad?'

Allegra took a deep breath. 'The thing is, I feel like they've got my whole life mapped out for me. I know they only sent me here because they didn't know what else to do but coming here has been the best thing that's ever happened to me. In New York I felt stifled. I don't think they even see me as a person, just someone they need to marry well so they can feel better about themselves.' She looked at Etienne, scared she'd said too much.

'Why don't you come home with me for Christmas instead?'

'I couldn't. They'd kill me.'

'No, they won't. Not if you tell them the truth. Perhaps not the part about marrying you off.' He smiled. 'But just say you're happy to stay here and that you've been invited to spend Christmas with my family.'

'I haven't told them about you yet.'

'Why not?' Etienne's face fell slightly.

Allegra was suddenly embarrassed. Why was she so afraid of telling her parents?

'I'm not sure. We just don't really talk about things like that.' She thought about Etienne with his family, how happy they all were when they were together.

'Well, I think you should. Write and tell them you're going to Provence for Christmas. And even better, tell them you're going on a road trip. That's an American thing, isn't it?'

Allegra couldn't help but laugh a little. 'Yes, it's an American thing I guess.' She sighed. 'You're right, I need to just tell them. I'll write to them tonight.' She folded up the letter and put it back in her pocket. 'Are you sure you want me to come with you?'

Etienne kissed her on the bench in Place Dauphine and with that, she knew the answer.

'Hold it!'

They both turned to see Elizabeth standing behind them,

her camera in one hand. She waved to them, then joined them on the bench.

'Given that it took you two so long to kiss each other in the first place, you really haven't stopped since,' she said, teasingly.

Etienne and Allegra both blushed. It was true. Since that first kiss in the vineyard in Provence, they'd barely been able to stop.

'We're just making up for lost time,' said Etienne, shrugging his shoulders.

Allegra reached for Elizabeth's hand. 'So, what would you like to do? How about a walk along the river?'

Elizabeth sighed. 'You two are too kind to me. I'm sure you don't always want me tagging along.'

Etienne offered her a cigarette. 'We miss him too,' he said.

'You know what we need?' said Allegra.

'Ice cream?' Elizabeth looked hopeful.

'Exactly.' Allegra stood up, pulling her coat around her. 'Let's go to that new place; the sorbet there is insane. I've tried to get the recipe out of them but it's a secret. It's just a couple of blocks down from here.'

'You can take the girl out of New York...' said Etienne, teasing her.

Allegra had written to her parents to tell them she wouldn't be returning for the winter break and had heard nothing back, not even a phone call to admonish her. She'd felt immediately lighter having done it, wondering why it had taken her so long to just say what she wanted, but the lack of contact unnerved her. Still, she tried her best to put it out of her mind and simply enjoy the trip.

The morning Allegra and Etienne left Paris for Provence, they'd had to scrape ice from the windscreen of Etienne's car. Allegra had spent much of the first part of the journey wrapped in blankets, the car was so cold. The plan was to break up the drive halfway with an overnight stay with Etienne's uncle, a winemaker in Fleurie, before doing the second part of the drive the following day.

Allegra loved watching the landscape as they drove along the newly opened autoroute, past the rolling hills of Burgundy and on through the Rhone Valley. The further south they went, the more mountainous and dramatic the landscape grew. They stopped to fill up with fuel, feasting on the baguettes and various cheeses Allegra had bought from the market the day before and when she'd gone to fetch the basket from the boot, she couldn't help but notice a small package tucked down by the side of one of Etienne's bags, wrapped in brown paper. A book, no doubt. She smiled to herself, thinking of the present she'd bought for him. It was hidden away in her bag, a drawing she'd found in the Paris flea market they'd visited the previous weekend, now rolled up in a tube.

They arrived at the farmhouse by the early evening, their bodies aching after hours spent in the car, but Allegra couldn't have cared less. She was so happy to be back in Provence. Everyone came out to greet them, the pack of dogs at Etienne's mother's feet as ever. Camille hugged Allegra like a long-lost sister and both Nicolas and Agnès were clearly thrilled to see her.

'Etienne, how could you make the poor girl come all the way from Paris in that?' said his mother, shaking her head as she gestured to the car. She turned to Allegra. 'How are you feeling?'

'I loved it,' laughed Allegra. 'But yes, I think I might pay for it later.'

'Well, if you're not too tired we have friends coming for dinner tonight,' said Agnès. 'Let's get you inside, it's chilly.'

Allegra noticed a slight nip in the air but thought it was wonderfully mild compared to the weather they'd left behind in Paris.

'Who's coming?' asked Etienne.

'Serge and his wife,' said Nicolas. 'Hopefully he'll bring some of his red wine; it's the best I've tried in the region.'

'They've got vineyards nearby,' explained Agnès to Allegra.

'With their own *cave*. It's what we should do,' said Camille.

'What's a *cave*?' said Allegra, looking at Etienne.

'Their own winery, so they can make their own wine without having to rely on the co-operative,' he replied.

'That's all very well but there's one drawback,' said Nicolas to his daughter. He rubbed the tips of his fingers together.

'*Je sais, je sais*,' said Camille to her father, rolling her eyes. 'But one day we must do it.'

'Serge is also a sculptor, a very good one. So much so, he can afford to make his own wines now,' said Etienne.

'We don't have to talk about this *maintenant*,' said Agnès. 'I'm sure Allegra doesn't want to know about this... boring stuff.' She winked at Allegra.

Allegra was shown to her room by Etienne, the same one she'd shared with Elizabeth the last time she was there. She looked at the bed her friend had taken before, her absence acute. 'I worry about her,' she said, to herself more than anyone else.

'I know you do.' Etienne kissed her head. 'I'll just go and

put this in my room.' He held up his bag. 'Meet you downstairs.'

Allegra nodded. She sat on her bed and looked out of the window, across to the glimpse of blue in the distance. 'Can we drive to the sea one day whilst we're here? Have we got time?'

Etienne was obviously surprised. 'I thought after all those hours in the car I'd never get you back in there again.'

'I loved it. And now we're so close, I don't think I could bear driving back to Paris without seeing the sea. Properly, that is.'

Etienne sat down next to her on the bed and reached for her hand. 'I have a better idea.'

'What?'

He shrugged. 'You'll have to wait and see.' And with that, he smiled and turned. 'See you downstairs.'

That night, as they sat round the long table in the kitchen, the warmest room in the house, feasting on the most delicious beef en daube Allegra had ever tasted, she listened as they talked about the vintage – who'd had the best grapes, whose were the worst – along with discussions about everything from philosophy to politics and religion, mostly in English for her benefit. Every now and again they'd slip back into French and although she couldn't follow every word, Allegra realised how much her French had improved. She couldn't ever imagine having the same open conversations with her parents around the dinner table. The closest they'd ever come to talking about anything remotely similar was the time they'd argued about whether their neighbours in the apartment downstairs were Catholic or not.

'How did you make this? It's so good,' said Allegra to Agnès before taking another mouthful of stew.

'Nicolas made it,' she said, smiling at her husband. 'Tell her your secret, *mon chéri*.'

'You put everything together one day, cook it the next and eat it the next,' said Nicolas, shrugging his shoulders just as Etienne did, thought Elizabeth. 'My mother's recipe.'

'Very good wine, Serge,' said Etienne, raising his glass.

'*Merci*,' said the old man at the end of the table. Allegra thought he looked like a friendly giant, with his wild white hair and thick beard. His wife Mimi, next to him, was completely the opposite. She looked like a little bird, her dark eyes darting about the table, cigarette permanently between her bony fingers even when she was eating. When she spoke her voice was high and the words tumbled out so quickly Allegra wondered how anyone could follow a word she was saying.

'Mimi wants me to tell you that she thinks you look like Catherine Deneuve,' said Etienne.

'Who's that?' said Allegra.

'A young French actress; she's going to be the next big thing,' said Camille. 'And she's beautiful, by the way.'

Allegra thanked Mimi, then raised her glass to them. '*Le vin est délicieux*.' She blushed, realising everyone's eyes were on her. This sent Mimi into fits of laughter for some reason.

'Did I say it wrong?' she whispered to Etienne.

'No, don't worry.' He took a sip of his wine. 'She's always like this.' He nodded at Serge. 'He was the reason I fell in love with sculpture. Perhaps I'll ask if we can go to his studio. He's quite private about his work but he knows how much I love seeing it. I think you would too, especially with your new-found appreciation for art.' He grinned, knowingly.

After they'd finished their plates, Agnès placed a cheese-board on the table. The discussions continued long into the night and every time Allegra went to pick up her wine glass, she found it had been topped up. By the time she climbed into bed, her eyelids were heavy. Despite the curtains being drawn, moonlight flooded the room through the cracks. She thought of Etienne lying in his bed across the hall and wondered if he was still awake.

There was a soft knock at the door. Allegra went to open it and, as if she'd summoned him with her thoughts, found Etienne standing there. 'Couldn't sleep,' he said. 'Thought I might walk down to the vineyards. There's a full moon tonight.'

Despite feeling tired, she couldn't resist. 'Why not? I'll just put some clothes on.'

They crept out of the house so as not to wake anyone, bribing the dogs with biscuits as they passed through the kitchen and out of the back door to the path. The light outside was like nothing Allegra had ever seen, the moon a giant spotlight on the vineyards below them. Walking hand in hand, they talked about the evening's events, laughing at the thought of Mimi and her infectious giggle. Suddenly there was a rustling in the vines just to the side of them.

Allegra jumped. 'What the hell was that?' she said, looking around.

'A wild boar, probably.'

'Are you serious?' Allegra didn't like the sound of that at all. 'Are they dangerous?'

Etienne laughed. 'Only if you get in their way when there are grapes on the vine. But there's nothing on them now, they're too late. And you really don't see them very often here. They're quite rare.'

They made their way down the hill towards the stone hut at the top of the lower vineyard. As they approached, Allegra thought back to that night just a few months before when they'd danced until late. She looked at the old oak, backlit by the moon and bare of leaves now.

'Why did it take you so long to kiss me for the first time?' Allegra kept her gaze ahead.

He thought about it for a moment. 'The thing is, I had wanted to kiss you from the moment we first met. I walked into the bookshop and it was like, *Ah. There you are.*'

'Really?' She turned to him.

'And then you have no idea how hard it was not to kiss you on that dance floor in the club that first time. You looked so beautiful, but I didn't want to... scare you if that's the right way to say it.'

'Be too forward?'

'That's it. Not with you. I didn't want to lose you by being too forward. But then, that night, I knew you felt it too.' He put his hand gently on her chest. 'Right here.'

Allegra's heart was beating fast. She continued to look straight at him. 'And what would you say if I asked you to follow me now?'

Etienne blinked, as if he'd misheard her.

Allegra took his hand and led him into the hut. They stood facing each other and slowly, she removed her jumper, pulling it over her head. Dropping it onto the straw-covered floor below, she then placed her hands on his hips before moving them around to his back and lifting his jumper. As he took it off, she started to remove the shirt she was wearing.

'Stop,' he said.

'What?'

'The light on your body. Just let me look at you for a few seconds.'

She smiled. 'Don't. I'll get embarrassed.'

'You shouldn't.' He reached out his hand and ran a finger along her collarbone before moving his hand down towards her breast, the feeling of his fingers brushing her skin making her gasp. A million tiny electric shocks ran through her body and she found herself sinking to the floor, pulling him down with her. She unbuttoned his shirt, kissing every part of his neck as she did so.

Etienne looked at her, stroking the hair from her face. 'Are you sure you want to do this?'

Without taking her eyes off him, she guided his hand down her stomach towards the top of her trousers. 'Quite sure,' she whispered.

Afterwards, as they lay side by side on the straw, the moonlight casting a silver glow across their bodies, Etienne held her hand up in the air. 'You have beautiful fingers.'

'Thank you, so do you. Very adept.' She grinned, then kissed him again. This hadn't been Allegra's first time, but with Etienne she finally understood why it was called making love.

Just before dawn, they walked back up to the house, the sky behind the mountains streaked with colour. The air was still.

'We could drive to Cannes today if you like?' said Etienne, as he led her back through the vines. 'There's a Christmas market and we can pick up some presents.'

'Can we go to the beach? The one we went to before?'

'You want to swim?'

'God, no. I want to put my toes in the sand again. Remember when Elizabeth and I did that when we came here? It was the first time I'd ever seen the Mediterranean and I just wanted to feel the water on my skin. I loved that so much.'

'You know what I remember most?' Etienne stopped and turned to face her.

'Our first kiss?'

'Yes, that. But there was something else and I don't think I'll ever forget it. Luc and Elizabeth had obviously had an argument about something before the party that night.'

'She told him she loved him.'

'And he didn't say it back.'

'Exactly.' Allegra pulled a face. 'Awkward.'

'But the thing I remember most about that was how you took her dancing. I watched you, making her laugh, and that's when I knew.'

'Knew what?'

'That I loved you.'

A small smile was on Allegra's lips. 'You do?'

Etienne nodded. 'I do.'

'Well, that is a shame.'

'Why?' Etienne's expression collapsed.

'Because I love you too. And now we're going to have to figure out how to make this work.'

'What do you mean?'

'Etienne, it may have escaped your notice but I'm an American.'

'And?'

'I live in America.'

'You live in Paris.'

'Currently, yes. But I'm going to have to go back to America at some point.'

'Not if you stay here and marry me, you don't.'

Allegra wondered if she'd heard him right. 'Did you say…?'

Etienne dropped to one knee. 'Allegra Morgon, will you marry me?'

It was such a shock it took her a few seconds to speak. But standing in that hut in the vineyard where they'd first kissed, she looked at him and her future suddenly seemed crystal clear. She knew there was only one answer.

'Yes, I will marry you.'

'You will?'

'Yes.' Allegra laughed. 'Of course I will!'

They kissed and hugged each other tightly, laughing as tears of joy streamed down their faces. By the time they got back to the house, Etienne's mother was already in the kitchen making coffee. She took one look at them and shrieked with delight.

She immediately went to the door and shouted up the stairs. 'Nicolas!' she yelled. '*Viens ici!*' Turning back to the beaming couple, she stood with her hands on her hips. 'Do you have something to tell me?'

Etienne nodded and before they could even get the words out Agnès threw her arms around them both. She then took a step back and took a hand from each of them.

'You know your father and I married at your age. Living your life with someone you love is a gift. I'm so happy you have found it too,' said Agnès.

'Thank you,' said Allegra, her voice shaking with the excitement of it all.

'What's happening in here?' Nicolas appeared at the door in his pyjamas, scratching his head.

'Papa, I asked Allegra to marry me, and she said yes,' said Etienne, looking from his father to Allegra.

'You did?' Nicolas sounded surprised. 'Well, that is good news!' He came to hug them both.

'*Qu'est-ce qui se passe?*' asked Camille, as she walked into the kitchen in her dressing gown.

'They're getting married!' said Agnès, beaming. 'Nico, go and fetch a bottle of champagne from the cellar. Etienne, get some glasses.'

'Congratulations.' Camille kissed Allegra three times on the cheek, then went to hug her brother. 'I don't know what she sees in you,' she said, winking at him.

As they sat around the kitchen table toasting the newly engaged couple, Allegra was so happy she thought her heart might burst. The only stone in her shoe was knowing she would have to tell her parents sooner rather than later. She resolved to call them, perhaps when she and Etienne were in Cannes that afternoon. She knew they'd be furious but now she was eighteen years old she could do as she pleased, couldn't she?

After a long morning where seemingly every neighbour dropped in for a drink, the two of them sneaked away to exchange Christmas presents. They sat on the rug in front of a roaring fire in the hall, various dogs at their feet.

'I got it from George's bookshop; I thought you'd like it,' Etienne explained as she opened hers first, a copy of a new art book showing a collection of paintings by Picasso.

Allegra carefully opened it, the vibrant colours jumping out from the page. 'I love it, thank you.' She kissed him on the cheek. 'Well, I'm just hoping you like your present. I think you will.' She put the book down and handed him the cardboard tube, a bright red ribbon tied around the middle. He opened it at one end and slowly removed the piece of paper inside. He gently laid it on the rug and unrolled it, holding it down with his fingers to reveal a pencil drawing of a woman. He stared at it in disbelief, then looked at her. 'Where did you get this?'

'At the flea market in Saint Ouen. I went up there with Elizabeth.'

'But this is too much; you know who this is?' He looked at her, his eyes wide.

'It's Rodin.' She beamed at him.

'But...' He held the paper up in his trembling hands '...this isn't a print. This looks like an original.'

'What? Don't be ridiculous. I didn't pay that much for it. It just can't be.' She laughed.

'I'm being serious, Allegra. Look.' He pointed at the paper. 'A print would have a number on it somewhere. This one doesn't.' He turned it over carefully. 'Did it come with anything else?'

Allegra picked up the cardboard tube and peered inside. 'No, nothing. Are you sure?'

Etienne shrugged. 'I think so. We need to show Serge, he would know.'

'He's coming over later to eat with us, your mother said.'

Etienne whistled. 'If this is what I think it is, you have something very special on your hands.'

'Which I've just given to you,' Allegra reminded him.

'I don't think you understand. It's worth a small fortune. Enough to change your life.'

Allegra felt immediately uncomfortable. She really hadn't paid much for the gift but, so far, she had deliberately kept details of her family's vast wealth from Etienne. She liked the fact that here, away from her parents, she could be herself rather than the Morgon girl from the Upper East Side, as she'd been called to her face by parents of her friends back in New York. 'Well, if it is then I guess we've struck lucky but to be honest I bought it because I thought you'd like it.'

'I love it,' he said.

'But you love me more, right?' She grinned at him.

'More than you know.'

15

PRESENT DAY

Maggie looked at the photo of the couple on the bench in Place Dauphine. 'I love the story behind this one.'

'I love that your grandmother took it,' said Allegra.

'And I can't believe you were engaged! That's the most ridiculously romantic proposal I've ever heard.'

'Was yours?' asked Allegra.

Maggie laughed. 'Not at all. I mean, we'd been together for a while and were both at that age where we felt we should get on with it. I think he suggested it just after we'd taken the bins out.' The clocktower chimed again as it did every fifteen minutes and Maggie looked at her phone screen to check the time. 'It's almost midnight. I don't want to keep you up but please can you just tell me what happened with you and Etienne? Obviously, you didn't get married...'

'It was a crazy time. I made a long-distance call to my parents the day after Etienne proposed; I remember going to Cannes with Etienne to do it. My father was furious, as expected. He yelled for what felt like forever, then put the phone down. He wouldn't let me speak to my mother. It was awful but I was determined I was doing the right thing. I didn't care if they didn't approve. Then we got back to Paris.'

'My grandmother must have been so happy for you,' said Maggie. 'That must've helped?'

'By the time we got back, she'd gone,' said Allegra.

The sadness in her voice was palpable. 'When I got back to my room, that box was on my bed—' she put her hand on the small brown case between them '—with a letter from her explaining that they'd been asked to leave. She was obviously worried about taking the box with her, she said it contained her most precious photographs and maybe because Luc was in some of them, maybe she thought it would make matters worse. So, along with her camera, she left the box with me to look after. In the letter she made me promise I would use that camera on her behalf until we met again. But, of course, I couldn't bring myself to. I felt it belonged to her and I wanted to keep it that way. My job, as I saw it, was just to keep it safe until I saw her again.'

'Oh, Allegra, I'm so sorry. It must've been devasting to come back to find that your best friend had gone.'

'We'd gone from such happiness and went back to Paris expecting to spend New Year's Eve with Elizabeth and some other friends. The plan had been to go to the Bal, of course. With Elizabeth gone, we almost didn't go but I remember Etienne persuading me that she would have wanted us dancing, not sitting about being miserable. So, we did go and for a few hours we forgot everything that was going on. It was so busy. We danced and drank, then I stayed at his. The next morning, I walked back to my apartment to go and change, I remember I had Etienne's jacket around my shoulders. It had turned really cold.' Allegra shivered at the thought. 'I looked up and noticed the light was on in my apartment. I should've realised something unusual was going on but for some reason, I just went on up. When I opened the door to my room, my father was sitting on my bed.'

Maggie gasped. 'What did you do?'

'What could I do? He was right there in front of me, sitting on the bed, holding my passport in his hand. He looked right at me and told me I was coming home.'

'I can't bear it.' Maggie put her hands to her face.

'He said I was to pack my things right there and then, that we had a flight home later that day. There was an almighty row. He said I was making a huge mistake getting married. I told him I wasn't a two-year-old he could just drag back home; I was eighteen and could do as I pleased. That's when he told me that my mother was ill.'

'I'm so sorry. What was wrong?'

'He said she had cancer. He hadn't wanted to tell me on the phone. He said that he couldn't tell my mother I was engaged as it would make her worse.'

'But that's emotional blackmail, isn't it?'

'At the time I felt so guilty. It was all such a shock. He made me feel like the most selfish person in the world.'

'So, you went home?'

Allegra wiped a tear from her face. 'I didn't see how I could do anything else.'

'That's so awful.' Maggie's words were barely audible. She put her hand on Allegra's arm.

Allegra took a deep breath. 'It was all such a long time ago, but you never forget moments like that. I can see his face now, the veins on the side of his temple pulsing...' Allegra's words tailed off.

The bells from the clocktower rang out once more, telling them it was midnight.

'I think you should sleep now,' said Maggie. 'We can talk more tomorrow. Thank you, though. I hope you don't think I'm being too nosey.'

'Not at all. It's so rare nowadays that anyone's interested in folks as old as me.' Allegra laughed gently.

'I don't understand why that should be so. You seem to have all the best stories,' said Maggie.

They made their way back down the stairs, Maggie carrying the empty glasses and Allegra with the box of photographs.

'Sleep well, Maggie. I'm so glad you're here.'

'Me too,' said Maggie. And she meant it. She couldn't remember the last time she'd just sat and talked like this with someone, not checking her watch or worrying where she had to be next. Her mind felt clear, her shoulders relaxed. As she sank into the bed, the soft duvet around her, she thought once more of the couple on the bench – that stolen moment, captured forever – before drifting off to sleep.

* * *

Maybe it was the sea air or the warmth, she couldn't be sure, but that night Maggie slept deeply. Even the bells from the clocktower didn't rouse her. It wasn't until she heard a soft knocking at the door that she woke, Allegra's voice on the other side.

'Maggie, are you awake? There's tea for you here but don't get your hopes up. I'm an American. I'm just off to get some bread.'

'Thank you,' called Maggie from her bed, stretching her arms out wide. 'Shall I come with you?'

'No, you stay and drink your tea. I won't be long. We can

have breakfast upstairs when I'm back. Put some coffee on; there's a cafetiere on the side and the coffee is in the fridge. Back in half an hour.'

Maggie waited for a moment, then got up and opened the door. She looked down. Allegra had been right to manage Maggie's expectations; the tea was the colour of porcelain. She smiled to herself and went to open the windows, pushing the shutters aside. Her room was at the back of the house, over-looking the hills beyond the town. The terracotta-topped buildings of the Old Town gave way to modern white apart-ments and hotels further out, creeping up towards the wooded slopes behind. The pale blue sky was completely clear of cloud, the air already warm. She listened to the quiet hum of the town waking up below, the sound of scooters and cars on the boulevard in the distance.

Climbing back into bed with her mug of tea, Maggie thought back to the conversation the night before. She had loved hearing about Allegra and Elizabeth's time in Paris but there was so much more Maggie wanted to know. At the same time, she didn't want to pry.

Her phone vibrated on the table beside her bed, alerting her to a message. She picked it up and looked at the screen. It was from an old contact at a production company she occa-sionally worked for. Opening the message, she read through the details. There was a producing job available on an upcoming reality series, set in a manor house in the Cotswolds. She knew the programme; celebrities competed to win a trophy through a series of increasingly ridiculous tasks and plenty of tactical voting. It was an eight-week job with pre-production starting in two weeks' time. Clearly someone else had pulled out at the last minute for her to be asked so close to the start of filming but Maggie wasn't proud. And as painful as it sounded – she'd done too many reality shows over the years to find it fun – at least it was a decent chunk of time. Her parents could keep Tiger for her, and she could even rent out her flat for a few months in the meantime.

Maggie was just about to respond with a resounding yes when she remembered Jack. What if he was working on it too? Deciding she knew the contact well enough to ask without it being awkward, Maggie typed out a reply, asking if he was on the same job. The response came back immediately. Yes, he was, and so was Lottie.

Maggie's heart sank. She'd had a feeling about Jack but having them both there, with Lottie's growing bump for all to see and no doubt talk about, was almost too much to bear. However, turning down the job – or rather, the money – wasn't an option. Maggie would just have to put her game face on and get on with it. She replied and asked for details to be emailed over, trying to ignore the knot in her stomach.

After taking a quick shower, Maggie threw on a T-shirt and shorts and went to make some coffee as instructed. By the time she took the cafetiere and a couple of cups up to the terrace, Allegra was already there, dressed in a flowing cobalt blue kaftan with a blue patterned silk scarf around her head. Large black sunglasses shielded her eyes from the bright morning sun and even at this early hour, Allegra sported a slick of deep red lipstick.

Maggie thought she looked impossibly glamorous. She, on the other hand, was dressed pretty much like her teenage self. On the table was a plate with some sliced fresh peaches, a bunch of grapes and a basket of croissants, along with jam and butter.

'I didn't hear you come back,' said Maggie. 'I would have done all this.'

'The exercise does me good,' said Allegra, putting a croissant on her plate. 'Help yourself, they're still warm.'

'They smell divine,' said Maggie, pouring out two cups of
coffee and passing one to Allegra.

'So, given we've only really got today, I've arranged a little
surprise for you this morning. Afterwards we can pick up
some food at the market for our lunch, then perhaps go out
for something to eat later depending on how you feel. How
does that sound?' Allegra tore off a strip from her croissant
and curled it elegantly into her mouth.

Maggie nodded, swallowing the mouthful of fresh peach
she'd just taken. 'Really? You didn't have to do that. Whatever
it is, it sounds great, thank you,' she said, genuinely thrilled.

'Did you sleep well?'

'Like a log,' replied Maggie. 'I honestly haven't slept that
well for months, possibly years.'

'You've had a tough time,' said Allegra.

'Not really.' Maggie took a sip of her coffee. 'I'm way more
fortunate than most. I have a good job. My parents are both
still alive and well, for the most part.'

'What about friends, do you have good friends around
you?'

'Yes, I do. I mean, most of them I know through work. Most
of my old friends got married, had kids, moved away. Since the
divorce, I've had my head down with work. It's not that I've lost
them, I just don't really see them as much.' As Maggie said this
out loud, she realised it sounded pretty lame. The truth was,
she'd cut herself off voluntarily. The last thing she ever wanted
was to be a burden or, worse, pitied. 'I guess I keep myself busy
enough to not be lonely.' Maggie thought about the endless
evenings she'd had in by herself in recent months, lying on the
sofa before falling asleep to something mindless she'd been

watching. Why did she get the feeling Allegra knew Maggie was fooling herself? 'Was it easy to make friends here?'

Allegra nodded. 'It's a small town, really. Once the tourists have thinned out, everyone knows everyone. It's sad that no one lives next door on either side now, the houses are rented out. Different people come and go but that suits me. It's quiet most of the time and I can keep myself to myself. I still have friends who come to stay, especially from the old days when I ran a gallery.'

'When did you run a gallery?' Maggie topped up her coffee, then offered the cafetiere to Allegra.

'Thank you,' said Allegra, pushing her cup across the table. 'I had one for years, back in New York.'

'Oh yes, you went back.' Maggie's face fell at the thought of Allegra being dragged away from Paris, from Etienne, against her will.

'Not for one second did I think I wouldn't be going back to Paris. As far as I was concerned, I assumed I was returning with him to New York for however long it took, help nurse my mother through her illness, then return to Paris. I thought it was just a matter of persuading them that marrying Etienne wasn't a terrible idea.' Allegra took off her sunglasses and put them on her head. 'But as we know, life doesn't always go to plan. Shall we walk and talk? I can tell you on the way. Go and grab your swimming costume, you'll need it.'

Maggie took a last gulp of coffee. 'You really are full of surprises.'

16

NEW YORK, 1962

Allegra sat in the window seat in the first-class section of the plane, next to her father. He'd barely spoken to her since they'd left her room and climbed into the taxi, her small suitcase stuffed with her belongings. Her father had disappeared to see the principal for ten minutes, instructing her to pack whilst he was gone. Allegra had contemplated making a run for it but with the news of her mother, not to mention the fact that she didn't have a passport in her possession, she couldn't bring herself to do it.

Scrawling a note to Etienne, Allegra briefly explained what had happened but promised she would be back as soon as possible. She left her address in New York, asked him not to worry about her and told him she loved him. Knocking on the door of the girl across the hall, Allegra begged her to deliver the note to Etienne, writing his address on the front of the envelope. After some persuasion and a small monetary incentive, the girl had reluctantly agreed to do it and Allegra had thanked her, diving back into her own room when she heard her father returning.

The journey to the airport had been horrendous. She knew her father was furious, but his silence was unbearably oppressive. Allegra wished he'd just shout at her, get it out of his system. A few hours into the flight her father fell asleep, largely thanks to the three enormous whiskies he'd had before take-off. As he snored loudly beside her, Allegra imagined Etienne reading the note, hoping he'd do as she asked and not worry.

She tried to sleep, but it was no good. Her mind raced, different scenarios playing out in her head. Much as Allegra didn't always particularly like her mother as a person, the thought of her being unwell was awful. She had no idea what sort of state she would find her in and despite asking her father about her mother's illness, he said they would talk about it when they got home.

When they touched down in America eight and a half hours after leaving Paris, her father's chauffeur-driven car was waiting for them outside the airport. As they drove towards the familiar Manhattan skyline, Allegra's heart ached more and more with every passing mile. The grey skies reflected her mood as they crawled through the New York traffic and by the time they turned off Fifth Avenue and crossed Madison, Park and Lexington to their apartment on East 72nd Street, it was already dark.

As they made their way in the elevator up to the fifteenth floor – their apartment ran over the entire floor – Allegra readied herself for greeting her mother. But when the door to their apartment was opened, Allegra couldn't believe her eyes. There was her mother, coiffed hair high on her head, dressed and made up as immaculately as ever.

'Hello, darling!'

'Mom, you look...'

Her mother threw her arms around her. 'I know, I look so well! Come on in.' She waved Allegra into the apartment.

As soon as she stepped through the front door, Allegra felt a sense of unease.

'Well, thank goodness we got her back here before she did something really stupid,' said her father.

It was as if Allegra wasn't even in the room. 'I don't under-stand.' She looked from her father to her mother. 'I've been so worried, Mom. Dad said you were really unwell.'

'Oh, it's not that serious.' Her mother waved Allegra's concern away. 'The doctors say they can treat it and I'll be back to normal in no time. Would you like something to eat? You must be starving after your journey. Come and sit down and tell me about Paris, I want to hear all about it. You must've had quite the adventure.'

Allegra wondered if her mother even knew about Etienne and their plans to marry. If she did, she was hiding it very well. 'It's wonderful. I love it there.'

Her father pecked her mother on the cheek with a perfunctory kiss. 'I'm going to my study. What time is dinner?'

'I've asked Ida to have it on the table for seven o'clock.' Her mother smiled at him. 'Is that alright?'

'Bring it forward by an hour,' he called over his shoulder as he left the room.

Her mother sighed and turned back to Allegra, fixing a smile back on her face. 'Oh, I knew you would love it. Did you see the Eiffel Tower?'

She hated the way her father spoke to her mother. 'Every day,' said Allegra, smiling. 'It's not like here where everything is hidden behind another building.' She waited until she heard the door of her father's study close. 'Dad said you have cancer.' She felt sick even saying the words. 'Please can you tell me what's going on?'

Her mother dropped her gaze and smoothed down the front of her bouclé jacket. She nodded. 'It's breast cancer.' She looked at Allegra, that smile still in place. 'But I'm having surgery and then some radiotherapy and the doctors say I have a very good chance.' She put her hand on Allegra's and squeezed it. 'I don't want you to worry. Now, tell me more about Paris.'

'But I do worry, Mom. How long until you have surgery?'

'Next week, then I'll be home before you know it.'

Allegra saw a vulnerability in her mother's eyes and for the first time for as long as she could remember, her mother hugged her.

'I'm so sorry, Mom.'

'Oh, don't be dramatic, darling,' said her mother. 'It'll be fine. Now, I understand you had a boyfriend. What was he like?'

Allegra stared at her mother. Obviously, her father hadn't mentioned that she planned to marry him. 'Well, it was pretty serious. In fact, we…'

'Oh, Ida, there you are,' her mother called over to their housemaid. 'John is very tired after the journey, can you make sure we have dinner on the table at six rather than seven?'

'Of course, ma'am.' Ida nodded. 'Hello, Ms Morgon.'

'Hi, Ida, how are you?' said Allegra, getting up to give her a hug.

'Look at you!' Ida put her hands to Allegra's face. 'You look so grown up. Paris suits you.' She winked, then left the room.

'I do wish you wouldn't be so familiar with the staff,' said her mother disapprovingly.

'Mom, I've known Ida all my life. Of course I'm going to be familiar.'

'Well, I've got to get a few things done so I'll leave you to unpack. Perhaps you might want to freshen up before dinner?' And with that, she was gone, leaving Allegra on her own in the vast drawing room. If her mother was aware of her plans to marry, she clearly didn't want to talk about it.

Allegra desperately wanted to bring up the subject of Etienne with her mother again after that first conversation, but with her mother's illness and plans being made for her to go into hospital, she decided that it would have to wait. Instead, she wrote Etienne a long letter explaining she would have to stay in New York and help her mother through her recovery but would be back just as soon as she could. Every day, she would go down to the apartment building's reception in the hope of finding letter for her with Etienne's familiar writing on the front, but nothing came. Still, she was sure a response would arrive in due course.

Being back in New York after her time in Paris made Allegra see the city through new eyes. Compared with the wide boulevards and grand bridges of Paris, Manhattan felt small by comparison. Crowded, too, with rivers of people walking as if their lives depended on it. After her mother returned from surgery to recover at home, Allegra made herself as useful as possible, spending hours by her bedside reading to her or simply sitting with her. The full-time nurse her father had organised dipped in and out of the bedroom every half an hour or so but most of the time it was just Allegra and her mother. At her mother's insistence, Allegra would leave the apartment every now and again and she used the opportunity to visit an art museum on nearby Fifth Avenue, either the Met, MoMA or the Guggenheim with its stark concrete walls. Before she'd gone to Paris, Allegra had walked past these buildings often. Never once had she wanted to go inside.

Etienne had opened her eyes to a whole new world of creativity both on canvas and in sculpture. Before, and much to her embarrassment, her mother's love of art had simply bored her. Now, when her mother was up to it, they discussed paintings and artists at length. Allegra longed to tell her mother about Etienne but, worried that the thought of her leaving again would be too upsetting, she held back.

Of course, she thought of him constantly, especially when walking through the vast rooms of the museums. The art around her comforted her, as she imagined what Etienne would make of this painting or that sculpture. She played out entire conversations in her head, returning to the apartment to write him long letters detailing what she'd seen and loved that day. Allegra continued to write every few days but with no other way of contacting him, all she could do was wait. And hope.

Her mother died in her sleep, six weeks after she'd first come home from hospital. Allegra had gone to see her in the morning, with a glass of water and a book as she'd done almost every morning, to find her father sitting by the bed, holding her mother's hand. On the other side of the bed sat the nurse, her head bowed.

Her father didn't notice her standing there until Allegra realised what had happened and dropped her water to the floor. The shattering of glass brought Ida running into the room, where she took in the scene and immediately went to put her arm around Allegra. The next few weeks went by in a blur as her father organised the funeral, not once asking Allegra for any input despite her regular offers of help. She felt numb, not quite knowing what to do or say around her father. The apartment was so quiet without her mother and slowly, as the weeks went by after the funeral, the flowers disappeared too, leaving it drained of colour. Any hopes that her mother's death might bring her and her father closer were soon forgotten as he settled quickly into life without his wife of almost twenty-five years. As far as Allegra could tell, he couldn't have been less interested in how his daughter was feeling and he certainly didn't want to talk about her mother, changing the subject whenever Allegra tried to do so.

One evening, as they sat eating dinner at the table in the dining room overlooking Central Park, Allegra decided it was time to bring up what she might do next. It had been almost a month since her mother's death and she desperately wanted to return to Paris. The distance and silence between her and Etienne were unbearable. She wasn't sleeping, could barely eat. To take her mind off her aching heart, that day she'd gone to a small gallery that had not long opened just two blocks up from the apartment, one that her mother had told her to go and visit. They were to exhibit the works of Andy Warhol later that year and according to her mother, he would one day be a household name.

Allegra broke the silence by asking if her father had had a good day. He'd nodded without even looking up, shovelling more food into his mouth. Determined to make him speak to her, Allegra persisted, telling him about her visit to the gallery.

'I didn't appreciate how much Mom knew about art. She

really loved it, didn't she? I learnt so much in Paris, I loved talking to her about it,' said Allegra.

Her father slowly put down his fork, and continued chewing. He didn't look at Allegra, saying nothing.

She felt a rushing sound in her ears. Deciding she had nothing to lose, she just came out and said it. 'This has been a horrible time for our family, especially for you. I'm so sorry, Dad. But I do need to think about what I do next.' She dug her fingers into her palms. 'What I really want is to go back to Paris.'

He banged his fist on the table with such force, the cutlery rattled on their plates.

Allegra jumped in her seat. Ida, who'd been hovering at the door, slunk back into the kitchen. Finally, her father looked up at Allegra, his face red. She braced herself for an onslaught. As he started his tirade, she was reminded of the times she'd heard his raised voice from her bedroom as a little girl, the sound of her mother's voice begging him to stop. Allegra tried to breathe slowly, keeping a steady gaze.

His words came thick and fast. She was selfish and stupid. She was far too young to know what was good for her and the idea of her getting married was a joke. Frankly, she was an embarrassment to him.

The sound in Allegra's ears grew louder. She closed her eyes for a moment, then opened them. Her father's face was contorted with anger.

'Well, what have you got to say for yourself?'

Allegra stood up from the table and put her napkin on her plate. 'Goodbye, Dad.' She turned and made her way to the door.

'Where do you think you're going?' screamed her father. 'Do not walk away from me!'

'Thank you, that was delicious,' Allegra said to Ida as she passed her in the hall, where she'd clearly been hiding to not miss a word.

Ida kissed her on the cheek. 'You look after yourself.'

'I will,' she said, grabbing her coat from the cupboard by the front door.

She left with nothing but the clothes she stood up in and never set foot in that apartment again. Over the coming years, she would sometimes catch a glimpse of her father as he made his way from the apartment to his waiting car, careful to stay out of view. Only once did they bump into each other, quite literally, on Fifth Avenue. He looked at her, anger in his eyes.

'Excuse me,' he'd said, before walking on as if she didn't exist. Those were the last words she ever heard him speak.

* * *

That night, Allegra ran from the apartment and, ignoring the tears streaming down her face, found herself standing on East 74th Street near the corner of Madison Avenue. Pulling her coat around her, she wondered what to do next whilst she caught her breath. The initial relief at getting out of the apartment was soon replaced by the enormity of what she'd done. She sat down on the stone steps in the doorway of a building and wept. What was she supposed to do now? With nothing except a few dollar bills in her purse, she couldn't even afford to get a bed for the night. She tried to think of someone she could go to, but couldn't face turning up unannounced at anyone's house in the state she was in.

'Are you okay, honey?'

Allegra looked up to see a woman peering down at her, a concerned look on her face. She had curly brown hair that obviously didn't like being pinned in place. She wore a big red and brown checked coat with a bright yellow scarf wrapped around her neck and her huge eyes stared at Allegra.

Realising she needed to give an answer, Allegra tried not to sob. 'I'm fine, thank you.'

'You don't look fine to me. Can I help?'

Allegra shook her head, suddenly embarrassed.

'Well, what are you going to do? This might be a nice neighbourhood but even around here it isn't safe for a girl on their own once it gets late. Do you live near here?'

'Yes, on East 72nd.'

'Want me to walk you home? I can go that way.'

'I don't want to go home.' The words were out of her mouth before Allegra could stop them.

'Then what are you going to do?'

Again, Allegra shook her head. 'I'll be fine, really.'

The woman sat down on the step beside her. 'Won't your mother be worried sick?'

'She died,' Allegra whispered, desperately trying to hold back another flood of tears.

'I'm sorry.' She put a hand on Allegra's arm. 'How about your father?'

'He's the reason I left.'

'Oh, okay.' The woman thought about it for a moment. 'Why did you come here?'

Allegra looked up at the door, realising she was on the steps of the gallery she'd visited earlier that day. 'My mum told me about it before she died.'

'That was you in the gallery today? I thought you looked familiar. Except for the tears, that is.' The woman held out a tissue for Allegra.

'Thank you,' said Allegra, taking it and wiping at her face. 'Is this your place?'

'It is. You like it?'

'Like it? I love it.' Allegra sniffed.

'Here,' said the woman, holding out another tissue. 'My name's Valentina. Call me Val. I always feel like I'm in trouble when people call me Valentina.'

'It's a beautiful name.'

'Thank you. What's yours?'

'Allegra.'

'Okay, you win.'

Allegra shrugged. 'I always hated it growing up; I wanted to be called Susan. Just a nice, normal name.'

'It's good to be different. So, you like art?'

'I do. I was in Paris last year. I hope to go back soon.'

'I lived in Paris for a while when I was about your age. Such a beautiful city.'

'My fiancé is there,' said Allegra, unable to hold back a huge sob as soon as the words were out.

'Ah, I see. Is that what the argument with your father was about?' Val's voice softened.

'Kind of. He won't let me go back.'

Val placed a hand on Allegra's arm. 'Shouldn't you try and fix things with your dad before it gets any worse?'

Allegra sighed heavily. 'I'm not going back to that apartment.'

Val took a packet of cigarettes out of her pocket and lit one. 'How old are you?'

'Eighteen.'

'So, if you want go back to Paris, you'll have to get there on your own somehow.'

'You're right, I need a job. That's what I'm going to do tomorrow. Get a job. And I'll work for as long as it takes to get myself a plane ticket. I'll sort myself another passport somehow and then go back to Paris.' She was saying it to herself as much as to anyone else.

'I think I have a solution to both your problems.'

'You do?' Allegra looked at her, wide eyed.

'I had to fire the janitor of the gallery today. Which was annoying because he was a very good janitor. Unfortunately, he was also a thief. So, you can start tomorrow, and I will pay you a weekly wage. You can stay with us for a bit, just until you find somewhere to rent. My husband is at home; he's a writer so you'll need to make yourself scarce during the day but you'll be at the gallery so that's fine.'

Allegra couldn't believe what she was hearing. 'Are you a guardian angel or something?'

Val took one last draw on her cigarette and blew out the smoke into the cold New York air. 'Definitely not,' she said, stubbing it out on the step. 'But I was in your position once, so I know what it's like. Leaving is the easy bit. Making it on your own is the hard part. People helped me when I was down so the least I can do is help you get started.' She stood up and offered Allegra her hand.

Allegra took it and pulled herself up from the step. 'I don't know what to say. Thank you.'

'Let's just hope you're not a terrible janitor.' Val stepped out into the road. 'Taxi!' she yelled, just as one pulled up. She called through the open window. 'Jones Street, please. Between Bleeker and West 4th.'

'You live in the West Village?' Even though it was just a few miles away Allegra had only been a few times, without her parents' knowledge obviously. They barely travelled south of Central Park.

'Well, I certainly don't live on the Upper East Side,' laughed Val, holding open the door of the cab for Allegra. As they turned onto Park Avenue and headed downtown, Allegra felt lighter with every block they passed.

17

PRESENT DAY

Allegra and Maggie set off down the hill from the Old Town towards the harbour below, making their way through the narrow streets and into the main square. The cafés in the back streets were busy with locals, those in front of the harbour busy with tourists. As Maggie walked along beside Allegra, she realised the woman who claimed to keep herself to herself clearly knew everyone in the town.

Crossing the road to the quay, Maggie saw an older grey-haired man in a small white motorboat waving at them.

'Bonjour, Henri! *Ça va*?' said Allegra, waving back. 'This is Maggie, Maggie meet Henri.'

'Bonjour,' said Maggie. 'Nice to meet you.' She turned to Allegra. 'Are we going on this?'

'By the smile on your face, I'm hoping you're happy with that idea,' said Allegra, laughing.

Maggie looked at the boat, astonished. 'Absolutely! Where are we going?'

Henri pointed at the islands out in the bay. 'Over there. Please,' he said, offering his hand to Maggie.

She stepped down on to the teak deck, then helped Allegra do the same. They both sat on the long, cushioned seat behind Henri as he started the engine. Soon they were heading out into the deep blue waters of the Mediterranean and with not a breath of wind, the sea was calm. In his thick French accent, Henri told Maggie about the islands to which they were headed.

'There are four islands, but only two are inhabited. The smaller one has a monastery; the larger one in front has the fort on it,' he said, pointing it out.

Maggie looked out across the water as they sped towards the islands, taking in the impossible blues of the sea and sky around her.

'It gets very crowded by lunchtime, even now. So, I thought we'd come early before the rush and we can have a swim between the islands,' said Allegra, shouting over the sound of the engine.

Maggie leant towards her. 'So, is he—' she looked at Henri, his back to them as he helmed the boat,'—an old friend of yours?'

'He's an artist. I used to look after him here.' Allegra smiled enigmatically. 'He's a very good friend.'

'Right,' said Maggie, wondering just how friendly they were.

'I happened to bump into him this morning at the boulangerie; he lives at the bottom of the hill. He asked why I was buying two of everything. I told him about you visiting and he offered to take us out.'

'I'm very glad he did,' said Maggie, hair blowing in the wind. She grinned at Allegra.

'Me too. Now, look up ahead and you'll see the fort. We'll round this point and with any luck it'll still be relatively quiet.'

Henri slowed the boat down and navigated them gently into the turquoise blue waters between the islands. They found a relatively empty spot close to the shore of the smaller of the two islands, away from the handful of people already sitting on the decks of their boats or on the rocks.

'Maggie, can you go up to the bow and put the anchor over the side?' said Henri.

She did as she was asked, glad to be of use, and watched as it sank gracefully into the water before coming to rest on the pale sand below them.

'Ça va?' he said, looking at Allegra. She nodded and he cut the engine.

'Are you going in?' Allegra stood up and started lifting her kaftan over her head.

'Race you,' said Maggie, whipping off her T-shirt.

They heard a splash and looked down to see Henri already in the water, swimming below the surface.

'Too late,' said Maggie, before leaping off the side of the boat into the sea.

Henri climbed back onto the boat and the two women made their way to shore, swimming carefully through the rocks to a stony beach, Aleppo pines rising behind it.

'This is so glorious. Thank you,' said Maggie as she dropped down gently onto the stones.

'It's my pleasure. As I said, you came all this way. It's the least I can do. It's just a shame we haven't got longer but let's make the most of it.'

They lay on their backs, their faces up to the sun, listening to the sound of the water for a while. Maggie felt so far away from her everyday life, it was as if she could see herself from afar. She thought about what they'd talked about that morning. If she was honest with herself, she had to admit she was lonely. Keeping busy was her way of coping with it but all it did was push the problem to one side. It certainly didn't make the loneliness go away and, sooner or later, it would catch up with her. Maybe it already had. Still, she'd have to take that job whether she liked it or not. There wasn't anything else on the horizon and she had bills to pay.

'Penny for them,' said Allegra.

Maggie turned on her side. 'I've been offered a job, and I don't really want to do it.'

'Any particular reason?'

'It's complicated,' said Maggie.

'Try me.'

'My ex-husband and his new girlfriend, pregnant girlfriend if I need to remind you, are both working on it. I'm not sure I can cope with that, but I don't think I have a choice.'

'There's always a choice,' said Allegra. 'I can say that. I'm old enough to know.' She smiled at Maggie. 'Come on, there's another little cove bit further along; we can lie on the sand for a bit.'

They swam on, Maggie following Allegra as she navigated her way through the rocks towards a small strip of sand ahead. Once again they lay side by side, letting the warm sun dry the water from their limbs. Maggie watched as a kestrel hovered overhead, clearly on the hunt for something to eat in the woodland behind them. A heron sat on a rock a little further out in the bay, elegantly watching the scene. For a short while, the only thing disturbing the peace was birdsong.

Maggie's eyes were closed when she heard Henri call over to them.

'Time to go back; he did say he needed to be back just after midday,' said Allegra, shifting herself up.

'Is it that late already?' said Maggie. She'd lost track without her watch or phone to hand.

They swam back to the boat and climbed up the ladder at the stern, Allegra making it look much easier than Maggie did. Given she'd struggled to keep up with Allegra in the water, she made a mental note to finally do something about her fitness when she got back to London, much as she loathed going to the gym. As they sped back across the flat sea towards the mainland, into the wide bay, Maggie thought about the choices she faced. Maybe it was time for her to make some different ones?

* * *

Having said their goodbyes to Henri, Allegra and Maggie crossed the road and walked back into the streets behind the harbour. Somehow Maggie had completely missed the covered market the previous day, quite a feat given the size of the building. As they walked through the earthy red brick-coloured archway into the market, Maggie's senses were immediately hit by the colour, smell and noise of the place. Row upon row of stalls heaving with vegetables of every colour ran as far as the eye could see. There were glass-fronted cabinets with shelves stacked with cheeses, fresh meat and charcuterie, flowers stalls and honey stalls alongside displays of herbs and spices. Great trays of ice were laden with fresh fish of all sizes, piles of shellfish alongside. Stalls with olives, olive oils and tapenades and tables stacked with melons and green, red and yellow tomatoes, were all doing a roaring trade. The place was rammed, with locals and tourists alike. The former were easy to spot, with their baskets and colourful attire making the tourists with their backpacks and faded T-shirts and shorts look positively pedestrian. Maggie watched as two deeply tanned older women in full make-up, one wearing lime green, the other in purple, arms heavy with bangles, busied themselves feeling the produce and bargaining with the traders as they filled their baskets with their chosen items.

Maggie followed Allegra through the crowd as she made her way straight to a particular cheese stall.

'Which ones do you prefer?' asked Allegra, pointing at the display.

'You choose but let me pay for them,' said Maggie, reaching for her wallet.

'Absolutely not, this is on me,' said Allegra. 'Pick some more fruit for us to have tomorrow morning for breakfast before you go.'

Maggie walked on through the market, watching the people as much as the produce. She bought some more peaches and a bag of fresh figs, so plump she thought they might burst before they got back to the house. After they'd finished at the market, Allegra suggested stopping at a small café on their way back up towards the Old Town, a run-down looking place in a back street.

To Maggie's surprise, it served the best coffee she'd tasted for as long as she could remember. 'That was such a wonderful morning,' she said. 'I know I've only been here for a day, but I feel like I've had a week's holiday.'

'I think you needed it,' said Allegra, before taking a sip from her tiny cup.

'I've been thinking about what you said. And about that job...'

Allegra raised that eyebrow of hers. 'And?'

'I've got to take it. Unless something else comes along in a hurry, I really do need it, but I *have* decided I'm going to look to do something else in the long term.'

'You are?'

Maggie slowly nodded her head. 'It's time I made some changes. I'm not as happy as I could be and I think stepping away from it all, even just for a few days, has made me realise I've got to do something about it.'

'Nothing changes if nothing changes,' said Allegra. She smiled at Maggie, her green eyes sparkling. 'As I said, I'm old enough to say things like that.'

'Only just,' said Maggie, laughing.

They walked up the hill arm in arm towards the clock-tower, away from the busy market and into the peaceful streets behind. Allegra put down her basket as she reached for her key under the pot by the front door.

'Let me take these bags up to the kitchen,' said Maggie, taking one from Allegra.

'Thank you, I'm just going to go and change, I'll see you up there.'

Maggie closed the door behind her and watched as Allegra made her way up the stairs.

She stopped to look at the painting on the wall, a window looking out to the bluest sea beyond. Just then, she heard a yelp.

Maggie took the next flight of stairs two at a time to find Allegra on her side on the floor.

'Allegra! What happened?' said Maggie, as she bent down to try and help her up.

'I tripped on the damn step.' Allegra's voice shook a little.

Maggie could tell she was in pain. 'Don't move for a second. We need to make sure nothing's broken. Where does it hurt?' She noticed a cut on the side of Allegra's head, a small trickle of blood falling slowly down her face. 'Hang on, I'll just get something to stop that bleeding.' She rummaged in her basket for a tissue.

'My arm doesn't feel right,' said Allegra.

'Okay, that doesn't sound great,' said Maggie, looking at the arm underneath Allegra. 'Let's not move from here for a moment, I'm going to call for an ambulance. What's the number?' She got her phone from her bag.

'Just use the phone on the side there, dial the number fifteen and repeat what I say,' said Allegra.

Ten minutes later an ambulance was outside the house. Maggie showed the two medics in and listened as they spoke to Allegra in French, then helped her downstairs into the waiting ambulance.

'Shall I come with you?' asked Maggie.

Allegra nodded. 'Just lock up behind you and put the key back under the pot. And please can you go and put the cheese and figs in the fridge before you do, I can't bear them to go to waste.'

Maggie couldn't help but smile. 'Sure. I'll be right back.'

18

NEW YORK, 1962

'Can I help you?' said Allegra to the man who'd wandered into the gallery without so much as acknowledging her as she sat behind the desk at the back of the room.

He was older, around her father's age she guessed, and about as short and round. 'I'm looking for something for my wife; she told me to come and buy her a painting.' Not once did he look at Allegra when he spoke. 'How much is this one?'

Allegra got up from the desk and went to join him as he stood, looking at the picture. 'That's a wonderful piece, painted by a young up-and-coming artist.'

'But it's just a blue canvas, isn't it?' The man put his face close to the painting.

'Well, yes... if that's what you want to see. For some, it's the colour of melancholy and despair but for this particular artist, it's the colour of the cerulean blue skies of the Mediterranean. He was born in the South of France.'

The man shrugged. 'I don't get it.' He pointed to another painting beside it. 'What about this one?'

Allegra steeled herself, concentrating on keeping the smile

on her face. She looked at the canvas, one of her favourites currently in the gallery. It showed streaks of different colours from green to blue, red to yellow, varying in shape and texture. Some were fine lines, others seemingly smeared across the canvas. For Allegra, simply looking at it made her feel more connected to the world around her. 'The artist is a landscape painter, she's American but has been living in France for a few years. She's very much influenced by the great French Impressionist painters of the nineteenth century, particularly Matisse.'

The man stepped back and cocked his head to one side, squinting as he looked at the painting in front of him. 'That's a landscape?' He shook his head. 'I really don't get it.'

Allegra was about to give up and go and sit back at the desk, leaving him to no doubt dismiss all the other works of art hanging on the walls, when he reached inside his jacket pocket and pulled out a chequebook.

He waved it in front of Allegra. 'How much?'

'The price is right there, on the little sign below.' She tried not to show her surprise.

He leant in and whistled as he read it.

Allegra smiled as he turned back to face her.

'I'll take it.'

'Really? That's wonderful!' Allegra couldn't believe she'd misread him. Normally her ability to identify a serious buyer was spot on thanks to watching and learning from Val over the last few months.

'She likes those colours. If you like it, I think she will too.'

'I can give you more information about the painting, I'm sure your wife would like to know. Please, come and have a seat and I can take your details.'

The transaction done, Allegra closed the door of the

gallery behind him as the man walked back onto the street, turning left towards Madison. When Val came back from her customary lunch with her husband, Allegra couldn't wait to tell her about the unexpected sale.

Looking at the ledger book on the desk, perfectly filled in with the details just as she'd taught Allegra to do, Val closed it and put her hands on Allegra's shoulders. 'That is wonderful news. I knew you had an instinct for it.'

'But that's the funny part. I hardly said a word,' said Allegra, her eyes wide.

Val laughed. 'The thing is, people either like buying from you or they don't. You've just got it, along with a natural feel for the artists' work.'

It had been almost three months since Allegra had started working for Val. Her birthday had been and gone and as desperate as she was to get back to Paris, Allegra had barely any money to her name – not to mention no passport. She often wondered if Etienne had gone to the place they'd agreed to meet, picturing him standing in the spot under the Eiffel Tower just as he'd looked that first night when they'd met.

Instead, Allegra had thrown herself into her work, resolving to return just as soon as she was back on her own two feet. She'd quickly worked her way up from general gallery dogsbody, cleaning the floors to making coffee, to helping Val with the paperwork and organising the transportation of artworks between artists and buyers. Now, here she was being left in charge of the gallery every now and again and this had been her biggest solo sale to date by quite some way. Allegra thought she might cry with happiness on the spot.

'Thank you,' she managed.

Val hugged her tightly. 'We are very proud of you. I think

we need to celebrate tonight. Let's go to Lutèce for lamb and lots of red wine,' she said, laughing.

The French restaurant around the corner from Val and Robert's apartment had quickly become Allegra's favourite place to eat, not least because it reminded her of the food she'd eaten when she'd been in France. Almost everything came cooked in butter and garlic was a given.

When she'd received her first pay cheque from Val, Allegra had already started to look for an apartment to rent nearby in the West Village but Val, who'd insisted on coming with her to view them, had refused to let her spend her hard-earned money on such miserable digs. Instead, Val and Robert had persuaded her to stay with them for a while longer and save up some money, insisting they loved her company. Their three-storey red-brick house had plenty of space and an almost constant flow of visitors, often artists and friends. The long oak dining table in the low basement kitchen was a carousel of conversation, from the first coffee in the morning to the last whisky (always Scotch for Robert) at night.

Allegra loved the way Robert and Val could communicate without words, their actions so clearly borne out of love and respect for one another. The atmosphere at home with her parents had been cold in comparison. They had only ever conveyed facts, never feelings, as far as she'd been able to tell. As they sat around the table in the restaurant that evening, Allegra retold the story of her first sale to Robert as instructed by Val and he promptly ordered a bottle of champagne. They toasted her success and Allegra thanked them, as she did often, for their kindness.

Their food arrived, along with a bottle of Bordeaux ordered by Robert and more toasts were made. 'I honestly don't know what I would have done without you,' said Allegra, looking from one to the other.

'Don't be silly, we love having you. Now,' said Val, as she heaped another spoonful of potatoes dauphinoise onto Robert's plate before putting more on her own, 'I know you don't like talking about it, but have you thought about going to see your father?'

Allegra put her fork down on her plate. 'I have been thinking about it.' She wiped her mouth with her napkin. 'But I just don't think I can.'

Robert topped up their glasses with more red wine. 'You should try and make peace with him. Go and see him, explain what you've been doing, what you want to do.'

'And,' said Val, 'you can ask him for the letters from Etienne.'

Allegra had written every week without fail since being back in New York, long letters telling Etienne what she'd been doing, her work at the gallery and how much she missed him. She loved describing the paintings in the gallery, the new artists she was discovering through her work there and the people she was meeting. But still she hadn't heard back from him, despite giving him her new address. There was no way of knowing if he'd written back to her at her home address without seeing her father and much as she had told herself she would be happy if she never saw him again, she knew deep down he would always haunt her. She should at least try, especially now that she had a job and was on her way to being able to have enough savings to return to Paris, even if it was going to take a little longer than Allegra had hoped.

'I know, I will,' she said. 'Tomorrow. I'll go tomorrow.' Maybe it was the wine making her feel brave but suddenly it seemed clear and she knew what she had to do.

* * *

The following morning Allegra left the house before either Val or Robert had surfaced and decided to walk across town through Washington Square Park and take the 6 Train uptown. Despite the slight chill, spring was definitely in the air and the park was coming alive with bulbs peeking through the grass on the ground. A few brave daffodils had already revealed their petals to passers-by, not that many seemed to notice. She sat for a moment on the bench by the fountain collecting her thoughts, then walked under the arch and across to Lafayette and the subway station.

Allegra's plan was simple: she would go to the reception at her parents' home and ask them to call her father to let him know she was there to see him. Then it was up to him whether to allow her to come up or not. If the answer was no, she would leave knowing she'd tried. And as much as she was desperate to have any letters that may have arrived from Etienne, it made no real difference one way or another. Allegra would return to Paris just as soon as she had enough money to do so.

Standing outside her old apartment looking at the forest green awning of the building, Allegra told herself to put one foot in front of the other but she felt rooted to the spot. Looking up at their floor, she felt the familiar knot in her stomach she'd had when thinking of her mother lying sick in the bed upstairs. The one comfort was the closeness they'd enjoyed just before her mother had died. Too little, too late. This time, she had nothing to lose.

Allegra was greeted with the usual cheery hello from the doorman as she walked through the heavy oak and glass doors into the building. She went straight to reception and waited for someone to appear.

'Hello, Ms Morgon,' said the old man on the other side of the dark wooden desk.

'Hey, Alfred, how are you?'

'Good thank you. We haven't seen you for a while, how've you been?'

Allegra smiled, grateful for him not asking why she'd disappeared so suddenly. 'Fine, thank you. I'm working round the corner now, at the gallery on East 74th.'

'Fancy! Good for you,' he whispered, winking at her. 'Now, you going up to see your father?'

'Can you call him and let him know I'm here?'

'Of course, one moment.' Alfred picked up the telephone on the desk and dialled the number. 'Mr Morgon, sir. I have Ms Allegra down here. Shall I send her up?'

Allegra watched as Alfred listened, nodding his head.

'As you wish, sir. I'll let her know.' He put down the phone and looked at Allegra. He was clearly reluctant to relay the message.

'It's okay, Alfred. Just tell me.'

'I'm so sorry, Ms Morgon, he says he's very busy.'

Allegra bit her lip hard, not wanting to let him know how much those words hurt.

'I'm sure he'll come round,' said Alfred, shrugging his shoulders.

'Thanks, I'll try another time perhaps.' She sighed and looked around the hall with its polished marble floors. The smell of the lilies in the vase on the table in the middle of the room reminded her of her mother. Suddenly she wanted to cry.

'There have been some letters for you,' said Alfred. 'Not

that I have them here, I'm afraid. Your father takes them with his post.'

Allegra's heart leapt. 'Did you happen to notice where they were from?'

'Obviously I don't look at the post in detail, it's not my place,' said Alfred. 'But—' he leant towards Allegra '—I happened to notice they did have an unusual stamp on them. I think they were from France.'

'Could I ask you a big favour?' She put her hand on his arm. 'Next time something arrives for me, please can you put it aside? I'll come and pick it up.'

He looked about. 'They were coming every week but there hasn't been one for a while.'

'Please? My father won't ever know. Besides, they belong to me. He shouldn't be able to keep things from me.'

Alfred thought about it for a moment, then nodded his head. 'Okay, sure. I will. But if I get into trouble...'

'You won't, I promise. Thank you, Alfred. I can't tell you how much I appreciate it. I'll come back next week.' Allegra turned to leave. Just as she got to the door, she heard him call her name.

'Ms Morgon?'

'Yes?'

'Look after yourself.' The old man smiled at her.

'Thanks, Alfred, you too.' She walked back through the revolving doors onto the quiet New York street and made her way to the gallery, happy in the knowledge that Etienne hadn't forgotten her. If her father had his way maybe she'd never get her hands on those letters, but it didn't matter. Sooner or later, she was going to return to Paris and there was nothing he could do to stop her.

* * *

New York sweltered as preparations were made for a new exhibition at the gallery. Allegra had been flat out for weeks organising the logistics that came with putting on a new show. There was already a buzz about it but Val had been tight-lipped about the artist in question, even with Allegra. It was to be a Minimalist sculpture show featuring works by a female artist and Allegra couldn't wait to write to Etienne, knowing how much he'd love the idea.

Late one morning, when Val had left for lunch with an artist she was trying to get on board for an exhibition later that year, Allegra was working at the desk cataloguing artworks. The gallery door was locked, as it sometimes was when she was alone. It took a few seconds for Allegra to realise someone was knocking gently on the glass window, trying to get her attention. Looking up, she saw Alfred on the other side, waving at her. At first, she didn't recognise him, used to seeing him in his uniform.

Allegra crossed the gallery floor and opened the door. 'Alfred, nice to see you. Come on in.'

'Hello, Ms Morgon. I won't stay long. I came to give you this.' He handed Allegra a small cardboard tube.

Taking it from him, she looked at the typed label on the front. She recognised the tube but couldn't quite place it. 'When did this arrive?'

'Yesterday, late afternoon.' He pointed at the stamp. 'It's from France. It was posted a while ago though, maybe it got lost on the way.'

Allegra took it from him and studied the postmark. 'Thank you so much, I'm truly grateful.'

He looked around the gallery. 'So, this is where you work?'

'Yes, I've been here for a while now. I love it.'

Alfred looked around at the paintings on the walls. 'Bet these are worth a pretty penny.'

'Hopefully but until they're sold, I get to enjoy looking at them. That's the best bit.' She hugged Alfred. 'Thank you, I really appreciate you coming.'

'My pleasure. Well, I'd better get going. And if your father ever asks, I wasn't here.'

'Never saw you,' she said, winking at him. 'Thank you.'

After locking the door behind him, Allegra went back to the desk and sat down. With trembling fingers, she lifted the brown wrapping paper from the tube, then carefully opened one end. Reaching inside, she slipped out the rolled-up piece of paper and unfurled it gently on the desk. She stared at the drawing for a few seconds before registering what she was looking at. 'Oh my God,' she whispered. There in front of her was the sketch she'd bought in the flea market for Etienne, the one she'd given to him that Christmas. She looked at the lines on the paper, the curves of a woman's body depicted with just a few strokes of the artist's hand. She instantly recalled his face when he'd first seen it. How she missed those eyes. He'd loved it, so why was he returning it?

She looked again inside the tube and saw there was an envelope. She took it out and tore it open, desperate to see his words on a page. As soon as she saw his handwriting, small and precise just as she remembered it, her eyes filled with tears. She read the words, her heart beating faster with every sentence. When she finished, she dropped the letter to the floor and wept.

'What's going on?'

Val had let herself into the gallery to find Allegra sitting on the floor beneath a painting, her knees to her chest, a faded piece of paper in her hands.

Allegra looked up, her face streaked with mascara. She held out the drawing to Val. 'It's from Etienne.' Her voice was weak.

Val took it from her and turned it up the right way. She stared at it, her mouth dropping open. 'Where did he get this?'

'I bought it for him in Paris. It was his Christmas present.'

'Where from?'

'A flea market, I forget the name.'

Val couldn't take her eyes off it. 'You know what this is?'

'A Rodin,' said Allegra, flatly.

Val went to the desk and sat down, placing the drawing in front of her. She opened the drawer and rummaged around for a pair of glasses. 'But how on earth did you get your hands on it?'

'That's what Etienne said when I gave it to him.' Allegra shrugged. 'I just bought it. I assumed it was a print.'

Val examined the drawing, a magnifying glass now in her hand. 'I think this is an original.'

Allegra laughed, but her face was stony. 'It is.'

'How do you know?'

'Because Etienne wrote to me.' Allegra held up a letter. 'I just got it. He checked with his friend, a neighbour of his parents. He's an artist. Serge said he's 99 per cent sure it's an original.'

Val was obviously confused. 'But then why are you crying? This could be worth a lot of money.'

'Etienne says I shouldn't go back to Paris.' Allegra wiped the tears from her face. 'He says he can't offer me the life I deserve there but wants me to have this so I can start the life I should be leading here instead.'

Val thought for a moment. 'Don't you think he's doing you a favour here? He must really love you to do this.'

Allegra closed her eyes. 'That's the point. He doesn't love me. That's why he wants me to stay here.'

'How do you know?'

'Because he says so.' Allegra pointed at the letter on the floor. 'Read it for yourself.'

Val picked up the letter from beside the desk where Allegra had dropped it and, without looking, simply folded it over. She stood up and went to sit down on the floor next to Allegra, handing her the letter.

Allegra took it, holding it in her long fingers. 'How could he be so cruel?'

Val put her arm around the distraught girl. 'Listen to me, honey. Letting you go back there would have been cruel. He's been honest and as painful as it might be right now, you'll be thankful one day that he was. And he feels guilty enough to give you a damn Rodin drawing.' She laughed and squeezed Allegra's shoulder.

They sat together on the floor for a while, Val gently soothing Allegra until there were no tears left to cry and later that night, as they sat around the table in the basement kitchen, Allegra sipped on the double measure of whisky as instructed. The Rodin drawing was propped up at the end of the table and as they ate supper, a chicken pie made by Robert, Val attempted to persuade Allegra that this could all be a blessing in disguise.

But Allegra knew better. Her heart had been broken twice over, first by her father and now by Etienne. And she was determined not to trust it to anyone else ever again.

19

PRESENT DAY

Lined with palm trees and clad with undulating white shutters, the hospital – less than ten minutes from Allegra's house – looked more like a hotel than a hospital to Maggie. She wheeled Allegra, now in a wheelchair at the insistence of the ambulance staff, through the front doors and into the airy reception. Inside, the space was calm and cool. They were directed straight up to another floor to wait for someone to assess the injury and, as suspected, the x-ray showed two broken bones in Allegra's left forearm. The painkillers she'd been given on arrival had taken the edge off according to Allegra, but Maggie could tell she was in more pain than she was willing to let on. Once the cast had been put on and all the medical checks completed, Allegra was discharged with instructions to rest and to keep the arm protected and elevated as much as possible. The nurse spoke quickly to Allegra in French, handing her a paper bag stuffed with tablets. Allegra nodded and thanked her.

'You are staying with Madame Morgon?' the nurse asked Maggie. Without waiting for a response, she continued. 'She will need looking after for the next few days. The instructions for her medication are all in there but it is very important that she rests and protects her arm as much as possible. This first few days are critical. And put something cold on that arm to help reduce the swelling.'

Maggie looked at the nurse. 'Of course.'

'But you're going home tomorrow, aren't you?' said Allegra.

Maggie looked at Allegra, incredulous. 'I'm not going to leave you on your own now. I can stay for a few more days, just until you're more comfortable.'

'I'm sure I can call on some friends to check in on me.'

'And I can change my flight when we get back. I'm not back at work until next week. Please, let me help.'

The nurse signed a piece of paper and asked for Allegra's signature, then turned to Maggie. 'I think it would be a good idea for you to stay for a few days if you can.'

'See?' said Maggie to Allegra. 'She agrees.'

Allegra sighed. 'I don't want to be a burden.'

'Don't be silly,' said Maggie.

'Well, that's very kind but you can only stay on condition that you let me pay for your flight if you can't get a refund.'

'We can argue about that later,' said Maggie. 'Let's get you home.'

It was late afternoon by the time they got back to the house and Allegra was already feeling the soporific effects of the painkillers. Maggie helped her up the stairs and onto her bed, then fetched her some water.

'Are you comfortable?' asked Maggie, as she opened the windows to let in some breeze.

'Thank you, I'm fine. I think I'm going to close my eyes for a little while.'

'How about a pillow under your arm?'

Allegra agreed and once settled, Maggie left her to sleep. She didn't want to go to the terrace just in case she couldn't hear Allegra from there, instead settling at the table by the kitchen with a cup of tea. She searched for different flight options on her phone, then fetched her laptop to clear down her emails. She'd had three from the production company doing the reality show, despite not committing to the job yet. Ignoring them, she emailed her father instead, knowing he'd print it off and read it out to her mother as they sat in the garden with their evening drinks. Maggie described the Old Town and the house, their visit to the islands and the food market and, of course, the fall. Maggie thought of her parents, her biggest cheerleaders.

As the bells in the clocktower rang out at six o'clock, Maggie went to check on Allegra, relieved to find her still sleeping. Realising she was now starving, Maggie went back up to the kitchen and broke off some of the fresh baguette Allegra had bought earlier that day. She looked in the fridge and took out the creamy white cheese, cutting a slice and putting it on a plate. Then she poured herself a small glass of rosé from the open bottle in the fridge and carried it all carefully upstairs to the terrace. As the sun started its descent behind the hills to the west of the bay, Maggie savoured the food in front of her. She swirled the glass of rosé and stuck her nose in as she'd seen people do on a Saturday morning cookery programme. With no one around to make her feel self-conscious, Maggie took a long, deep sniff. The scent of red grapefruit filled her nose and when she took a sip, it was as if she were tasting it in high definition. She savoured every sip and mouthful and once she'd finished both what was on her plate and in her glass, Maggie returned downstairs to check on Allegra.

Finding her still sleeping, Maggie went to the kitchen and topped up her wine glass, taking a picture of the label with her phone before putting the bottle back in the fridge. She spotted the box of photographs on the table and sat down, her glass of wine in reach. She lifted off the lid and took out the camera from the top, placing it carefully on the table. Taking out the first few photographs, she lay them down flat and looked at the images again. Allegra and Luc sitting at the table in Etienne's flat, their faces so joyous Maggie could almost hear their laughter. Then there was the photograph of Etienne standing on the street, scarf draped around his neck with a book in his hand. There was the photograph of Allegra and Etienne, that stolen kiss on the bench caught on camera by Elizabeth. Taking out the next few photographs, Maggie slowly turned them over and placed them on the table like a giant jigsaw, each piece a part of Allegra's story. Another showed Allegra and Luc dancing in a tiny bar, a man in the corner playing the accordion and, just out of shot, the side of Etienne's head as he watched with a smile on his face. Allegra looked so carefree, mid-spin, dressed in black trousers and a short trench coat, her ponytail swishing up in the air behind her. Then there was one with Etienne and Allegra in what looked like a wine cellar but must have been a jazz club judging by the posters on the wall behind them. They had their heads close, Allegra speaking as Etienne listened to her intently. Maggie turned the photograph over to read the back. In pencil, she could make out what she now knew to be her grandmother's writing. *E & A, Bal – 1961*. What a time that must have been for them all, thought Maggie. She couldn't help but smile to herself, the images so full of life – and love.

By now, the light was starting to fade. She got up to close the windows, then heard Allegra's voice. 'Coming,' she called.

'Just a second.' Leaving the photos where they were, Maggie went down the stairs to Allegra's room to find her awake and propped up on her pillows. 'How are you feeling? You've been asleep for quite a while.'

Allegra shifted herself up a little more. 'Much better. Those painkillers were most effective.' She laughed, then winced.

'Where does it hurt?' asked Maggie, gently sitting on the end of the bed.

Allegra touched her arm. 'It doesn't hurt so much as just ache. It's fine if I keep it still.'

'Are you hungry? I was starving when we got back. I hope you don't mind but I had some bread and cheese.'

'Actually, that sounds good.'

'I'll go and fetch you some. Is there a tray I can put it on?'

'Yes, in the cupboard to the left of the sink.'

'More water? Tea? Martini?' Maggie laughed.

'I would but by your own admission your martini making needs work. Just some more water for now, thank you.'

Maggie went to put a plate together for Allegra, slicing some more bread and putting cheese and pâté on it together with a small bowl of green olives. She carried the tray downstairs and put it down on the table next to the bed.

'Here, let me help you,' she said, placing the plate closer to Allegra. Picking up the water glass, she refilled it from a large water bottle she'd brought down with her, leaving it on the floor next to the bed.

'Did you have a look at flights?' said Allegra, as she slathered a thick bit of butter onto a piece of baguette.

'I'll have a look tomorrow, once we know how you're doing. The nurse suggested I stay for the next few days so unless you really don't want me here, that's what I'm going to do.'

Allegra laughed gently. 'Maggie, I'm thrilled you're here. I'd much rather have you than one of my friends fussing over me. They'd be no use with these stairs anyway.'

'I've been looking at some more photographs whilst you've been sleeping. There's a lovely one of you and Etienne in a jazz club. The Bal, it says on the back.'

Allegra smiled at the very mention of the name. 'Yes, that was our favourite.'

'Can you tell me what happened after you went back to New York?'

The smile faded from Allegra's face.

'How stupid of me. It's probably the last thing you want to talk about.'

Allegra lifted her gaze to Maggie. 'No, I'd love to tell you. Where did we get to?'

Outside, the clock chimed.

20

NEW YORK, 1963

'I'll take it.' Allegra looked around the tiny apartment, the kitchen so narrow you could only get one person in it at a time and a bedroom that barely fitted an actual bed in it. She couldn't have been happier. It was hers – at least, she was able to pay the rent on it herself – and as much as Val and Robert had tried to persuade her to stay, she knew it was time to get her own place.

It had been almost a year since Allegra had first started working at the gallery and, after receiving the devastating letter from Etienne, she'd thrown every part of herself into her job. It seemed like the best way to deal with her heartbreak. She was learning so much from Val about the ever-changing art world and not long after their ground-breaking sculpture exhibition, they'd secured one of the most famous pop artists of the day to exhibit at the gallery. Predictably, this led to more artists and collectors knocking on their door and by the end of the year barely a week had gone by without a glowing write-up in a newspaper or magazine about the gallery and the woman behind it.

Behind the scenes Allegra was doing more of the day to day running and adored dealing with the artists but much as she loved what was happening in the world of pop art, her heart belonged to a more classical, Impressionist style. She didn't care if it was unfashionable; to her it was eloquent, not to mention breathtakingly beautiful to look at.

Standing in what was about to become her first apartment on Washington Street on the Lower West Side, in an old red-brick two-storey building on the floor above a dry-cleaning business, Allegra shook hands with the landlord and handed over a month's rent. It was a ten-minute walk further south from Val and Robert's house (they certainly weren't keen on the idea of Allegra walking down Greenwich Street on her own at night) but with the money she was earning she could afford to take a cab after dark.

The following week, she moved in with her few belongings and set about making it feel like home. Val had insisted on giving her some bedding and Robert had brought round a box of books, insisting it wasn't a home without books no matter how big or small the space. The floor was split into two apartments, and even though she was told she had a neighbour, it would be almost a week before they met.

One morning, Allegra had been woken by the sound of banging. She lay in her bed, trying to figure out exactly where it was coming from and what was making it. She looked at the small alarm clock by her bed, the faintly illuminated hands telling her it was just after five o'clock. She listened again, deciding the noise wasn't coming from downstairs as she'd first suspected, but from her next-door neighbour. Allegra reluctantly got out of bed and threw a jumper on over her pyjamas, then opened her door to knock on the one opposite. At first, she knocked gently but there was no response. The banging continued, not so much as pausing at her attempt to get their attention. Allegra knocked again, this time more loudly. Still, nothing. On the third attempt, she continued knocking until the banging sound behind the door stopped. She waited for whoever was there to come and answer it, but no one came. She knocked again, explaining that she was their new neighbour and maybe they hadn't realised she was there but if they could just keep the noise down for an hour or so, she'd be grateful. Allegra put her ear to the door, hoping for some indication that she'd been heard.

'Okay, thank you, I'm going back to bed now.' She went to go back into her apartment, then turned back to speak through the closed door. 'Hope to meet you soon, maybe not quite so early though.' She was about to tell them her name, then thought better of it given she had no idea who this person might be.

The same thing happened the following morning, and the next and the next until, not knowing what else to do, she decided she had no option but to lie in wait for them to leave or come back to the apartment and confront them about the noise. One evening, having had dinner with Val along with an upcoming artist she was hoping to represent, at a new French restaurant that had just opened not far from the gallery, Allegra arrived back at the apartment. Noticing the lights in the apartment next to hers were off, she took up her position on the steps of the building opposite and waited in the shadows.

It was still cold at night in the city and despite being suitably wrapped up to keep out the chill, after an hour she was ready to give up. But just as she went to cross the road, a figure appeared around the corner wearing a hooded coat and carrying a large piece of wood under their arm, dragging a broken chair with their other hand. Allegra watched as the figure rummaged for their keys, then went inside, leaving the piece of wood propped against the wall whilst they carried the chair inside.

Once Allegra saw the light come on upstairs, she crossed the road and went inside the door, waiting at the bottom of the stairs for whoever it was to come back down. She heard their footsteps and braced herself for a confrontation. When she saw the face beneath the hood, she was surprised to see it was a woman standing there.

'Can I help you?' said the stranger.

Allegra smiled awkwardly. 'Hello, I'm your neighbour. I've been knocking on your door for the last week asking if you could be quiet.'

The woman stared at her, then removed her hood. She had long dark hair and her skin was pale. 'I'm so sorry. I really didn't hear you.'

'Are you serious? I almost broke your door down!'

The woman started to make her way down the stairs. 'When I am working, I don't hear a thing.'

'Working? What are you doing at that time in the morning? And what's with the wood?'

'I make sculptures from anything I can get my hands on really.'

Allegra's interest was immediately piqued. 'You do? What kind of thing?'

'If you help me get that piece of wood up the stairs, I can show you.' The woman looked at Allegra, her face impassive.

'Sure,' said Allegra, intrigued. 'I guess this is why you're out at night finding materials?'

The woman didn't answer, instead extending her hand to Allegra. 'Pleased to meet you. My name is Eve.'

'Eve,' said Allegra, taking her hand. 'Nice to meet you too. I'm Allegra.'

With some careful manoeuvring they managed to get the long piece of timber around the corner at the top of the narrow staircase without too much trouble. Eve opened her door, apologising for the mess as she did so. 'I'm hoping to get some proper studio space soon.'

Allegra looked around the room, the layout of the small apartment the same as hers but this one had no furniture at all. Instead, every bit of space was taken up with various objects. It looked like a junk shop save for one thing. In the middle of the room was a plinth, standing like an island in the chaos. On it was a sculpture, the distorted figure of a woman curled in a ball, made from wood, metal and coloured glass. It was, Allegra thought, one of the most extraordinary sculptures she'd ever seen.

She stared it at for a moment. 'Can I take a look?'

Eve nodded.

Allegra picked her away around the random objects on the floor and circled the sculpture, marvelling at the way the artist had created movement from the still materials. 'What was your inspiration?'

'I wanted to create something beautiful from the mundane.' Eve shrugged her shoulders.

'It's astonishing,' whispered Allegra. 'Seriously, I've never seen anything like it. Where did you train?'

Eve looked at her blankly.

'I mean, who taught you how to do this?'

'No one. I taught myself.'

Allegra peered closely at a piece of carved wood so black it looked charred. 'How did you get that colour?'

'It's a particular pigment. I like working with it at the moment.'

'Do you have any more finished pieces?' Allegra looked around.

'Yes, at another studio not far from here but like I said, I need to get my own space.'

'Can I see it?'

Eve looked at her neighbour suspiciously.

Allegra suddenly realised she was asking too many questions without context. 'I'm sorry, I should have said. I work in a gallery on the Upper East Side.'

Eve's eyes widened. 'The one on East 74th?'

'Yes, that's the one. You know it?'

'It had the Marisol sculpture exhibition last year.'

Allegra smiled. 'Yes, that's the one. Did you see it?'

'Of course,' said Eve. 'She's such an inspiration. So, you work for Valentina?'

'I do,' said Allegra. 'She's been very good to me. The first time she met me I'd just run away from home. Well, I'd only gone two blocks, but I knew I didn't want to go back. She gave me a job and now I'm here.'

'With a horribly noisy neighbour.' Eve grimaced.

'Yes, but now I know why.'

'I'll try and keep it down from now on.'

Allegra looked around the room again. 'I don't know how you create anything in this space. You're right, you do need your own studio.'

'One day, maybe.'

'I really want Val to see what you're doing here. Can we have a look at some of your other work?'

'Sure,' said Eve. 'But female artists are hardly in demand right now.'

'Val put on the show you came to and that opened the door to Indiana and Warhol.'

'You've met Warhol?'

Allegra nodded. 'I have. Only very briefly and he didn't say much. He's always watching, observing those around him. It's a bit unsettling, to be honest.'

'And what was Marisol like?'

'Enigmatic,' said Allegra. 'And very beautiful. Listen, I've got a bottle of wine that Val and Robert gave me when I moved in but they refused to let me open it with them. Do you fancy sharing it?'

As they sat on the floor of the corridor between the two flats, sipping warm white wine from the bottle and talking about everything from art to heartbreak, they both found the friend they needed, just when they needed them.

* * *

Val was already in the gallery, sitting behind the desk with her glasses on her nose as she looked through the daily newspaper, when Allegra walked through the door. 'Someone had a late night,' she said, without even looking up.

'How do you know?' asked Allegra, shaking herself out of her coat.

'Because I think this might be the first time since you've worked here that you're in after me,' said Val. 'Were you out? I'm hoping so.'

'No, I just met my neighbour and you will never guess what...'

'Don't tell me, she's an artist.' Val looked up at Allegra over her glasses.

'How did you know?'

'Because they're all in that part of town now. It makes the West Village look hideously bourgeois.' Val laughed at her own observation.

'She is but, Val, she's really good. She's called Eve, she's a sculptor.'

Val looked up. 'Really?'

'She's mostly working in her apartment now because she has so little space in the studio she's renting. I've only seen the piece she's got in her flat, but she's got some other finished – or almost finished – pieces in the studio. Honestly, Val, I've never seen anything like it. It's incredible.'

Val closed the paper on the table. 'Don't bother taking your coat off.'

'Why? Where are we going?'

'To see her now before anyone else gets to her. Come on.' Val stood up and pulled her long grey cape around her shoulders, fastening it at the neck.

'But... what if you don't think it's very good?'

'Honey, I know you well enough to realise that you have an instinct for art. Not everyone does, even if they think they do. Ready? Let's go.'

They made their way downtown in a yellow cab via 5th and then 9th Avenue, sitting in gridlocked traffic for much of it.

'We could have gone later, on our way home,' said Allegra, looking up at the billboards as they passed through Times Square, the smell of car smoke and candy apples in the air.

Val blew the smoke from her cigarette out of through the gap at the top of the cab's slightly open window. 'I've missed out on too many artists by waiting. If you want the good ones, you must go to them as soon as you can. I'd like to see her work, talk to her about it and see what she says.'

By the time they got to Allegra's building it was almost eleven o'clock. Allegra went up the stairs first, followed by Val. She knocked on the door. 'Eve, it's me, Allegra.'

'One second,' called Eve. The door opened slowly. She looked at Allegra, then Valentina. Her face registered her shock as soon as she realised who it was. To Allegra's surprise, Eve promptly shut the door again.

'I told Val about your work. She really wants to see it,' said Allegra, through the door.

Eve's muffled voice came from the other side. 'Is this some kind of joke? If so, it's not funny.'

'Of course it's not. Why would I do that?' Allegra looked at Val as they waited for an answer.

Val signalled to Allegra to let her speak. 'Eve, this is Valentina. I'm sorry to turn up unannounced like this but I really wanted to come and see you. Allegra told me about you this morning. If you'd rather I didn't see your work yet that's obviously up to you but maybe we can just have a conversation? We could go and get some coffee, or lunch if you haven't eaten.'

The door opened slowly, Eve's face appearing round it. 'Remember I haven't finished this one.' She beckoned them in.

Allegra waited as Val walked ahead, stepping carefully across the object-strewn floor. When she got to the sculpture in the middle of the room, Val turned to Eve. 'May I?'

Eve nodded and Val walked slowly round it, taking in every detail. She then took a step back and stood looking at it for a while longer. 'I love how you've done that,' said Val, pointing at the figure's hands, interlocked over her face. 'And this here,' she said, 'using the glass to reflect the light like that.' On she went, telling Eve her thoughts about the sculpture in front of her. Finally, she turned to the artist. 'I'd love to know what inspired you to create this.'

Allegra looked at Eve's face, waiting for her to speak. She almost didn't dare breathe.

'I'm not sure I even know. I just create what I'm feeling,' said Eve, as casually as she might order a coffee.

Val let out a sigh of relief. 'That's exactly what I was hoping you would say. Now, I know you need to get your other work out of your studio, Allegra told me on the way here. Can we help you move it to the gallery? I want to put on a show of your work.'

Eve gasped. 'But you haven't even seen it?'

'I don't need to,' said Val. 'This—' she gestured to the piece in front of them '—tells me all I need to know at this point. You were right, Allegra. It really is incredible.'

Eve walked over to Val and shook her hand. 'Thank you, I would love that.'

Three months later Eve's show opened to great acclaim, selling almost every piece on the opening night. The exhibition cemented the gallery as the hottest in town and instead of having to charm the collectors, Val was having to fend them off. So, it caught Allegra completely off guard when Val announced, over martinis at The Carlyle, that she planned to retire.

'But it's going so well!' Allegra couldn't believe what she was hearing. 'Why would you give it all up now?'

'I always said I would do this for as long as I loved it. And I do love it, so much.' Val reached across the table and put her hand on Allegra's. 'But we're not getting any younger. Robert and I want to travel, go to Europe. Maybe I'll get to see all those paintings in Paris you're always telling me about. We've lived in this city for almost our entire married life. I'm not leaving this place for the last time in a coffin.'

Allegra tried not to cry. 'I'm happy for you, really I am. But I don't know what I'm going to do without you.'

'It's funny you should say that because I have a plan. Waiter?' Val called over to the barman. 'Two more of those please. Vodka, dirty, three olives.' She turned her attention back to Allegra. 'Ready?'

21

PRESENT DAY

Maggie had slipped out early that morning, hoping to get to the boulangerie and back before Allegra awoke. She walked down the cobbled steps from the house and through the narrow streets to the place on the corner Allegra had pointed out to her the day before. Opposite was a small café, one she remembered walking past on her first morning here just a few days ago. With its red awning and small round tables and chairs outside, it was already busy with locals catching up over an early coffee. Having been told there was a five-minute wait for fresh croissants, Maggie decided to join them and sat at a table, ordering her coffee from a passing waiter as she did so.

She listened to the conversations around her while she waited. No one was in a rush, everyone seemed happy to see one another. It made her think of her usual morning ritual back home, standing in line in a large coffee shop chain where people avoided making eye contact, let alone conversation. Everyone just wanted to grab their coffee and go.

The young waiter brought her drink to the table. 'How is Madame?' he said, as he placed the bill in front of her.

Maggie looked at him, quizzically. Was he asking after her?

'Madame Morgon, someone told me this morning she had a fall yesterday.'

'Oh, yes, she did. You know her?'

The waiter smiled and nodded. 'She lives here a long time. Is she okay?'

'She's broken her arm, unfortunately. Two bones broken. She has a—' Maggie indicated to her arm '—cast? I don't know the word, I'm sorry.'

'*Plâtre*,' he said, nodding. 'Ah, *dommage*. Are you family?'

Maggie smiled to herself, wondering how to best explain it. 'I'm related to an old friend of hers. I just came to visit for a few days but now I'll stay for a few more, at least until she's up and about.'

'That's good. She is a very good person.'

'Yes, she really is.'

'Let me know if you need anything else,' he said.

Maggie thanked him and went to take a sip from her cup.

'Excuse me? Hello?'

Maggie looked up to see a man standing just to the side of her.

'I'm sorry, I didn't want to make you jump, especially not as you're about to have that.' He pointed to her cup.

The man had curly dark hair, greying at the edges, with dark brown eyes and (Maggie couldn't help but notice) killer cheekbones. But despite his handsome, tanned features, he looked like he'd slept in a bush. His T-shirt was covered in dirt and his shorts were not much better. She realised she was yet to say something. 'Sorry, can I help you?'

'I just came from the boulangerie over there; they said to tell you the croissants are ready.' He held up a brown paper bag. 'Got mine.' He smiled at her, the creases at the side of his eyes making his face even more attractive.

'Oh, thanks.' Maggie gulped her coffee, practically burning a hole in her throat as she did so, bringing on a coughing fit.

'Let me get you some water.'

Maggie wanted to tell him not to but before she could get the words out, he'd disappeared. She tried to regain her composure, not that anyone around her seemed remotely bothered. A moment later she was handed a glass. She took a few sips, nodding her thanks to him as her coughing subsided.

'Are you okay?' He put his hand gently on her shoulder.

Maggie immediately twitched and he quickly removed it.

'I'm sorry, I didn't mean to... I was just... I hope you are alright now.'

Maggie felt suddenly embarrassed. 'Yes, sorry. Thank you.' She took another sip.

'Okay, don't forget to go and get your croissants before they all go again,' the man said. He gave her a small wave, then turned and disappeared down the street. Maggie sat for a moment, processing what had just happened. Why would the simple touch of a concerned stranger make her react like that? She'd literally shrugged him off. Putting her money on the table to pay the bill, she finished the last of her – now not so hot – coffee and got up to walk over to the boulangerie, thanking the waiter as she left.

By the time she got back to the house and started up the stairs, Maggie could hear Allegra talking to someone on the phone in her bedroom. She waved through the open door as she passed, indicating the croissants in the bag and went up to the kitchen on the top floor. After she'd laid out plates and cutlery on the table, Maggie made a fresh pot of coffee and poured some orange juice into a small jug. She put the still-warm croissants into a basket along with some butter and a pot of apricot jam, then sliced up a fresh peach, the juices running from the board as she cut into it.

She went back down to check on Allegra, who was sitting on the edge of her bed, still in her nightdress.

'How are you feeling?' said Maggie.

'I can't even get this off on my own.' Allegra was clearly frustrated.

'That's why I stayed, to help you. Here,' said Maggie. 'Let me get your arm out, then you can do the rest. I can lay your clothes out for you if you let me know what you'd like me to get.'

'Thank you, in that cupboard there.'

'I'll run you some water in the sink but I think you should wait a few days until you have a shower or a bath.'

Allegra waved the thought away. 'Don't, I feel so old suddenly.'

'You've got a broken arm. You're going to have to accept my help, like it or not,' said Maggie. 'Now, how about this one?' She held up a long red silk kaftan and grinned at Allegra. 'I think you should style this injury out.'

They sat and had breakfast together, Allegra's arm resting on a pillow on the table, the colour coming back into her cheeks as she ate.

'I had a coffee this morning when I got these,' said Maggie, holding up a piece of pastry taken from the top of her crois-sant in between her fingers, 'and the waiter at the little café on the corner, the one with the red awning, asked how you were.'

Allegra smiled and popped a slice of peach into her mouth.

Maggie laughed. 'You really do know everyone, don't you?'

'Not really, it's just that people are friendly. No one is too busy to say hello. But you can live here and keep yourself to yourself quite happily. As I do, most of the time.'

'Is there anyone you want me to speak to, to let them know about your arm?'

'I was just on the phone to my late husband's daughter, and she said...'

'We haven't even talked about your husband! I'd almost forgotten you had one.'

Allegra laughed. 'Darling, I just haven't got there yet.'

'Okay, so last night we got up to the part when you took on the gallery from Val. Which, I have to say, I didn't see coming at all. Did you keep in touch with them?'

'Absolutely. Robert and Val were like my surrogate parents right up until they both died. I don't know what I would have done without them, to be honest. My father died just a few years after my mother, I only found out when the family lawyer got in touch. The sad thing is, my father knew where I worked so he must've kept an eye on what I was doing. He just couldn't bring himself to forgive me for leaving.'

'Did you ever find out what happened to the letters from Etienne?'

Allegra shook her head. 'God only knows. They were never found. My father left me some money in his will. I didn't want it but it allowed me to take on the gallery earlier than I perhaps would have done otherwise.'

'And so, you ran the gallery and I'm assuming it was a great success?'

'Well, I don't know about that. We had our moments, that's for sure,' said Allegra.

'We? Was that with your husband?'

'No, actually. That was with Eve. After that first sell-out show, she almost instantly lost the love for creating her art.

She always said it was because she got happy.' Allegra laughed, the thought clearly amusing her. 'But I think she just wasn't interested in making money from her art. She was happiest helping me bring on other artists and because she was one herself she had the best connections. We made such a good team. We got to the point where we needed to expand so eventually, when the dry-cleaner's below our apartment came up for sale, we bought it and turned that space into a sister gallery focusing just on sculpture. We both lived above, me on one side, Eve on the other. I focused on more classic Impressionist styles in the uptown gallery, but all our artists had their own space. No one in our stable was competing, they were all complementary.'

'And your husband, when did he come along?' Maggie poured Allegra some coffee as she spoke.

'That was all quite unexpected. He was the kindest man I ever knew. That's him, there.' Allegra pointed to a photo in a frame on a small table under the mirror on the far wall.

Maggie got up to have a closer look. She picked up the frame and studied his face. 'He even looks kind.' He was tall, with light-coloured hair and gently sloping eyes.

'That's Leo, he came into my life much later. I'd given up on ever falling in love again after Etienne. It took me years to move on from that heartbreak. I just couldn't bring myself to put my happiness in anyone else's hands after what happened. But before she died, Val wrote to me and told me something which made me think. She'd met Leo, another art dealer, years before. He was a widower. His wife had died when their young daughter was very young. Just like they'd once been, we were two lost souls with broken hearts in New York City. Val waited until the right moment, then put us together. I wasn't sure about it at first but then eventually, I fell in love with him.

Ours was a different kind of love, not like with Etienne. This was deep friendship and companionship, really.'

'What did Val say to change your mind?'

A slight smile came to Allegra's face. 'She said if it weren't for second chances, we'd all be alone. Leo was my second chance at happiness.' She sighed, gently. 'We were together for almost thirty years.'

'And you're still close to his daughter? Your stepdaughter I should say.'

'Very, she's wonderful. Her name is Nancy. Sadly, I don't see her very often because she lives in the States, but she comes over with her family, usually once a year. There they are, in that photo.' Allegra pointed at another photograph on the side.

Maggie picked it up and looked at the smiling faces in the picture. Allegra stood in the middle next to a younger woman, also tall, with eyes just like her father's. In front of Allegra were three late teenage-looking children, two boys and a girl, all laughing at whoever was taking the photograph. 'What a gorgeous picture.'

'That was taken a few years ago now. Her husband took the photo. I adore them all.'

'I hope you don't mind me asking but you didn't have children of your own?' said Maggie, her eyes still on the photograph.

Allegra shook her head. 'I never really wanted kids of my own. I mean, maybe once, fleetingly. We got married when I was in my early thirties but for whatever reason, it didn't happen for us, and I was okay with that.' She paused. 'Eventually.'

Maggie closed her eyes for a second. 'Hearing you say that out loud makes me think I might get there one day too. Feeling okay with it, I mean. I thought I was, but I'm not sure I'm quite there yet.' She sat back down at the table.

'It takes time,' said Allegra, patting Maggie's hand with her good arm.

They sat in comfortable silence for a moment, eating their breakfast. After they'd finished, Maggie cleared the plates, ordering Allegra to stay put whilst she did so. Then, much to Maggie's delight, Allegra suggested a walk down to the beach.

It was still relatively quiet as they walked along the Croisette, the tourists yet to arrive on their day trips to Cannes. The sky was blue and cloudless, just as it had been the day before and the day before that.

'How far would you like to go?' said Maggie, her arm held gently underneath Allegra's sling.

'How about we go as far as The Carlton.'

'The hotel at the end? Isn't that from the film with Grace Kelly and Cary Grant?'

'I love that you know that!' said Allegra. 'Do you fancy having a look inside? It's beautiful.'

'Only if you promise you won't make me have a martini,' said Maggie.

'Of course not,' said Allegra. 'It's way too early for that. We'll have *une coupe de champagne* instead. I lived there for a while. I'll get us a good table.'

Maggie looked up at the majestic white hotel, the grey turrets on the corner glinting in the sunlight, adding a fairy tale touch to the Croisette. 'Sorry, did you say you lived there? At The Carlton?'

Allegra laughed. 'You'll love it.'

22

NEW YORK, 2003

'Darling, are you coming? We're going to be late if we don't leave soon.' Leo stood at the bottom of the stairs, Allegra's coat over his arm.

'Just a second,' she replied. Allegra finally descended the stairs of their West Village townhouse, dressed in a long green dress, her auburn hair falling around her shoulders.

Leo let out a long wolf whistle. 'How do you do that?' he said, eyebrows raised.

'You always say that,' said Allegra, laughing. She kissed him on the cheek. 'Ready?'

Of all the numerous dinners Leo and Allegra had hosted with various collectors over the years, this was the one she looked forward to the most. The couple in question, Bert and Carole Donnell, had been prolific collectors for at least thirty years and owned one of the most enviable art collections in all of New York. But rather than hoard their art like hidden treasures, they shared what they couldn't fit inside their modest Upper West Side apartment with various museums around town. The only stipulation was that the museum had to offer free entry for visitors in order for the Donnells to loan them their pieces. Over the years, the two couples had become firm friends, regularly meeting up to discuss what was happening in the art world and the inevitable gossip that came with it.

Allegra had picked one of her favourite French restaurants, legendary for both its notoriously grumpy chef patron and real star of the show, an impossibly light soufflé with streaks of spinach running through the egg inside. The room itself had been given something of a makeover since their last visit, switching its white tablecloths for paper ones and plush red velvet dining chairs for wooden seats that, in Allegra's opinion, looked like they belonged in a classroom. But despite the brasserie makeover the food was just as good, or so she'd heard.

They were shown to their usual table – fourth on the left from the entrance, the best one in the house naturally – and Allegra ordered a bottle of champagne whilst they waited. The ice bucket was delivered to the table just as Carole came through the door, turning heads as she did so. Allegra thought her the most elegant octogenarian in all the city, her long white hair slicked back, revealing exquisite diamonds in her ears. She waved to Allegra, gently shaking her coat off her shoulders into the arms of a waiter. Bert followed as Carole crossed the black and white tiled floor, the heels of her impressively high shoes clicking as she walked.

'What are we celebrating?' said Carole, spying the bottle in the ice bucket. She took a seat next to Allegra. 'I'm not sure about these chairs, are you?'

'Don't,' said Allegra. 'Why they felt the need to make it look like every other place in town, I'll never know.'

'Dining rooms are out, apparently. So last decade,' said Carole, rolling her eyes.

'We certainly are celebrating,' said Leo. 'Darling, do you want to tell them?' He poured out their glasses, filling each one right up to the top.

'I do wish you wouldn't do that, Leo. It loses its fizz,' said Allegra, gently disapproving.

'Well then, drink more quickly,' he replied, winking at her. 'Go on, tell them.'

Bert sat down and kissed Allegra on the cheek. 'You're looking beautiful, as ever.'

'Thank you, as do you both.' Allegra picked up her glass. 'We're celebrating because after forty very happy, mostly busy years I've decided it's time to finally sell the galleries.'

'I think that's wonderful,' said Carole, clapping her hands. 'You've worked so hard but life is short! Time to put yourselves first.'

'My daughter is getting married next year in Paris so instead of coming back straight after, we thought we'll just keep travelling through Europe and see where we end up,' said Leo, his eyes shining.

Allegra looked at him; he looked so happy. Until now, she'd been the one always pushing to do more. Another artist, another exhibition, another sale. The idea of not working had never even occurred to her. But turning sixty had made her think of Val quitting at the top of her game. At the time she couldn't understand why – surely there was more to be done – but now she could relate to her old boss' decision. As much as Allegra loved her life in New York, there was so much more she wanted to do and see. As soon as she'd voiced her desire to quit to Leo, he'd been so relieved. Eve had effectively retired a few years before and now lived with her husband upstate. It had taken a while for Allegra to admit she just didn't love the business as much as she used to and now, decision made, she couldn't be more excited for the next stage in their lives.

'Congratulations, darling,' said Carole, raising her glass to Allegra's and clinking it gently.

'So do you have a buyer for the galleries?' asked Bert.

Allegra shook her head. 'Not yet, you're honestly the first people we've told. We didn't want to say anything until we were sure.'

'You'll have buyers queueing up once word gets out,' said Carole.

'Where will you go first?' asked Bert. 'After Paris, that is.'

Leo filled up their glasses. 'The idea is to travel on through France to Spain, then Italy and perhaps down to Greece. Who knows? We haven't got that far yet. We're thinking we do a three-month trip and see where we end up.'

'Didn't you live in Paris years ago?' said Carole, fixing her dark bird-like eyes on Allegra.

'A long time ago, yes.' Even the mere mention of the name of the city was enough to transport her back to the banks of the Seine. She thought of the evening light on the stone bridges. And there, always hidden in the shadows of her mind, was Etienne.

'I want her to show me where she used to hang out back in the day,' said Leo. 'Apparently there isn't a jazz club in the 14th arrondissement that Allegra hasn't frequented.'

'I didn't go to every single one,' she laughed. 'Just most of them.' She looked at Leo, thinking how lucky she was to have him love her as he did. 'I can't wait to show you around.'

'Well, here's to wonderful adventures ahead,' said Bert, raising his glass for another toast. 'To you both.'

They drank and ate and laughed and reminisced. By the time Allegra climbed into the cab she'd hailed whilst Leo settled the bill, she was tired but happy, knowing they'd made the right decision. The galleries had been her life for so long but it was time to see the real world, not just the one depicted on canvas by other people.

'Where to?' said the cab driver over his shoulder.

'West 11th Street, please. Between 4th and—'

'I got you,' said the driver. 'Are we waiting for someone else?'

'Yes, my husband is just inside, he won't be a minute.'

'I got to run the meter, ma'am, I'm sorry.'

'That's fine, he won't be long. I just didn't want to miss you.'

Allegra checked her phone for any messages as she waited. There was one from Nancy, asking if they would be at home that weekend as she would be passing through New York and did they fancy dinner on Saturday night. As Allegra typed a response, a knock on the window of the cab made her jump. She looked up to see the waiter standing there and wound down the window. 'What is it?' She wondered if Leo had forgotten his wallet.

'I'm so sorry madam, it's your husband. He's inside...'

Before the waiter could finish his sentence, Allegra was out of the cab and through the doors of the restaurant. The maître d' took her arm and gently led her through the restaurant towards the restrooms at the back. As she crossed that same black and white tiled floor, she remembered the sound of Carole's heels on it only a few hours earlier. This time, all she heard was the sound of her own heart beating.

* * *

Allegra moved through the following days and weeks as if in a dream. If hadn't been for the kindness of Nancy, Eve and friends like Carole, she might never have left the house. Leo's funeral was a small family affair with only their nearest and dearest present. The celebration service the following month saw a gathering of some of the biggest names in the art world and the uptown gallery was transformed for the occasion with many of Leo's oldest clients gifting pieces of art to be auctioned off to raise money for charity in his honour. It was a touching gesture and Allegra was grateful for the small comfort it gave her, knowing how much her husband had meant to people he'd worked with over the years. To lose anyone to a sudden heart attack was shocking but it seemed especially cruel for it to happen to someone so seemingly fit and well despite his advancing years.

One morning, as Allegra sat at the table in her kitchen trying – and failing – to write thank you letters to the artists who'd donated their work, the doorbell went. Allegra looked up at the clock; somehow it had got to almost twelve o'clock without her noticing and she was still in her dressing gown. She peered at the screen on the wall, relieved to see Nancy standing on the doorstep.

'I'm glad it's you,' she said as she opened the door and embraced her stepdaughter. 'I'm sorry about—' she gestured to her attire '—this.'

Nancy dismissed it immediately. 'Please don't apologise. How are you? Silly question, I know.'

Allegra still had no idea how to answer that question truthfully. 'Oh, you know...' was all she could manage.

'I bought you these.' Nancy held up a bag from Allegra's favourite deli.

'Bagels.' Allegra smiled. 'You are kind. Let's go up.'

Nancy followed Allegra back up the stairs to the kitchen. She put the bagels on a plate and placed it on the table. 'Please tell me you're not writing to everyone by hand,' said Nancy, pointing to the pile of letters on the table.

'That's not even half of them,' said Allegra over her shoulder as she made them some tea.

'You really don't have to write to everyone, they wouldn't expect it.'

'It gives me something to do. Eve's handling the sale of the galleries and I'm not ready to go through Leo's things yet.'

'Are you sure that's still what you want to do?'

This wasn't the first time Nancy had asked.

'Honestly, I think it's time. According to our lawyer, New York is yet to get the memo that the property market bubble is about to burst. Better to get out now, apparently. I have been thinking about what to do next though,' said Allegra, picking at her bagel.

'That's good news. What are you thinking?'

'I'm going to do that trip after your wedding, just as your father and I had planned.'

'You are?' Nancy couldn't hide the surprise in her voice.

Allegra took a sip of her tea. 'I need to get out of the city.'

'You could just come and stay with us for a while, you know that?'

'Thank you, but I need a real change of scene. I think I'll go sooner rather than later.'

Nancy put her head to one side. 'Allegra, are you sure? That's a big decision to make whilst you're still, you know…'

'Grieving. I know, but I think it's the right one. It's too painful being here without him.'

'Obviously it's up to you but just don't feel you need to make any big decisions now, that's all I'm saying.'

Allegra took Nancy's hand and squeezed it. 'I won't, I promise.'

Nancy peered at the envelope on the top of the pile of unopened post in front of them. 'Who's this one from? The postmark says Nice. Isn't that in France?'

Allegra reached out to take it. 'I hadn't got to that one yet. Must be from one of Leo's artists, although I can't think who off the top of my head.'

'I can't believe you're not more curious; I'd be ripping that one open,' said Nancy, reaching for a bagel. 'Do you mind?'

'Help yourself,' said Allegra. 'How is everyone?'

Nancy spoke through a mouthful of food. 'All good.' She nodded at the pile of envelopes again. 'Please open that one, I really want to know who it's from now.'

Allegra opened the letter and read the words in front of her, her mouth moving a little as she did so.

'What does it say?' said Nancy, looking at Allegra expectantly.

Allegra turned the letter over to make sure she hadn't missed anything, then read it again. She wiped a sudden tear from eye. 'It's from a woman called Camille, I knew her years ago.'

'You've gone pale. Shall I get you some water?'

'No, I'm fine, I just can't believe what I'm reading.'

'Go on,' said Nancy. 'Only if you want to, of course.'

Allegra went to speak, then stopped and closed her eyes for a few seconds. She took a breath, then began to talk. 'Camille was the sister of a man called Etienne. I met him when I lived in Paris when I was eighteen. I guess you could say he was my first real love. Your father knew all about him. I was still in a bit of a mess about it when we got together. His family lived in the south, in Provence. His parents were winemakers. Anyway, Camille says she saw my name and picture in the newspaper in France. There must have been something in there after Leo died, I suppose. He had several French artists he looked after over the years so they must have done an obituary or something. She realised it was me and says they've been trying to track me down for a while because her brother left me something in his will.'

'Oh, I'm so sorry. When did he die?'

'Just over a year ago, she says.' Allegra looked from the page in front of her to Nancy, her face a picture of disbelief. 'He left me a house.'

'What? Where?'

'In Cannes.'

'Cannes, as in Cannes, France?' Nancy put her hands to her mouth.

Allegra handed her the letter. 'That's what she says.'

Nancy scanned the letter. 'I don't believe it.'

'Me neither. Why on earth would he leave me a house? The last letter I ever had from him was telling me not to return to Paris after my mother died.'

'Seriously?'

'Yes, he said he didn't love me after all, which is why none of this makes sense.'

'You need to speak to her, find out what's going on,' said Nancy. 'Look, she's written a number here. Although from what she says here, it sounds pretty straightforward. You've been left a house by your first love and if that's not the most romantic thing I've ever heard then I don't know what is.' Nancy laughed.

It took Allegra a few days to pluck up the courage but eventually, spurred on by regular messages from Nancy, she dialled the number on the letter. It was about eight in the morning in New York so by her reckoning it was around mid-afternoon in France.

'*Oui*?' said a voice.

'Bonjour, it's Allegra Morgon.' She panicked, her mind going blank. 'Please can I, sorry...' She was about to hang up when she heard her name.

'Allegra, is that really you?'

'Camille?'

'Yes, I'm so happy you called! We have been trying to find you!'

'Camille, I can hardly believe it. I'm so sorry to hear about Etienne.' Saying his name after all these years felt strange.

'I saw your name in the paper... oh, I'm so sorry. Forgive me, we are very sorry to hear about your husband.'

'You knew him?'

'My husband knew him. Do you remember Serge, our neighbour?'

Allegra remembered him and his tiny wife, laughing in the kitchen in Provence all those years ago, the memory of that night seared into her brain. 'Yes, of course. How was he connected to Leo?'

'Serge's son sold some his pieces to Leo long before you were married, I think. They had to sell some to keep the vineyard going after a run of bad vintages. Anyway, Leo was apparently very kind to him and so they kept in touch. I didn't know any of this until Serge's son emailed me the newspaper cutting. He knew I'd been trying to find you since Etienne died. I'm sorry, Allegra, it's a lot to take in I know. But I will try and explain as best I can. Etienne had to leave Paris because my father got sick. He gave up his place at art school and moved back at my mother's request but insisted he didn't want you giving up your life to move so far from anywhere or anything you knew, just to be with him. He said you wouldn't have listened if he tried to explain so instead he told you not to return.'

Allegra was stunned. 'But... how do you know all of this?'

'When he told me he didn't love you any more, I knew he was lying. I used to see him reading your letters over and over again, thinking I hadn't noticed. I tried but I couldn't make him change his mind. I thought about not telling you that part but him leaving you the house in Cannes doesn't make sense unless you understand that.'

'And how did you find me?'

'The article in the paper, the one about Leo, mentioned you and the galleries you ran so I emailed one of them and eventually a lady called Eve emailed me back. She gave me your address, I hope that's okay. I told her why I needed to get in touch and she agreed it was something you needed to know.'

'I see,' said Allegra. She had a million questions but all she wanted to really know was why. Why had Etienne decided what was best for her without even asking?

The answer was obvious, even if Allegra didn't want to admit it. He'd done it because he'd loved her. And as frustrating as it was to learn the truth all these years later, Allegra knew it was too late to do anything but accept it.

23

PRESENT DAY

It had been three days since the fall and Allegra was feeling much better. As she was getting used to managing with just one arm, Maggie agreed to stay on until the weekend, returning home the following Monday. They'd developed quite the routine. In the morning Maggie would get bread, grabbing a quick coffee in the café on her way back. After breakfast on the terrace, they walked into town taking different routes so that Maggie could get to know the area a little better, picking up food on the way home from the market. Later they'd take a walk down to the beach once the day-trippers had gone home before returning to the terrace for sunset drinks.

That evening, as they sat with a glass of rosé each, the bay below soaked in golden light, Maggie wondered aloud if she might be able to find a bottle when she was back home.

'This wine?' asked Allegra. 'It's from a vineyard not far from here but I doubt you'd get it in England. I think they sell pretty much everything they make here.'

'I'd love to go to a vineyard before I leave,' said Maggie. 'I've never been to one, not even at home.'

'They make wine in Great Britain?' asked Allegra.

'They do. Some of them are pretty good. The sparkling wine is as good as champagne, apparently.'

'I never knew that,' said Allegra. 'I'll have to try some. It's a shame Camille, Etienne's sister who I told you about, isn't here. She's a winemaker but she moved to Burgundy with her husband years ago. We keep in touch, of course.'

Maggie took a sip of her wine and shook her head. 'I still can't believe what Etienne did.'

Allegra sighed. 'I know, it seems so sad when things could have been very different but that's the point. You can't change the past. Only the future. Which is exactly why I got on a plane a few months after I got Camille's letter. I sold the house and moved to Cannes. Not straight away, of course. I took that trip through Europe and I have to say, I loved every minute of it. There were times when I wondered what the hell I was doing but I got to see the most beautiful places, not to mention artwork in some of the galleries. You know, you can look at paintings in books, but nothing beats seeing them in real life.'

'What happened to their family home in the end?'

'It was sold after Etienne's father died, sadly. They couldn't afford to keep it all, the house and the vineyards. Etienne's other sister Isabelle wanted to sell so they had no choice.'

'Is that when he bought this place?'

'Exactly, Etienne bought it as a wreck and obviously meant to do it up over the years, but he worked all over the world as a winemaker. Camille told me he came back here every now and again. I guess this was his investment. He never married though, which makes me sad. I asked if he ever talked about me or thought about coming to find me, but Camille said that he always felt he'd made his decision and the last thing he wanted to do was crash back into my life years later. Obviously, I then met Leo but there will always be a part of me that will wonder what if... I think maybe that's why Etienne left me the house. It's where we might've ended up if our story had been different.'

Maggie topped up their glasses with the last of the rosé. 'So did you plan on moving here without even seeing it?'

'Not at all. In fact, I almost put it straight on the market. It was still pretty much a wreck when I first saw it. I got to Cannes and stayed at The Carlton, as you know.'

'I still can't believe you lived there for a while,' laughed Maggie.

'I know, it was quite extravagant of me but then again, I was on my own. Looking back, I was quite lost still. I'd gone on this adventure thinking it would help heal the pain, but you take it with you, as I'm sure you know.'

Maggie winced a little. 'So, what made you decide to stay?'

Allegra looked out across the bay, the sun now casting the last of its light on the water, the sky a canvas with thick brushes of orange and pink across it. 'This.'

Maggie took in the view in front of her. 'It is beautiful.'

'More than that,' said Allegra. 'I found peace here. The house connects me to Leo because we dreamt of coming here together one day. And it connects me to Etienne and what might have been. I love my simple life here. I see friends when they come and stay but I'm just as happy when I'm here alone.'

Maggie raised her glass to Allegra. 'Thank you for having me. I've loved being here and I'm just sorry it took your fall to make me stay.'

'Well, the timing was perfect,' laughed Allegra.

They sat for a while, watching the sun creep out of view,

then returned to the kitchen where Maggie made them a big salade niçoise to share along with some baguette, cheese and fresh figs.

'I thought I'd make you something you can eat easily with one hand,' said Maggie as they sat down at the table.

'Thank you,' said Allegra. 'Truly, I'm so glad you stayed.'

'Me too,' said Maggie, raising her glass. 'Right now, I'm not sure I ever want to leave.'

The next morning Maggie got up early, threw on her T-shirt and shorts and made her way down the hill to the boulangerie to pick up bread and croissants as usual. Deciding she had time for a quick coffee, she took a seat at the little café on the corner and ordered an espresso. She'd been awake since around five for some reason – she couldn't quite work out why – and thought a quick shot of coffee might help sharpen the mind. Just as she was about to take a sip, she heard a familiar voice.

'Excuse me?'

Maggie turned to see it was the same man she'd met a few days before.

'We met the other day. Well, we didn't meet exactly. I made you choke on your coffee.' He put his hand out. 'My name is Nico.'

She looked at his outstretched hand, noticing the dirt under his fingernails. She shook it. 'I'm Maggie.' She felt her heartbeat quicken at his touch.

'It's funny to see you here twice.'

'I guess,' said Maggie, laughing.

They held each other's gaze.

'May I?' said Nico, pointing at the empty chair opposite her.

'Yes, of course.' Maggie hoped her delight wasn't too obvious.

'So, you're on the strong stuff this morning.' He looked at her espresso.

'Yes, couldn't sleep. Need a shot today.'

'I haven't been to sleep yet.'

'You haven't?'

He shook his head of dark curls. The waiter put a coffee on the table in front of him. 'I work on a vineyard not far from here. We were picking grapes early this morning before sunrise.'

'Why so early?'

'It's better for the grapes to pick them before it gets too hot. It helps keep them fresh.'

Maggie gestured to his hands. 'That explains the state of you.'

He laughed, those same creases Maggie couldn't help but notice last time appearing again.

'Yes, I am sorry. No matter how much I try, I always end up like this.'

'So, what are you doing here in Cannes?'

'The Domaine where I work is just behind those hills you can see there.'

'Do they not have coffee?' Maggie suddenly realised she probably sounded quite rude. 'I mean...'

'I had to pick something up from a garage in town, a tractor part. It's just round the corner. And I needed a proper coffee.'

'Got it.' She wanted to look at him and not look at him all at the same time. 'So, are you a winemaker?'

'Not quite, I look after the vines.'

'So, you're a... vigneron? Isn't that the name?'

'Almost. That's someone who owns their own vines. One day I hope to but for now, I'll have to make do with looking after someone else's. What are you doing in Cannes?'

'Staying with a friend. Just for a little while. In fact, I was hoping to visit a vineyard before I go home, I've never been to one.'

Nico nodded enthusiastically. 'This is the perfect time to see one, when the grapes are being picked. You could come and visit the one where I work, if you like?'

'Actually I was really hoping to visit the vineyards that my friend, the one who I'm staying with, used to go to as a teenager. She's in her eighties now.'

'Whereabouts, do you know?'

'It's towards Fréjus. She said the Domaine is at the foot of a hill.'

'That doesn't really narrow it down but there are plenty out that way; you'll find somewhere I'm sure,' said Nico, laughing. He picked up his cup and drained it in one. 'Well, I wish you luck today. Let me know how it goes.'

Maggie laughed too. 'And good luck with... your grapes.' She wondered what on earth she was saying.

Nico smiled, putting a five-euro note on the table. 'These are on me.'

'No, please, you really don't have to...' said Maggie, but he'd already gone.

By the time she got back to the house, Allegra was sitting at the table with a glass of water. 'You've been already?'

Maggie put the basket down, the smell of freshly baked baguette filling the air. 'I have.' She reached for some plates from the side and put them on the table. 'You know, I was being serious yesterday. I really would like to visit a vineyard whilst I'm here. I just spoke to a guy at the café who's been picking grapes already today.' Much as Maggie wanted to tell Allegra about this handsome stranger, she decided it would sound ridiculous. After all, he'd only bought her a coffee to be nice.

'Well then, how about we take my car out – you'd have to drive obviously – and we go and find you a vineyard.'

'Are you sure you're up to it?'

'I've got a broken arm, darling. I'm not completely incapacitated.'

'Okay, I'm sorry,' Maggie laughed. 'In which case, yes. I'd love that. Do you think we can go and see Etienne's old family place, the one you went to?'

Allegra thought for a moment. 'I guess it would be nice for you to see it, then you can tell your mother about it. Your grandmother and I had such a wonderful time there. We came down on the train together, from Paris, on a whim. It was one of the most thrilling trips of my life.'

'Can you remember where it is?'

'I'm sure if we find the right road, we'll drive past it.'

Maggie reached for her phone. 'What's the name of the village?'

'I can't recall exactly but if we head towards Fréjus I know roughly where it is.'

'The DN 7 road?' said Maggie, looking at the map on her screen.

'That's the one. It'll be interesting to see it after all this time.'

'It won't bring back sad memories?'

Allegra smiled. 'No, only happy ones.'

After clearing the table, Maggie put together a picnic of

leftovers from the fridge and took everything downstairs. Allegra's car was in a garage at the bottom of the street and when Maggie removed the dustsheet, she couldn't help but practically squeal at the vintage blue convertible Mercedes underneath. 'Allegra, this is my dream car! Are you sure you trust me to drive it?'

Allegra smiled. 'Of course! Get in, I'll see you out.'

Maggie eased herself into the beige leather seat and put her hands on the steering wheel. She looked back at Allegra. 'Ready?'

Allegra waved her out and soon they were on the road, heading into the hills behind the town.

As they wound their way up through the wooded landscape, it wasn't long before Maggie glimpsed her first vineyard, the rows of vines looking full and lush with bright green leaves and heaving bunches of grapes beneath them. They drove on, Allegra pointing out various landmarks as they went. They stopped briefly by the side of the road at one of the viewpoints, the hills dropping away to the coast beyond.

Looking at the map on her phone, Maggie showed Allegra their location. 'Do you think we're nearby?'

Allegra squinted at it. 'It's off this road to the right, another couple of kilometres and we're there.'

Maggie drove on, trying not to rubberneck at the passing hilltop villages, almost too beautiful to be true.

'I think we just passed it,' said Allegra, looking back over her right shoulder. 'I'm sure those were the gates. I remember those cypress trees.'

Maggie drove on until she found somewhere to turn the car round, then took a left into the drive only to find a heavy chain and padlock in place.

Allegra opened her door with her good arm and walked up

to the gates and shook the padlock. She looked back at Maggie. 'This is definitely it. If you look from here—' she pointed up ahead '—you can just see the house.'

Maggie turned the engine off and went to join her. She looked at the vineyards in front of them, clearly in a state of disrepair. There were wires hanging loose from posts and the vines were out of control, long tendrils swaying in the gentle breeze. Bunches of grapes hung below, the thick trunks of the vines just visible. Maggie looked up towards the house, pale orange stone peeking through the thick line of olive and cypress trees surrounding it. The faded blue shutters at each window were closed, some hanging precariously, others missing all together. 'It looks abandoned, don't you think?'

'Sadly, I think it does,' said Allegra, her voice quiet.

'I'm so sorry, I was really hoping it would be as you remembered it. It must be sad to see it like this.'

Allegra nodded. 'Camille didn't know who bought it. I think she found it too painful to think about. So sad, really. That house was so full of life when they lived there.' Allegra turned and looked across the road. There, just as she thought, was another small road leading off down the hill. 'You know, if we drive down there, I think it takes us to another vineyard on the other side that used to be Etienne's family's too.'

'Down that track?' Maggie looked at the dirt road, grass growing in the middle.

'Let's go and have a look.'

'You sure you want to take the car down there?'

'Absolutely, come on.'

They made their way slowly, Maggie avoiding the potholes as best she could. Almost as soon as they left the main road, the track veered off to the right, then down a short way and there in front of them was another vineyard, as ragged as the one by the house. The vines in this one looked different. There were no posts, just small bush-like vines planted in rows of sorts.

'Look at that sweet little stone hut up there,' Maggie said, pointing to a small pale stone building not far in front of them.

Allegra looked at it, removing her sunglasses. 'This is definitely it,' she said.

'I'm going to have a look,' said Maggie, turning off the engine again. 'Are you coming?' She opened her door.

'In a moment, you go ahead.'

Maggie walked up to the stone hut and in through the doorway. The timber roof was half missing and all that was left of the door were two huge metal hinges on one side. She peeked inside; a few rusting old tools were propped against the wall. She turned back to the vineyard in front of her, the soil dry and cracked, full of jagged rocks and stones. Walking over to the nearest vine, she picked at one of the bunches of grapes hanging beneath the canopy. It was covered in a white bloom and one wipe of her finger revealed a dark purple-black grape beneath. She put it into her mouth and bit into it, tart juice filling her mouth. She'd rather a black seedless, she thought, as she spat the grape onto the ground.

As Maggie walked back to the car, she looked at Allegra sitting in the passenger seat with her eyes closed, the sun and a small smile on her face.

Maggie called over to her. 'Are you okay?'

Allegra opened her eyes and looked at Maggie. 'Happy memories, that's all.'

'What a beautiful place. It's just such a pity it's been left like this. And I'm sad we can't see the house.'

'I guess some things are best left in the past,' said Allegra. 'I tell you what though, how about we have our picnic under that old oak tree before we leave? I reckon we've got the best views from here, and we've got them all to ourselves. There's a rug in the boot.'

'Leave it to me,' said Maggie.

Under the shade of the tree, they feasted on cheese and charcuterie, breaking off wedges of baguette over the grass. As they ate and chatted, Maggie felt her shoulders drop. 'There is something quite magical about this place,' she said, cutting off a thin strip of aged Comté cheese bought from the market. 'Want some?' She offered it to Allegra.

'Thank you. Yes, there really is. It's where the harvest party took place every year. I think I told you about it.'

'Oh yes, of course.'

'There was a full moon that night, I remember.'

'Is that what you were thinking about just now?'

Allegra nodded as she took a bite of the cheese. 'It's funny, I look back now and at the time I thought I knew how life was going to work out. Then, when it didn't, I spent a long time thinking I'd lost what should have been mine. I mourned a life with someone I believed I was destined to be with. But really life is about living in time, wherever you are, at that precise moment. Promise me something, Maggie.' She reached across and took Maggie's hand. 'Stop living in the past. Your life is here, now. And the day after. And the day after that. Do you see what I'm getting at?' Allegra stroked Maggie's hand gently.

Maggie nodded. A tear rolled down her cheek. 'I do,' she said. 'And I know you're right.'

'Of course I am. I'm old,' said Allegra, laughing gently.

24

PRESENT DAY

The sound of a single bell toll from the clocktower woke Maggie from her sleep. She looked at her phone, surprised to see it was already quarter past seven in the morning. Realising she hadn't woken once in the night, she laid her head back onto her pillow and sighed. No wonder she felt so rested. Then she remembered. Tomorrow she'd be returning home. Her heart dropped. She really, really didn't want to leave just yet.

Deciding to make the most of the time she had left, Maggie got out of bed and put her swimming costume on under her T-shirt and shorts, scribbled Allegra a note telling her she'd gone to the beach and that she'd be back with croissants by eight o'clock. Less than ten minutes later Maggie was in the sea, the beach almost empty bar a couple of other swimmers a little further down from her. As she lay on her towel on the sand drying off, she thought about what they'd talked about the day before. Living in the now. As thoughts of returning to work started to flood her mind, Maggie filed them away one by one. 'I will deal with you tomorrow,' she said out loud. A shadow crossed over her.

'Deal with who?' said a voice.

'Jesus!' Maggie shouted, opening her eyes. It was Nico.

'I'm not following you, I promise,' he said, then rolled his eyes. '*Merde*, that sounds worse.'

Maggie sat up. 'You gave me such a fright.'

'Sorry, I didn't mean to. Can I sit?'

'Go ahead.' Maggie hugged her knees to her chest. 'Are you sure you're not following me?' She glanced at him, trying not to smile.

He paused. 'Not this time.'

Maggie narrowed her eyes. 'What do you mean not this time?'

'I really needed to jump in the sea this morning. We finished picking about an hour ago and I don't have to be back until ten this morning. I had no idea you'd be here.'

'Right.' Her eyes swept down across his tanned, toned body. She could feel herself blushing and quickly looked away. 'So which time did you follow me?'

'I didn't follow you, just to be clear. But yesterday, when I said I was getting something for the tractor? That wasn't entirely true. Well, it was but I didn't have to do it. It's not my job but I offered because I wanted to come back to the café and see if you were there. Which sounds ridiculous, I know. We met for, like, two minutes before.' He shrugged his shoulders.

Maggie couldn't help but notice the sea water glistening on his skin.

'I wanted to see you again.'

'I don't know whether to be flattered or freaked out, to be honest.' She shielded her eyes from the glare of the sun.

'I'm really hoping you go for the first choice,' he said, holding her gaze.

They looked at one another for a moment. Despite the oddness of the situation, Maggie thought it strangely familiar too. Truthfully, far from being freaked out, she felt calm. Before she could change her mind, Maggie opened her mouth to speak. 'Have you got time for a coffee? I need to pick up some bread.'

They walked back along the beach towards the old harbour, then made their way through the streets behind to the café. As they took their seats at a table against the wall, the waiter gave Maggie a knowing look. They ordered their coffees and for the first time since they'd met, neither quite knew what to say.

'So, are you...' said Maggie.

'Tell me...' said Nico, speaking at the same time.

'You first,' said Maggie.

'Sorry, you go...'

'Please,' she laughed.

Nico smiled at her. 'I wanted to ask how your trip was yesterday. Did you find the vineyard?'

'We did, but sadly it wasn't the visit I'd hoped. My friend who I'm staying with stayed there years ago, I think I told you, but when we found it, it looked pretty deserted. The gates were locked and the vineyards obviously hadn't been looked after for a while. Still, we had a really lovely picnic looking at the view. It's really beautiful.'

'Where was it exactly?' Nico put his coffee cup down.

'Just off the road to Fréjus, not the main one, the other one. I took a few photos. Hang on, I can show you.' Maggie reached for her phone and tapped on the screen a few times. 'That's the entrance gate, you can just see the house behind the trees there.'

Nico leant in towards her and looked at the screen. 'Have you got any more photos?'

Maggie swiped through them. 'There's the view down to the bay and this is the other vineyard.'

Nico stared at the photo. 'Was there a stone hut?'

'Yes, here.' Maggie swiped the screen again. 'It's not got much of a roof or a door any more.'

She waited for him to say something. 'Do you know it?'

Nico shook his head. 'I don't believe it. I think that's my mother's old family home.'

Maggie gasped. 'Wait, is your mother called...'

'Camille.' Nico looked at Maggie, his dark eyes wide. 'What is the name of the lady you are staying with?'

'Allegra Morgon. She's American but she's been living here for about twenty years. She lives just up there in the Old Town.'

'In the house left to her by...'

'Etienne. Oh my God, are you...?'

'Camille's son.' Nico nodded.

'But... how come you know this place? I thought they sold it years ago.'

'They did. I think it changed hands a few times but I had no idea it was empty. That's so sad.' Nico looked at the screen again. 'My mother loved it there.'

'So, you know Allegra?'

'No, I mean I've heard about her from my mother – they keep in touch I think – but my parents are winemakers in Burgundy. I've lived there all my life. Like my uncle did, I work all over the place but I wanted to do a vintage down here this year, so I got a job at the vineyard I told you about. The one just outside Cannes towards Mougins.' He looked back at the screen. 'Go back to those vines a minute.'

Maggie put her fingers on the screen and zoomed in on the photo. 'These ones?'

'Exactly.' Nico studied the image. 'Those old bush vines must be at least eighty years old, probably planted by my grandfather.'

'That's insane!' said Maggie, laughing. 'I can't wait to tell Allegra. In fact, you've got to meet her. I know she'd love to meet you.'

Nico was still looking at the screen. 'I still can't believe it.'

'You should send the photos to your mother. I can AirDrop them to you.'

'I think she might find it too sad seeing it like that. I wonder who owns it now. There wasn't a for-sale sign or anything like that?'

'Not that I noticed. It was just locked up.'

'I'll ask the team where I'm working, I'm sure someone will know.'

'So, will you come and meet Allegra? We could have a drink later maybe?'

'Definitely, I have to work tonight but I can come before then. Let me take your number… if that's okay?'

Maggie tried not to look too pleased. 'Sure,' she said. She put it into his phone and called hers before handing it back to him. 'I'll check with Allegra and let you know. I'd better get back.'

'Of course, I'll wait to hear from you,' said Nico. He drained his coffee. '*À bientôt.*'

Maggie walked back up the hill, fresh croissants in a paper bag and a baguette under her arm. The bells in the clocktower struck nine times as she opened the front door. The last hour had flown by without her noticing.

Allegra was already up and pottering in the kitchen upstairs. 'Did you swim?'

'I did,' said Maggie. 'And I have to tell you, I met someone at the beach. Actually, we'd bumped into each other before but just by chance. Apart from one time, when he'd planned it. But that's not the point...'

'Maggie, you're not making any sense at all. Sit down and start from the beginning.'

'Sorry, you're right, I'll start again.' Maggie sat down at the table. 'So, I met someone called Nico.'

Allegra joined her at the table. 'And...?'

Maggie took a deep breath. 'And you won't believe this but he's Camille's son.'

'Did you just say Camille's son, as in Etienne's Camille?'

'That's exactly who I mean,' said Maggie.

Allegra looked completely taken aback.

'I know, it's a lot,' said Maggie.

'But... how did you make the connection?'

'That's the thing, we'd bumped into each other a few times but had no idea obviously. Then this morning he was at the beach swimming and we went for a coffee. I'd told him I wanted to see a vineyard and he's working at one nearby but I'd said I wanted to go to another one that you knew. He didn't know it was you when I told him that. Anyway long story short, I described the house and the vineyard from yesterday and showed him some pictures and he knew pretty much straight away where I was talking about. He's never been but obviously his mother had told him about it.'

Allegra sat back in her chair. 'What's he like?'

Maggie pointed at the box of photographs on the table. 'He looks a bit like Etienne but with curly dark hair.'

'His grandfather Nicolas had curly dark hair.' Allegra thought for a moment. 'Can I see him?'

'I was hoping you'd say that! I do have his number; perhaps we could meet him for a drink later?'

Allegra looked at Maggie. 'I'd love him to come here.'

'Are you sure?'

'Absolutely. And I think by the look of you, you'd like that too.'

Maggie blushed. 'Is it that obvious?'

'Literally written all over your face, darling.' Allegra laughed. 'Tell him to come at six if that suits him.'

After breakfast, they walked down to the harbour, then on to the food market to pick up something for lunch. As it was to be Maggie's last night, Allegra insisted on booking a table for dinner at one of her favourite restaurants as they passed it on their way back up to the house. Maggie was on a flight the following morning, and as much as she tried to not think about it, the knot in her stomach was impossible to ignore.

Later that afternoon, Maggie lay on the sofa on the terrace trying to read her book when Allegra appeared at the top of the stairs, a straw hat in one hand.

'I thought you were going to have a nap,' said Maggie.

'I couldn't sleep,' said Allegra. 'I can't stop thinking about the farmhouse we visited yesterday. It really was so very sad seeing it like that. I just don't understand how anyone can leave a place like that to go to ruin. It's such a waste.' Allegra looked devastated.

Maggie changed the subject, hoping it would take Allegra's mind off the house. 'I've been meaning to ask, what's the story behind the Picasso downstairs? I'm sure you said he gave it to you.'

Allegra sat down at the other end of the sofa, stretched her legs out and put on her hat. 'Yes, he did. The Museum of Modern Art in New York had a show in 1962 to mark his eightieth birthday. Val knew the directors of the show, so we went to the opening. It had everything from his drawings and paintings to sculptures and ceramics. Think what you like of the man but his art is extraordinary. Impossible to label, really. I remember one particular painting, a woman by a window, painted in Cannes. Anyway, I got talking to someone at the party and said I was sorry not to see his painting called *The Pigeons* as I wanted to see it because it reminded me of the first time I laid eyes on the Mediterranean. It was like a door opening to a whole new world. When I eventually bought the gallery from Val, she gave me the signed limited edition print of the painting, the one downstairs. They got it from Picasso via an art dealer, a friend of theirs who'd had a gallery in New York about ten blocks down from Val's. Turns out the person I'd been talking to was the art dealer, not that I realised at the time.'

'Is it worth a fortune?' said Maggie. 'Sorry, that's really crass of me.'

Allegra lowered her voice. 'Not compared with the Rodin. That one really is worth quite a bit. It's been lent to various museums over the years but when I moved here, I decided I wanted it on my wall, so I could look at it whenever I wanted to. It reminds me of falling in love for the first time.'

'I love that,' said Maggie, sighing. 'You know, this trip has been like a door opening for me. Thank you so much for having me.'

'We're not done yet.' Allegra laughed.

The doorbell rang, making Maggie jump.

'Well, are you going to let him in?' said Allegra, raising that arched eyebrow of hers.

Maggie looked down over the side of the balcony to see Nico standing there, running his hands through his hair. 'I'll come down,' she called.

He looked up at her and waved.

Maggie sat back down, then stood up. 'I was going to change.'

'Too late,' said Allegra.

'Shall I get drinks? What shall I offer him?'

'Maggie, relax.' Allegra held out her hand with her good arm and took Maggie's in hers.

Maggie nodded. She walked down the stairs, checking her appearance in the bathroom mirror on her way past, wishing she'd at least had time to put on mascara. She inspected her teeth in the mirror to make sure she didn't have anything stuck in them then went downstairs. She opened the door to find Nico standing with two small bunches of flowers in his hand.

'I got you these,' he said, holding the bunch out to her. 'And one for Allegra.'

'Thank you. Come in,' said Maggie, taking the flowers. She was ridiculously pleased to see him.

Nico followed her up to the kitchen. 'What can I get you to drink?'

'Whatever you're having.'

'We were going to have a glass of this,' she said, holding up the opened bottle of rosé from the fridge door.

'Perfect.'

She poured out three glasses of wine and she offered him one. As he took it, their fingers touched briefly.

'Follow me,' said Maggie. 'We're on the roof.'

As soon as Allegra saw Nico, tears sprang to her eyes.

'Hello, I'm Nico. It's so good to finally meet you.' He held out the flowers. 'I bought you these.'

'You look so like your uncle,' whispered Allegra, as much to herself as to him. She held out her hand. 'I'm Allegra, it's lovely to meet you too. Please, come and sit down.'

'I told my mother I was coming; she said to send you her love and she hopes you are well. She says you were the one that got away and it was all my uncle's fault.' Nico smiled.

'I am quite well, apart from this damn thing,' said Allegra, nodding at her arm in the sling. 'The only good thing to come out of it is that it meant Maggie had to stay for a few more days. And as for the one that got away, that's a whole other story.' She laughed. 'So, tell me what you know about your parents' old house?'

'It is so sad, really.' Nico shrugged his shoulders. 'My mother, along with my uncle and aunt...'

'Isabelle, wasn't that her name? I never met her,' said Allegra.

'That's right.' Nico nodded. 'They inherited the Domaine when my grandparents died, the house and the vineyards, but by then Isabelle was married to a winemaker in Bordeaux and they weren't interested in somewhere in Provence, so she wanted to sell. My mother and Etienne couldn't afford to keep it without her, sadly. They had to sell and I found out from the people I'm working for now that it was eventually bought by a couple from Paris. They promised to do great things with it apparently, but after a few years decided winemaking wasn't for them and just left it empty. There's an ongoing divorce case, which makes things complicated.'

'Did you ever go when you were little?' asked Allegra, picking up her glass.

'No, they sold it before I was born so I've never seen it. My mother had me when she was in her forties so she'd long since left and was living in Burgundy by the time I was born. But after seeing Maggie's photos I'm going to drive up there and have a look. The vines look incredible, the vineyard is in such a good location. The *terroir* up there is fantastic for vines.'

'Allegra, tell Nico about the harvest party you told me about,' said Maggie. She turned to Nico. 'It sounded like something out of a film.'

'My family love a good party,' said Nico, laughing. 'I can just imagine.'

They chatted on as the sun started to set behind them and the bay emptied of boats.

When the bells rang out seven times, Nico got up. 'I'm so sorry, I've got to go. We're doing a night harvest tonight; we start in about an hour.' He turned to Maggie. 'When do you go home?'

'Tomorrow, sadly.' Maggie's eyes dropped to the floor.

'That is a shame,' said Nico. 'I don't suppose...' He paused. 'Obviously only if you want to but why don't you come with me? It's the last one tonight.'

'Oh, you should definitely do that, Maggie. What a wonderful experience!'

Maggie looked at Allegra. 'I can't leave you...'

'Of course you can! I've got dinner booked, remember? Don't you worry about me, I'll be fine.'

'There's a small party in the vineyard afterwards and

there's a harvest moon tonight.' Nico looked at Maggie hopefully.

'I'm not sure. My flight is in the morning. I've got to be at the airport by eight o'clock,' said Maggie.

'Nico, what time do you finish?' asked Allegra.

'Usually about five in the morning but you can leave at any time, really. Maybe just come for a bit?'

'You can sleep on the plane!' Allegra nudged Maggie with her foot.

'You're sure you don't mind about dinner?' Maggie felt awful leaving Allegra on her last night but one look at her host's face told her Allegra wasn't going to have it any other way.

'Darling, dinner on my own at that restaurant is one of my greatest joys. Honestly, you must go. I'll see you in the morning, just promise to come and wake me up before you leave.'

Maggie turned to Nico. 'What do I need?'

'A pair of secateurs. I've got some you can use.' He grinned and reached for her hand. 'Ready?'

By the time they got to the vineyard, barely fifteen minutes from the edge of town in the foothills behind Cannes, Nico had talked Maggie through what to expect from her first night harvest. They turned off the road and made their way up the steep drive to the chateau; in front of the house, people of all ages gathered ready for the last pick of the season. Nico introduced Maggie to a stream of people from the workers to the owners, along with friends and family all roped in for one last push.

Nico had patiently shown her exactly what to do, from selecting the right bunches of grapes to cutting the vine so as not to cause any damage. Maggie set to work, Nico coming back to check on her often as he moved through the vineyard overseeing the pickers. There was a rhythm to the work she found calming, her mind focused on nothing but the task in hand. The only thing that mattered was cutting the bunches from the vine as gently as possible so as not to damage the fruit.

Once the last of the grapes were placed carefully in the waiting crates and onto the waiting trailer to take them to the winery, everyone came together around a long table set up in front of the house for a candlelit feast that went long into the night. The atmosphere was one of celebration and joy, and once seated, Nico barely left her side. He happily translated the conversations around them as the wine flowed. At one point, the owner's wife joined them, putting herself between Maggie and Nico, telling her she mustn't let him get away, much to Nico's obvious embarrassment.

The music started as soon as the last of the plates were cleared and Maggie and Nico danced in the moonlight under a tree festooned with paper lanterns. Nico spun her around, then held her close, their bodies moving to the music as one. For the first time in a very long time, Maggie didn't want the night to be over. When all but a handful of guests were left, Nico took Maggie's hand and led her down to the garden beyond the house where they sat on a stone bench overlooking the vineyard, the lights of Cannes in the distance. Nico asked about Allegra and Maggie about Etienne, agreeing what a love story that must have been. They talked about their families, of Nico's dream of owning a vineyard of his own one day and Maggie's plan to write. Finally, he took her face in his hands and kissed her under the harvest moon, still visible in the sky above them. By the time dawn broke over the vineyard, their own love story had truly begun.

25

PRESENT DAY

'Any drinks or snacks?'

Maggie opened her eyes to see the flight attendant smiling at her, holding out a bottle of water. She took it and thanked him, then turned back to look out of the window, cotton wool clouds partially covering the landscape below. She didn't know whether to laugh or cry. On the one hand, Maggie had had one of the best nights of her life. On the other, never had she been so sad to leave a place – or person – behind. She was exhausted; her nails were filthy, her fingers sore from sorting grapes and as for her back, she wondered if she'd ever be able to stand up straight again. But for all her aches and pains, she'd loved every second.

Eventually, when they couldn't put it off any longer, Nico said they should get going if she was to make it to the airport in time. They walked back up to the house and he ran her back into town, waiting outside whilst she grabbed her bags and woke Allegra as promised to say goodbye, then insisted on driving her to the airport despite her saying she was happy to catch a train.

'I'm so glad you stayed for the harvest,' said Nico as they sat in the car outside the terminal. 'But I hate that you're leaving.'

'Me too,' said Maggie, trying not to cry.

He kissed her again. '*À bientôt.*'

As much as Maggie wanted to stay, real life was waiting for her back home. She had a job to go to, a flat to pay for, her friends and family were there. By the time the plane landed and she switched her phone back on, there were three messages waiting for her. The first was from the boss of the production company asking her to confirm whether she was taking the job. The second was from her father on the family WhatsApp group, a photo of Maggie's cat lying flat out on their kitchen table as if he owned the place and the third was from Nico. She opened it, her heart racing. She read his words and replied immediately.

I miss you too x

* * *

The following day, Maggie turned down the job. She felt sick as she pressed send on the email but as soon as she'd done it, she knew it was the right thing to do. Maggie had grown adept at hiding her feelings – she'd done it for the last few years of her relationship with Jack – but the idea of working alongside him and his pregnant girlfriend was just too much, however desperate she might be for work.

Maggie was halfway through typing an email to her agent when her phone rang. It was her mother.

'Mum! How are you?'

'Hello, darling, glad you're home safely. Did you have a lovely time?'

'Gorgeous.' Maggie smiled to herself. 'Allegra is wonderful. I wish Granny was still alive so I could ask her more about her time in Paris. It sounded amazing. I can just imagine the two of them together, they obviously had so much fun there.'

'She never really talked about it much; it probably felt like another lifetime to her,' said her mother, quietly. 'Did you bring the photos back?'

'Yes, and I thought I'd come up later this week.'

'I thought you said you had a new job starting?'

'I've turned it down.'

'Really?'

'I couldn't do it, Mum. Something else will come up, it always does.'

'That would have been a tough gig for you.'

'I'm emailing a few people now, actually.' Maggie looked out of the window at the grey London sky. 'How's Dad?'

'Oh, you know, same as ever.'

Maggie could tell her mother wasn't being entirely truthful.

'He does love having Tiger here, though. They're literally inseparable.'

'I saw the picture. He's obviously made himself quite at home,' said Maggie, laughing. 'I'll let you know but assume I'll be with you in time for drinks on Thursday.'

'Okay, we'll look forward to seeing you then. Don't forget to bring the photos.'

'I won't.' Maggie thought about telling her mother about Nico, then decided against it. At least for now, she would keep him to herself.

The next few days flew by as Maggie continued her

mission to find work but something felt different. At first, Maggie put it down to having been away; no one wants to go back to work after a holiday. Whatever it was, the feeling just wouldn't go away and Maggie knew her heart just wasn't in it like it used to be. She had the long drive up to her parents' house to think and by the time she reached Melrose she'd made a promise to herself to sign up for a creative writing course, something she'd always secretly harboured a desire to do.

The season was putting on a glorious display as Maggie crossed the bridge over the River Tweed, the trees looking like a fireworks display in shades of garnet and gold on either side of the blue-grey water. Her father was at the door when she pulled into the drive, Tiger in his arms.

'You have absolutely no loyalty,' said Maggie, stroking her cat under the chin and kissing the top of his head. Tiger narrowed his eyes at her. 'Hi, Dad.'

'Hello, darling,' said her father. 'Come on in, your mother's somewhere. Sylvie!' he called. 'How was your trip?'

Maggie followed him into the kitchen. 'Amazing, thank you. I can't believe I've never been to Cannes before. That whole area is just beautiful. Shall I put the kettle on?'

Her mother appeared, still in her overalls. 'Sorry, I was in the workshop. I didn't even hear the car. How was the drive?'

Maggie hugged her mother. 'All good. Lots to catch up on.'

'Is that cake? I'm starving,' said her father, hopefully.

Maggie had taken these familiar rituals for granted for so many years but now, as she watched her parents age, these were the moments she loved the most. They sat around the kitchen table, hot tea in their mugs and Maggie filled them in on her stay with Allegra. She put the box of photographs on the table and they went through them together, spreading them out before them just as Maggie had done with Allegra.

'So that's Luc, who was Granny's boyfriend at the time,' said Maggie, tapping the photo of them in Etienne's flat. 'In fact, it's a shame Granny isn't in any of them.'

'She was a very good photographer, wasn't she?' said her father.

'She really was. So that's Etienne?' asked her mother, pointing at the photograph of him standing on the street with a book in his hand.

'Isn't he gorgeous?' said Maggie. 'Theirs was a real love story, I think.'

'Why didn't Allegra ever go back to Paris?' asked her mother.

Maggie sighed. 'Honestly, it's so sad. They were engaged and Allegra went back to New York when her mother was ill. She assumed she'd return to finish the year, but her father refused as he didn't approve. Then Etienne told her not to come back either. He said he didn't love her but in fact, as Allegra found out years later, it was because he had to go back to his parents' house in the south and he didn't want her to give everything up for him. He didn't think he could give her the life she deserved.'

'Goodness, that is sad,' said her mother.

'What happened to him?' said her father, pointing to a picture of Luc.

'If it's the same man, I think he became a politician in France, quite a famous one as it turns out,' said her mother.

'Really? How do you know?' said Maggie.

'Google.' Her mother laughed. 'It's funny because I know they had to come back from Paris quite suddenly but I never really thought to ask why.'

'It was all to do with the demonstrations and riots going on in Paris at the time, according to Allegra.' Maggie picked up another photograph. 'I love this one. It's taken in one of the jazz clubs they went to.' She handed the photograph to her father. 'There was one photograph I left with Allegra. I hope you don't mind, Mum. Your mother took one of her and Etienne on a bench in a park just by the Notre-Dame. I left it propped up on her table before I left, along with a thank you note. I thought she'd like it.' Maggie thought of that photograph, how she'd wished she'd been kissed like that when she'd first seen it. And now, she had. Nico hadn't been far from her thoughts since they'd parted company and with each passing day, their messages had become more frequent. She hadn't checked her phone since arriving at her parents' house, but she knew there would be one waiting. Her heart skipped at the thought.

'Of course, quite right.' Her mother nodded. 'Talking of which, there's a letter for you here too. I think it's from Allegra. I recognise the writing.'

'For me? Why would she be writing to me so quickly?'

'I've no idea. It arrived this morning. Hang on, it's on the side there. Michael, can you grab it?'

'Not with this damn cat on my lap,' said her father.

'I know you love him more than you're willing to admit,' said Maggie, winking at her father. She got up to retrieve the letter, picking up the light blue envelope.

'Open it,' said her mother, pouring more tea.

'What does she say?'

'Hang on, Dad. I'm reading it.' As Maggie scanned the words, her mouth dropped open.

'What is it, darling?' said her mother. 'Is everything alright?'

Maggie read it again, then handed it to her mother.

'What is it, Maggie?' said her father.

Maggie looked from one to the other. 'She's bought a vineyard. And she wants me to have it.' Maggie felt so light-headed, for a moment she thought she might pass out.

'She's what?' said her father. 'Did you just say vineyard?'

Her mother took the letter from Maggie and started reading. 'It's not just a vineyard. She's bought a house. And who is Nico?'

'Sylvie, what does it say?' said her father, looking nonplussed.

'I think I need a drink,' said Maggie.

'I'll fix us some,' said her father, putting Tiger on the floor.

Her mother reached across and squeezed Maggie's hand. 'I thought you seemed different.'

'What do you mean?' said Maggie, picking up her cat and putting him on her lap. His purring started up like an engine in a waiting car.

'Start from the beginning,' said her mother.

Maggie took a deep breath and told them her story.

26

ONE YEAR LATER

'Do you think we'll have blue skies today?' said Maggie, looking out of the window. She stretched and yawned. 'Oh, hello you.'

A cat jumped onto the end of the bed and made himself comfortable.

Her mother turned from where she was standing at Maggie's bedroom window. 'I think it's going to be a beautiful day.'

'How's Dad?'

'He just can't cope with too much change. Today might be a bit confusing for him but he'll be fine. I'll make sure he gets some rest before this afternoon.'

'Okay, as long as you're happy. I'd better get up.'

'Darling, whilst I've got you to myself can I just say something?'

'As long as you don't make me cry, go ahead.' Maggie looked at her mother, a small smile on her lips.

Her mother sat on the edge of the bed. 'We are so, so proud of you, especially given everything you've been through.'

'Mum, I said you are not to make me cry,' said Maggie, tears welling in her eyes.

'I know, I'm sorry. I lied,' she said. 'We know there were times when you felt completely lost, as did we watching you go through everything you've been through. It was awful not being able to just make it all better. But this past year, you really have found the happiness you deserve.'

Maggie wiped her cheeks, laughing gently. 'Mum, stop.'

'Seriously, Maggie. You have made some big decisions, ones not everyone would be brave enough to make.'

'You know, when I first came here Allegra said something to me that didn't make sense, but now I get it. A friend of hers once told her that if it weren't for second chances, we'd all be alone. I remember thinking what's wrong with being on your own? And of course, there's absolutely nothing wrong with it if that's what you want. After Jack, I was better off that way.'

'But then Nico turned up...'

Maggie smiled. 'Then Nico turned up. It's funny, looking back I think Allegra knew I loved him before I did. I'd got used to staying on my own, keeping busy to avoid pain, but that wasn't the answer.'

'Do you think that's why she wrote the letter?'

'Exactly. She gave me a choice. I could say no, or I could give it a go.'

'Well, I'm so happy for you. This place is beautiful.'

'Mum, it's still a building site,' said Maggie. 'But we're getting there. To be honest, we're happy living in chaos for a while if the vines are in good shape.' She looked at her watch. 'Nico is out there already.'

'What time is everyone coming?'

'Five o'clock so we have plenty of time. I'm so pleased you're here for your first proper French harvest supper.'

Her mother nudged her daughter's arm.

Maggie grinned. 'And my wedding.'

'Talking of which, may I?' Her mother pointed at the large wooden cupboard in the corner.

'Of course, it's on the right.'

Her mother went over to the cupboard and carefully pulled out a long, pale gold sleeveless satin dress, hanging it on the door. She stood back and looked at it. 'Oh Maggie, it's beautiful.'

'Thank you, one of my friends in the next-door village made it. You'll meet her later. She's coming with her husband and kids.'

Suddenly, they heard Nico's voice calling for Maggie up the stairs.

'Nico, you can't come in, it's bad luck,' shouted Maggie, crossing the room to close the door.

'Wouldn't dream of it,' he said, from the other side. 'But I had to come and tell you, Maggie. The grapes on those old vines? They are unbelievable. We got the last of them in this morning.'

'I wish you'd let me come with you,' said Maggie, her face pressed to the closed door.

Nico laughed. 'I wanted you to have a night off. Did you have a nice dinner with your parents?'

'We did, thank you. There are some leftovers in the fridge if you're hungry?'

'I already found them,' he said. 'Thank you.'

'Okay, you have to go now. I'll see you down there at five.'

'Don't be late,' said Nico.

'I promise.' She turned and looked at her mother sitting on the bed, the cat on her lap, wiping a tear from her face. 'Oh God, don't you start, or we'll never get through today.'

* * *

At quarter to five there was a knock at the kitchen door. Maggie was standing barefoot in her dress, her hair tied up with strips of fabric in an attempt to get a wave in it and her face completely bare of make-up. 'Come on in, unless you're Nico,' said Maggie. She'd spent the day getting food ready at the house with her parents and a collection of friends coming and going, leaving Nico, at his insistence, in charge of setting up for the feast to follow in the vineyard.

Allegra appeared round the door, an enormous smile on her face.

'You're here!' cried Maggie, throwing her arms around her.

'Of course I am, I'm your chauffeur.' Allegra laughed. 'I asked your mother if I could drive you all down there, you and your parents, so you don't have to walk. They're in the car already.'

'You did?' Maggie looked out of the window to see Allegra's blue Mercedes in the drive, her father and mother tying cream ribbons on the front. 'I don't believe it! Thank you. Can you stay here tonight?'

'Camille and her husband are staying with me, so he'll drive us back. They've already gone down.' Allegra looked at the old clock on the wall, the same one that had been there when she'd sat round that same table. 'We'd better get going.'

'Okay, give me a second,' said Maggie, unwrapping her hair. 'I've just got to put on a bit of make-up.'

'Sit down, let me sort out your hair whilst you do it.'

Maggie did as she was told and hastily applied some blusher to her cheeks, a smudge of gold eyeshadow, mascara and a touch of pale pink lipstick. 'How's that?' she said, turning to Allegra.

'Beautiful,' she said, kissing the top of Maggie's head. 'Let's go.'

By the time they got to the far vineyard, it was drenched in the light of golden hour. The stone hut, now with a roof thanks to Nico's handiwork, was festooned with paper lanterns and huge bunches of lavender ran the length of the tables set for the feast. Everyone had gathered around and the car pulled up to spontaneous applause.

Maggie got out and looked up to see Nico waiting for her in front of the door, so smartly dressed she barely recognised him at first. When he turned and saw her, his face lit up. And as she walked towards him, she knew with all her heart she was where she was supposed to be.

EPILOGUE

Allegra's life in Cannes had been a very happy one but the last year with Nico and Maggie had been one of the best of her life. She hadn't been sure what they would make of her proposal at first, but as soon as she'd found out about the old Domaine and the vineyard that went with it she knew it was meant to be.

Selling the Rodin had been easy; she had enough old friends in the business to help her make a quick, not to mention discreet, sale. The sale on the house went through without too much difficulty; money talked.

The hardest part was convincing Nico and Maggie. At first, they'd said they couldn't possibly accept. When Allegra explained that she was doing it for selfish reasons – namely, it would make her very happy – they agreed to think about it. It was everything they wanted, and she would benefit from having them living not too far away. A win-win situation, surely.

Barely a month after Maggie had left, she was back in Cannes and in the process of letting her flat out in London, her and Nico rarely apart. But the real turning point as far as the Domaine was concerned had come when they'd all gone to visit the property together. As soon as Nico clapped eyes on those gnarly old vines, Allegra knew she had him onside. It was so long since it had been farmed, the soil was perfect. Plus, they found they had some rare varieties planted including Tibouren, impossible for Nico to resist. Maggie was still unsure, saying she couldn't possibly accept such a generous gift. After the tour of the house and vineyards, the three of them sat under the old oak tree and discussed it over a glass of wine. Rosé, naturally.

'Can I please just say one more thing?' said Allegra. 'I have no children of my own and more money than I know what to do with, despite giving most of it away. There was a time when it might have been me living here,' she said, looking at Nico. 'But that didn't happen, for whatever reason, and I'm fine with that, I really am. Life took me elsewhere. But I would very much like to give you both, two people I love so much, the opportunity to make this place your home and to make it wonderful again. Together.'

Maggie and Nico had looked at each other, and with a nod of their heads, had made Allegra almost cry with delight. They raised their glasses, pale wine glinting in the sunlight, and made a toast to happiness.

Returning home after the wedding, with her guests fast asleep on the floor below, Allegra stood in front of a framed black and white photograph of a young couple, kissing on a bench in Paris. A stolen moment. It now hung on the wall in place of the Rodin. She climbed into bed as the bells in the clocktower rang out twelve times and closed her eyes, Etienne waiting for her as ever in the shadows of her mind.

* * *

MORE FROM HELEN McGINN

Another book from Helen McGinn, *The Island of Dreams*, is available to order now here:

https://mybook.to/IslandOfDreamsBackAd

ACKNOWLEDGEMENTS

So many people have helped me get this book into your hands. Firstly, thank you to my literary agent Elly James at HHB and to my incredible publishing team at Boldwood, especially my editor Sarah Ritherdon. Sarah, you make me want to write the best book I possibly can. Every. Single. Time. Thank you to Amanda Ridout, Emily Ruston, Wendy Neale, Nia Beynon, Claire Fenby, Marcela Torres, Megan Townsend, Issy Flynn and team for all your support, always.

Thank you to Alice Moore for producing yet another beautiful cover and to Candida Bradford and Sandra Ferguson for your expert advice and eagle eyes.

To Alie, Charlotte, Gemma and Claudia – thank you as ever for your honest feedback on the book from the first draft to the last. And to my constant cheerleaders Amanda, Elizabeth and Bells, thank you for keeping me going in the meantime.

To the Cannes crew, thank you for the best research trip! Not that I knew it was that at the time (too busy drinking rosé and playing cards badly, the former not wholly unrelated to the latter).

To my children George, Xander and Alice; I am so very proud of you all. And to my husband Ross, I honestly couldn't do any of this without you. Thank you for your love, support and understanding especially when I say, 'I just need to finish this bit' (which is a lot).

Finally, my heartfelt thanks to you, my wonderful readers. Whether you found me through wine or fiction, I'm so glad you did. It means the world when I hear or read that my words have resonated with you in some way. Thank you for all your lovely messages and reviews, I so appreciate you taking the time to let me know what you think.

ABOUT THE AUTHOR

Helen McGinn is a much-loved wine expert and international wine judge. She spent ten years as a supermarket buyer sourcing wines around the world. Now, she's the drinks writer for the *Daily Mail* and regularly appears on TV's Saturday Kitchen and This Morning.

Sign up to Helen McGinn's mailing list here for news, competitions and updates on future books.

Visit Helen's website: www.knackeredmotherswineclub.com

Follow Helen on social media:

 facebook.com/knackeredmotherswineclub
x.com/knackeredmutha
instagram.com/knackeredmother

ALSO BY HELEN MCGINN

This Changes Everything

In Just One Day

This Is Us

The Island of Dreams

Under a Riviera Moon

Boldwood

Boldwood Books is an award-winning fiction publishing company seeking out the best stories from around the world.

Find out more at www.boldwoodbooks.com

Join our reader community for brilliant books, competitions and offers!

Follow us
@BoldwoodBooks
@TheBoldBookClub

Sign up to our weekly deals newsletter

https://bit.ly/BoldwoodBNewsletter